# THE HONEY TRAP

## THEO BAXTER

INKUBATOR
BOOKS

Published by Inkubator Books
www.inkubatorbooks.com

Copyright © 2024 by Theo Baxter

Theo Baxter has asserted his right to be identified as the author of this work.

ISBN (eBook): 978-1-83756-396-8
ISBN (Paperback): 978-1-83756-397-5
ISBN (Hardback): 978-1-83756-398-2

THE HONEY TRAP is a work of fiction. People, places, events, and situations are the product of the author's imagination. Any resemblance to actual persons, living or dead is entirely coincidental.

No part of this book may be reproduced, stored in any retrieval system, or transmitted by any means without the prior written permission of the publisher.

## PROLOGUE

I can see that he is struggling with something. He seems distracted and a little jumpy. It's putting me on edge after I've finally found some peace in my work. I don't normally pick up on cues like this in people, but his are too obvious to ignore. "What's going on with you?"

"I—" He stops and looks at me, clearly upset. "I don't know how to tell you."

"Are you leaving me?" I ask.

"What? No. That's not... I have to tell you something, and I know you're going to hate me for it."

That takes me aback. He's been with me for a while now. I don't know what would make me hate him, unless... I stare at him. "What is it?"

He shakes his head, and his face crumples. "She's having an affair. She wants you dead."

His words strike a blow to my chest. Betrayal. Hurt. Anger. All of those pass through my mind, through my heart, but I'm also curious. "Why tell me?"

"Because you need to know. I can't just sit by and do nothing. I won't."

He speaks some more, giving me details, and an idea forms in my mind. I should have known it would come to this. There were warning signs that I ignored. Others told me to be wary, but I didn't listen. I am listening now.

"I'm glad you've told me. I have a plan." I'm unsure of what I'm hoping for, his refusal or his acceptance to help me.

I share my plan with him. As I finish, I hear a door slam somewhere in the house. "I know she's here, waiting, probably hoping I'm already dead. Let's continue our previous conversation as though you never said anything."

He nods.

I lift the paper I showed him when he joined me earlier. "I do wish I could live with less."

Maybe I'll be getting my wish in the near future... It is almost freeing, I think, as I smile at him.

# 1

"See you tomorrow," the young woman at the front desk said cheerily.

"Have a good one," Chris Abrams said politely before exiting the discount fitness center. He walked to his car and opened the trunk, carefully laying a damp T-shirt and a pair of underwear on top of his duffel bags and camp stove.

From there, he would stop by the liquor store for whatever was on sale. He needed a drink, but he didn't want to get wasted. He only wanted enough to keep the nausea and shakes away. Some days exercise was enough, but it hadn't really helped this morning.

If Chris decided that he wanted to stick around, he could visit a different liquor store each day before anyone would recognize him as a drunk. Even in a state where no one knew him or his reputation, he didn't want to be perceived as a degenerate. After all, he was an educated medical professional. He feared he'd never use his training again, but something about that set him apart from the other vagrants he bumped into on his daily circuit to survive.

His phone buzzed in the cupholder, and he picked it up.

> Any luck finding a job?

His sister texted him.

Laura usually sent the same text about once a month. His little sister knew that it pained him to reply that he hadn't, so she didn't ask more often.

He replied.

> Not yet.

She replied back immediately.

> You know you could come home and live with me.

> I know, but I can't be there. I can't be around those people anymore.

Unfortunately, Chris had become notorious in Omaha. Though many people sympathized with him, there were too many others who blamed him and treated him as if he were a mass murderer.

It had been an accident. He'd been overworked and exhausted, and someone had put the medication on the wrong shelf. A beautiful, popular high school girl had died. On top of that, she'd come from a very wealthy family. One who had pursued litigation and ruined him.

Of course he felt bad that the girl had died. There was never a moment that he didn't regret her death. But part of him felt that had she been a criminal or maybe someone less connected and maybe ugly, he wouldn't have been dealt such a hard punishment. He supposed he was lucky he hadn't ended up in jail and had escaped with just being fired and having to pay monetarily. Something his former wife had resented.

As someone who'd had a career in helping people overcome their mental health struggles, it was a cruel irony that all Chris wanted to do was move back home, reconnect with his sister and the few friends who had stuck by him, and check himself into an outpatient center for his depression and alcoholism. Unfortunately, the shame and lack of money made that impossible.

After the trial, no medical facility in Nebraska would touch him. He'd even had trouble just getting job interviews.

He'd finally found a boarding school in upstate New York that hadn't balked at his history and offered him a job. While he hadn't been sure about being a counselor at a school for troubled kids, he'd needed employment and a new life. He even had a bed in a staff dorm on campus. He'd figured that when he had enough money, he would move on to something else—or even go back home. Once he'd proven himself to be reliable once again. So he'd packed up the few belongings he had left after the divorce was settled and headed east.

As he had pulled up to the campus for his first day, a reporter stopped him. Chris had been terrified that they were going to bring up his past, but was surprised when they asked him to comment on the abuse allegations at the school. It turned out that while he'd been driving across the country, the school had been shut down, and the headmaster had been arrested.

Then he had noticed the police cars and the buildings with boarded doors. Feeling sick, he had turned back to the closest town and found a dive bar, where he spent way too much money on vodka.

Chris had seen no point in turning his life around and persevering. He only wanted to do the minimum to survive. He just needed enough money to eat, and when that failed, to drink. He had decided that he would simply float along until he went under.

Putting all those thoughts of his past aside, Chris focused on the fact it was a warm, spring day—one of those days that offered a preview of summer with its bright sun and smell of plant life when the cool breeze shifted. After checking the gas gauge to ensure that he had enough fuel to make it, he drove to a nearby park that was tucked away in a wooded area. As he drove down the long gravel drive, he watched a family set up a picnic.

He parked as far away from them as he could and spread his wet clothes on a bench before cracking open a can of spiked seltzer that tasted like the cough medicine he used to take as a kid. Normally, he wouldn't choose something so artificially flavored and bitter, but it was the most effective option in his budget.

From his soft cooler in the trunk, he pulled out half of a gas station sandwich from the previous day and nibbled around the limp edges. He needed something solid in his stomach in order to drink without getting sick. Feeling calmer and somewhat sleepy, he pulled a blanket from the stuffed trunk, laid it on a soft patch of grass, and reclined on his makeshift mattress, allowing his eyelids to flutter, then close.

Chris dreamed that he was sitting outside his home in

Omaha, watching the sun set. He used to love the summer days that weren't so hot and humid that he could actually enjoy his little backyard in the city. Chris and his former wife, Maddie, would sit on their oversized porch swing together, his arm wrapped around her shoulders and her head nestled in his chest.

In his dream, Maddie told him that they were expecting a baby, which they were planning for in the near future. Chris had been ecstatic to hear this news, only to feel bitter disappointment when he was woken by the cold nose of a Labrador that had wandered from his owner to explore the park.

"Sorry about that," the owner shouted as he called the curious dog back.

Chris gave a forgiving wave and sat up on the blanket. He didn't want to get a reputation for being the drunk homeless guy loitering around public parks. Small towns called for more discretion.

It was time to consider where he would sleep for the night. During the day, he was careful to pack all of his belongings in the trunk so no police officer would see he was living in his car and try to shove him into a shelter. At night, he closed towels, blankets, and T-shirts in the windows so he would have some privacy. It was cramped and uncomfortable, but it was secure. He just had to make sure he found the right parking lot to sleep in, as he didn't want trouble from the authorities.

Chris figured that if he kept driving up the highway, he'd reach a good spot to settle in for the night, so he packed up his car and drove toward town.

He was only ten miles away when he saw a shiny black BMW parked on the shoulder. Its driver, an older man with silvery hair, stood precariously close to the road, crouched in front of the luxury car. Chris wasn't the type to stop for every flat tire along the road, but this seemed like an accident waiting to happen, and he was in no hurry to get anywhere.

Flicking on his hazard lights, Chris pulled to the side of the road, then backed up closer to the car.

The man didn't move except for his slim, heaving shoulders. Chris could see the man was upset. Was it more than a flat tire? Had something else occurred? Was he hurt?

## 2

As Chris grabbed his phone from the center console and got out of his car, an old rusty pickup slowed to a stop behind them. Chris headed for the older man hunched down at the side of his car.

"Are you okay?" Chris asked the stranded motorist.

The man sounded like he was hyperventilating.

The second good Samaritan rolled down the window of his truck. "I've got my cell phone with me. Want me to call the sheriff's department?"

The hunched-over man let out a strangled shriek and collapsed onto his knees.

Chris's training and work experience told him that this man wasn't mentally well, and feared that a police officer's presence wouldn't calm him and could make the situation worse.

"I think the gentleman is overwhelmed," Chris said, walking closer to the truck to talk to its driver. "Why don't you continue on, and I'll help him out."

He raised his eyebrows. "If this guy is crazy, are you sure you want to deal with this?" he said with a lowered voice. "Could get dangerous."

"I'm a psychiatric nurse," Chris said, neglecting to include that he was no longer practicing, and his license wasn't valid in this state. "If I can't get anywhere with him, then I'll call for backup."

"Good man," the guy said before driving off.

"Sir? My name is Chris, and I'm here to help you," he said gently, kneeling down next to the troubled man.

"Get away," the man whimpered, not looking up at Chris.

His labored breathing made Chris suspect that he was having a panic attack. In these instances, some people needed help close by, and in other times, they needed space. Chris shuffled a few feet away and tried to look for information that would help him out.

Quietly, he walked around the back of the man's car and stuck his head through the open passenger-side window. The check-engine light was on, confirming his original suspicion that the car had broken down, causing the man to break down. In the passenger seat, he saw a thin, leather portfolio case. He pulled the door open and reached in to grab the man's belongings.

An embossed business card had the name Perry Bryant on it and a phone number below. Chris pulled his own phone from his pocket and dialed the number. A screen in the cupholder lit up, confirming the first piece of useful information. The motorist's name was Perry.

Chris dug back into the briefcase, pulling out printed sheets with spreadsheets and pictures of art. At the bottom, he discovered a pill bottle with a prescription for anti-anxiety medication. He recognized the name and dosage as something one would take in an emergency. Jackpot.

"Perry, I found your medication in your car," Chris said gently. "Why don't you take it? It will make you feel better."

Perry thrust out his hand, and Chris dropped a pill into it. Perry placed it on his tongue and swallowed it dry, but didn't get up from his spot on the ground and didn't stop rocking or whimpering.

Chris jogged to his car and got out a bottle of water. He opened it and placed it into Perry's hand as he urged him to drink.

"Focus on the way the water feels in your mouth and throat," Chris suggested. "Notice how cold it feels—notice how it moistens your tongue and hydrates your body."

He waited beside Perry, making sure no cars hit him as he suffered through his attack. It felt like an hour had passed, but with time, Perry's breathing became more steady.

"Are you feeling better?" Chris asked cautiously.

Perry lifted his head, but kept his eyes locked on the pavement. "A little, yes."

"Can I help you up?" Chris asked, holding out his hand. He grasped onto Perry's forearm and gently pulled him to a standing position.

"Thanks," Perry murmured, now staring at Chris's chest. "You seem like you've helped people like this before."

"I have," Chris admitted. "It used to be my job."

"What do you do now?"

"I'm, uh, job seeking," Chris said awkwardly. "So, can I wait with you for a tow truck? It seems like we won't be able to get you driving right now."

"No," Perry said with a shudder. "I don't do well with strangers, especially in these types of situations. I just want to go home. I'll have an assistant deal with it."

Chris surveyed the scene. He was glad that Perry was in a mental state that he could get himself out of harm's way, but Chris was still concerned with the prospect of Perry waiting for help on his own.

"Can I drive you somewhere off the road where you can wait? I'm sure there's another gas station or rest stop a little farther up the way."

"There is," Perry said flatly. "But I'm not far from home. If you're going to drive me to the next rest stop, we're better off if you just take me home. I'll reimburse you for the gas and your trouble, of course."

Chris gave the man a strange look. "Are you sure?"

"I'm feeling drowsy, and I want to rest," Perry said, walking toward his car. He pulled his belongings out and walked to the passenger's side of Chris's sedan.

Chris wasn't necessarily comfortable with this arrangement, but he had nothing better to do, and there was compensation involved. He desperately needed to fill his gas tank, and a little extra could get him a good meal.

"Can you give me directions?" Chris asked. "My phone doesn't have much data left."

"Head toward the old dairy processing plant," he said. "You take the next exit after that."

"I'm not from around here," Chris said hesitantly as he started his car and slowly pulled back on to the highway.

"No?" Perry asked. "What are you doing in this area, then?"

"I came for a job, but it fell through," Chris answered. It

wasn't exactly a lie, but it had been several months since that happened.

"Oh. What now?"

Chris shrugged. "I'm not sure yet."

Perry didn't respond.

Chris drove in silence for a while before it was too much to bear. "So what do you do?"

"Art," Perry replied simply. "Mostly painting and drawing, some sculpting. My most popular pieces are maps and landscapes. I guess you could call me a plein air painter, but from memory."

"I'm not sure I know what that means," Chris replied, keeping his eyes locked on the road, searching for something that could have once held a dairy plant.

"It's when people sit outside and paint what they're currently submerged in, nature-wise. I do something similar, but the scenes are from memory. The ones that make the big bucks are commissions from people with a particular location in mind. Sometimes, I fly over the area in a helicopter, then paint by memory."

"That's very impressive," Chris said, amazed by the man's genius.

"I can show you some of my pieces when we get to the house. My wife says it looks like I'm too full of myself if I only display my work in the house, so she moved most of it to the guesthouse."

"You're married?" Chris asked. "Do you want to call your wife and let her know that you're okay and someone is bringing you home?"

Perry looked at his watch. "I don't think she would want me interrupting her Pilates class."

Chris chuckled at the absurdity of that statement. He had worked with patients who had that sort of absolute thinking where conditions didn't seem to matter. Perry must have bothered his wife over something trivial while she was in the middle of a class, and she had gotten annoyed, leaving Perry to think that under no circumstances should he contact her while she was in her class—even after becoming stranded on the road, panicked, and getting a ride from a complete stranger.

"Do you have a wife?" Perry asked obtrusively, jarring Chris from his safe anonymity.

Chris sputtered, "Nope."

Perry turned to stare at Chris's face. "You look like you're about the age that a lot of men get married by. You're in your late thirties?"

"Thirty-four."

"I shouldn't make such generalizations. I didn't get married until later in life. I had to find someone who understood and accepted me, knowing that they wouldn't be able to change me. When I first got to know my wife, she recommended therapists and doctors to try all of these experimental treatments and pump me full of medicine that didn't work for me. So I had my medical team explain to her that my brain wasn't going to completely rewire itself to make things easier on her. In the end, she decided that she would rather be with me—diagnoses and all."

"Wow," Chris said, feeling slightly uncomfortable from this major overshare. "That's lovely."

"I think so," Perry said confidently. "Turn right here."

Chris pulled off the highway onto a narrow road. Without Perry's direction, he would have been completely lost, so he was thankful to see that Perry had recovered.

"Now turn left when you get to the opening in the trees," Perry directed. "There's the driveway."

Chris turned onto a paved, gated driveway.

Perry got out of the car and punched a series of numbers into the lock, slowly springing the gate open. A moment later, Perry climbed back into the passenger seat.

Chris could just see the grandiose house at the top of the hill and felt a combination of excitement and nerves at the sight of it. The stone exterior and perfectly manicured landscaping reminded him of some sort of modern castle, as he had to drive past expertly trimmed hedges to reach the fountain in the front of the house. The other buildings farther back on the property were about the size of his first home after college.

"Pull around to the back of the house," Perry ordered.

Chris cruised through a covered carport that divided the main house from a five-car garage. Beyond the carport was a pool, complete with a waterfall feature, though it was still too early in the season to swim. He parked in front of a garage stall, stunned by where the day had taken him.

"Come inside," Perry said as he grabbed his briefcase and walked toward a back door.

Chris reluctantly followed Perry into his kitchen, which was spacious and decked out in white granite with small rivers of gold throughout. Instinctively, he slid his fingers across the smooth, cool surface. The entire room was immaculate, as if no one ever cooked or even ate in there.

"Our chef is cooking Chilean sea bass tonight. Is that okay with you?"

Chris turned toward Perry with a confused look on his face. "Oh, no, I'm just—"

"I insist you stay for dinner, unless you have prior engagements to attend?"

Chris racked his brain for excuses, but the hunger deep in his stomach told him that he would be an idiot to refuse a good meal. Plus, he had already eyed the wine rack by the pantry.

"I'll stay for dinner," Chris said, feeling out of place and uncomfortable.

"Good," Perry replied. "I'll tell the chef to prepare an extra meal."

PERRY TOOK Chris on a quick tour of his home, pointing out every piece of art along the way. His works were quite spectacular, even to Chris, who didn't have much of an eye for art. He could, however, find the beauty in the clean lines on the hand-drawn maps and the paintings of mountainscapes. Even more spectacular was Perry's home, as he never ceased to be surprised by each new outbuilding and specialty room in the main house. The sauna, the greenhouse, and the stables looked like they were just there for show, like they were part of Perry's art exhibit.

"And the gym is in the basement," Perry said, leading Chris down the stairs. "There's also an industrial refrigerator and freezer down here for storage and food prep. I thought Kara might take over the meal duties once she moved in, but between you and me, I couldn't palate her cooking. It's been worth it to keep a chef employed to cook for us."

Perry opened a door, revealing a wide room filled with gym equipment. It reminded Chris of the small gyms he would use to shower in, but much nicer and cleaner. In the corner by the long mirror, he saw a uniformed masseur kneading a woman's shoulders.

"We're almost done here, Perry," the young woman on the massage chair said, wincing as the masseur worked deep into the tissue.

"Okay," he said cheerily, and watched the woman on the chair.

Chris looked around the room, feeling uncomfortable as they silently watched the woman get a massage. She was dressed in a skintight exercise outfit with leggings and a matching bra top. The coral outfit suited her bronzed skin and bleached blonde hair, which was tied up in a high bun.

"I'll see you next week, Tobias," the young woman said to the employee before walking over to greet the men. "What do you need, Perry? I have a nail appointment in an hour, and I want to shower before then."

"I wanted to introduce you to our guest for dinner this evening," he said. "Kara, this is Chris. He helped me out of a tight spot today. Chris, this is my wife, Kara."

Chris extended his hand to Kara, who lightly grasped it with an already manicured hand. She was a gorgeous woman whom Chris estimated to be in her twenties. He was surprised to see that she was married to someone much older than her, and quite frankly, he found that unusual.

"It's always good to see Perry make a new friend," she said, though there was a hint of condescension in her voice. "Please excuse me. I have to get ready for my appointment."

"Will you be home for dinner?" Perry asked, concern etched across his face.

"I'll do my best," she said half-heartedly.

The initial thrill of being in a luxury home was wearing off, and Chris was starting to feel anxious. He wanted to return to his life of solitude because that was where he felt comfortable. He didn't want to wear the mask of a good Samaritan any longer than he had to. However, he had promised to stay for dinner, which couldn't come soon enough. There was something so earnest about Perry's personality that Chris couldn't bear to ditch him and go back to whatever parking lot he would call home for the night. Plus, he was still waiting on that cash from Perry.

To his relief, Perry invited him into his sitting room, which sat adjacent to his bar. Perry slapped his hands on the granite bartop and asked Chris what he wanted for his aperitif.

"Whatever you're having is fine with me," Chris answered honestly, though he hoped that Perry was having something strong.

"I'm going to have a bottle of sparkling water," Perry said, "but I want you to try this whiskey that was gifted to me by one of my clients. Tell me what you think."

He poured a generous portion into a crystal glass and passed it to Chris, who sat on a plush leather couch. He took a sip, letting the liquid burn his mouth and throat.

"It's very good," Chris said, waiting for the relief to kick in. He had a pounding headache and was slightly nauseated after walking around the grounds.

"I'm not much of a drinker," Perry said, a contradiction to his fully stocked bar. "I get a lot of interesting bottles as gifts. My wife enjoys collecting wine, and I enjoy traveling to vineyards with her on occasion, but I'd rather stay at home and work in my studio. I could disappear there for days. It's the reason I employ so many people around the house—I would forget to eat, drink, or take my medicine if no one intervened," he said with mirth.

"How many people do you employ?" Chris asked out of curiosity.

"I don't know if I could even tell you." He chuckled. "There's a ground crew, a few house cleaners, and our chef. I also have Morrie, my medical attendant. I've found that it is best for my mental health if someone is always on call."

Chris thought it was great that Perry had the resources to take care of himself. However, as someone who was broke and dealing with his own dark thoughts, it seemed a little indulgent to have someone on call to help with the slightest issue.

"I didn't have so many issues when it was just me in my little studio, selling my work on the internet. Now, though, if I want to keep my career where it is, I have to meet with clients and go to events. It's far too much for me, so I need someone who can help me when I get too overwhelmed to function."

"I see," Chris answered, wondering why Perry was sharing so much with him. He was a stranger to this man, and it seemed out of character, from what Perry had said, for him to even be talking to him like he was.

"You know," Perry added with a twinkle in his eye, "I've been thinking about hiring another employee to help me with my mental health. I'm never going to be what society says is normal. But I want to be more functional. I have a wife to provide for. I've built a certain lifestyle that I cannot go back from. I need to build my business, and I can't do that if I can't leave the house and go to meetings without having a panic attack. I can't do my art if I'm bedbound and not in the right frame of mind. I'd like to add additional therapy sessions and have someone close—maybe even have them travel with me."

Chris nodded along as he savored his beverage. Perry's plan was a good one, but why he was telling him had Chris bewildered. "Some people do report having success with increased therapy. It might be worth a try."

Perry stared at Chris's chest for a moment, clearly unable to look him in the face. His hands formed fists at his sides, as though he was working up the nerve to say what was on his mind. After a few seconds, he blurted, "I want you to work for me."

3
―――――

Chris coughed and choked on his whiskey. "Me?"

Perry nodded firmly. "It's not often that I find someone I'm comfortable around, and I feel a connection to you. You said you came here for a job that fell through, and I heard you tell that other man you worked as a psychiatric nurse. You're the right person for the job."

Chris froze in his seat. He hadn't been expecting to get a full-time job offer out of a little good deed. His immediate reaction was to decline. He didn't know Perry, and he wasn't interested in being responsible for someone's health again. It had been a mistake to leave the Midwest for a job in a similar field, and it would be a mistake to stay somewhere that he didn't belong. At his best, he was a solidly middle-class man. He didn't deserve to live in a mansion and work what would probably be an easy job.

On the other hand, he knew he didn't have any options. If he got back in his car and drove to a Walmart parking lot, he would never get his life back on track. He would keep drinking his pocket money away until there was nothing left.

He would surely die if he didn't take this job. Unfortunately, he had an apathetic view on life these days, so that didn't pull him toward making decisions that would be good for his future self.

"What would this job entail?" he asked as he finished his drink, regretting there wasn't more.

"You would be my private healthcare professional," Perry said plainly. "I'm prone to frequent panic attacks, and it's helpful to have someone near me to talk me through them or give me the appropriate amount of medication when necessary—just like you did today. I'm also agoraphobic, but obviously have to conduct business outside of my home. I need daily therapeutic exercises so I can manage my day-to-day tasks. You may also need to work with my psychiatrist to make sure I'm following her orders. The thing about my mental illness is that it's so hard for me to take care of myself if I'm not in the right mind frame."

"I can understand that," Chris said. "So you're basically looking for an on-call, live-in therapist you can access whenever you feel like it?"

"Exactly," Perry said, clapping his hands together. "I have Morrie, but I don't think he's nearly as effective as you are. I don't want to replace him, but I think he would like to spend more time at home with his family. You can have your own room in the employee quarters, as most of them stay when they need to, but they don't permanently live here. Your starting salary would be forty thousand dollars, and I'll pay for any medical care you need. You'll have days off as well as a lot of downtime, so you're free to use any of the facilities as long as my wife isn't entertaining guests. I do think it's a unique arrangement and would be beneficial for us both, don't you?"

The take-home pay was less than what he had been making in Omaha, but he would have free housing and healthcare. All of the money he made would go directly to his bank account—there were no other expenses. It was too good a deal not to at least try it. If things didn't go well, he always had his car and his trunk full of meager possessions.

"I'll take it," Chris said hesitantly.

"Excellent. You start now." Perry smiled. "Usually, the employees eat in the meal-prep area downstairs, but tonight, you're my guest. I'll have Morrie come by first thing tomorrow to show you the ropes."

"Great," Chris said breathlessly, wondering what he had gotten himself into. He felt like he was in a strange dream and would wake up in the back of his cramped car any minute now.

At precisely six o'clock, Chris and Perry sat down for dinner in the smaller dining room. The table was set for three people, and a bottle of white wine sat chilling in an ice bucket in the middle of the table.

"Will Mrs. Bryant be joining you tonight?" the chef asked as he appeared from the kitchen with a small tray in his hand.

"She may be late," Perry said, sounding disappointed.

"I'll keep her portion warm," the chef said, as if this weren't the first time Perry had dined without her. "We'll start things off with bacon-wrapped asparagus. It's the first asparagus from the garden this season, and it's very tender."

"I'm looking forward to it," Perry said, carefully inspecting the small plate.

Chris had finished his tiny portion before Perry even took his first bite.

The chef uncorked the wine, read the label to them, and

explained why he paired it with the meal. He poured a splash in Chris's glass to sample and approve.

A few moments later, a small ramekin filled with French onion soup and smothered in cheese was placed in front of him. Once they finished that, the main course of fish and roasted vegetables made its appearance. By the time Chris started eating the main meal, Kara showed up and took her seat, admiring her shiny pink nails.

"How was the salon?" Perry asked as he carefully cut into the fish.

"It was fine," she said flatly.

"Are you hungry?"

She shook her head. "My trainer is starting me on a new diet. I gave Darryl the recipe book, and he's going to bring me a juice and four ounces of steamed chicken breast."

Perry didn't seem to think anything about his wife going on a restrictive diet while they had a chef cooking gourmet meals. Chris, on the other hand, was outraged that a woman with a perfect body would have any need to diet.

"Chris agreed to start working with me," Perry announced.

"Doing what?" she asked.

"Remember how I said I was thinking about hiring a new medical attendant? It just so happens that Chris is a psychiatric nurse and is looking for a new job."

"Oh, that's good to hear," Kara said warmly, looking directly at Chris with a beaming smile. "I hope you'll stick around for a while."

"I'm excited about the opportunity," Chris said, feeling giddy after a few glasses of wine and a good meal in his belly. "It's not every day that you help someone with car trouble and get a job because of it."

Dessert, a chocolate brownie and a decaf cappuccino, was brought to the table, along with Kara's diet food. Chris thought it seemed cruel to eat the rich dessert in front of her, but she didn't seem to mind.

After dinner, Perry excused himself to his studio for the evening.

As Chris got up to wander toward the cottage, Kara reached for his shoulder, causing him to spin on the spot.

"Do you need anything?" she asked, looking concerned. "You just picked Perry up on the highway, and now you're staying for good without going home to get anything?"

Chris shook his head. "It's kind of a long story, but I actually have everything I need in my car."

"Okay," she said sweetly. "I think the house is pretty well stocked, but don't hesitate to ask me if you need anything."

"I appreciate it," Chris said, feeling a little more welcome, as if he hadn't made a mistake in taking a crazy job offer on short notice.

"Good night," Kara purred as she waved goodbye to Chris, then sauntered up the stairs.

Chris felt oddly breathless, but he chalked it up to new-job nerves.

CHRIS STRUGGLED to doze off despite the comfortable employee quarters being a massive upgrade from the back of his car. He had his own bedroom in the cottage and shared a bathroom, small living room, and kitchenette with whoever else needed a place to spend the night.

It had been a whirlwind of a day, no doubt, but he felt like he should have been happier to stumble into his current position. Chris was hesitant about being a medical caretaker for a man he didn't know well, and whose diagnosis seemed complicated. Chris was used to working under a head practitioner who gave him instructions to carry out. While it seemed Perry had a whole team of psychiatric services at his disposal, they weren't in the house giving him instructions. Not to mention, Chris wasn't even sure it was legal to accept a position after being fired from his old job. He'd planned to get his license to practice in New York, but at the moment his was invalid. If something went wrong, Perry could probably press charges or sue him until he was left with absolutely nothing. Not that he had even that much. He lay in bed fretting over things that hadn't even happened yet.

Around seven in the morning, Chris heard a sharp knock on the door. He hurriedly pulled on his clothes from the previous day and hustled to open the door. Perry stood at the threshold with a smile on his face and another person in tow.

"Good morning, Chris," Perry said brightly. "This is Morrie, the medical attendant I told you about."

The older man with toad-like features held out a thick, stubby hand for Chris to shake. Morrie's jowls pulled his face into a natural frown, and overgrown eyebrows enhanced his scowl.

"Morrie is going to spend a few hours with you to orientate you on the job and explain my care plan. I'll be in my studio." With that, Perry turned on his heel and walked away, leaving the grumpy Morrie in the living room.

"Right, so Perry told me about the car incident yesterday, but I still don't understand how you got here," Morrie said gruffly. "You're going to be nothing but trouble, I know it."

# 4

Chris shrugged. "I don't know why you'd say that. All I did was help him. I was working as a psychiatric nurse in Nebraska and came out here to New York for a change of pace and a job opportunity that fell through. I guess I got extremely lucky."

"But what did Perry say about needing more help?" Morrie questioned.

"He thought it would be useful to add a therapy session and have someone who could travel with him on work trips."

"Did he say anything about cutting my hours?"

Chris wondered if he was about to get himself into trouble with Morrie. "No, but he did mention that you have your own home and family."

"But he didn't say anything about replacing me?"

"No, in fact, he said he wanted to add someone who could live on-site and be around for when you couldn't be there."

Morrie seemed somewhat satisfied with his answer. "Okay, well, I don't know how much there is to tell you. The boss is filthy rich and often acts on impulse, which would explain how you landed a job after one chance meeting. I treat this job like a well-paid home health gig. I've been a counselor for thirty years, and I'm hoping to retire in the next five years. I've been working with Perry for a few years now, and while I don't always love running to the man's side every time he has a negative thought, I like the change of pace. Working here can be demanding at times, but it can also be a lot better than the hustle and bustle of a crowded psychiatric hospital."

"It's definitely a different scene than a hospital," Chris said, looking out the window at the flower garden.

"But the type of care provided is very different," Morrie warned. "In a hospital, you give patients what the doctor orders, and then you're done with them. You don't even have to be nice. Here, it's not like that. You have to keep Perry happy and be ready at all hours for him to page you. You can't expect his wife to have any part in his care. She won't comfort him if he is crumpled in a ball on the floor. That's your job to get him out of it."

"What's his official diagnosis?" Chris asked, remaining professional.

"A mixed bag, really," Morrie said offhandedly. "Autism spectrum disorder, sensory processing disorder, panic disorder, and extreme social anxiety. He knows he's not neurotypical and he's never going to be, but he sees how other people exist in the big, scary world and wants that for himself. It's a balancing act of doing what he wants and doing what he needs."

"Nothing I can't handle," Chris said. There had been times where he had been frustrated with his patients, but he generally treated them with a little more respect than Morrie gave Perry.

"I don't doubt that," he said. "It's not that hard a job. In a lot of ways, it's like taking care of a child. If Perry needs medication, you have to make sure he's getting the right dose. If he's in a certain state of mind, he effectively shuts down and can't take care of himself. That's basically all you need to know about this patient. Now, I'm going to go to the kitchen and see what Darryl has cooking."

A small wave of panic washed over Chris after the short job training. "So do I sit around the main house all day and watch Perry?"

Morrie turned and gave Chris a pitying look. "Would you want to be watched all day?" He tossed Chris a small pager exactly like the one clipped to his cargo shorts. "He's pretty good about calling for help if he needs it. But it doesn't hurt to be in the main house a few times a day to check in on him. Otherwise, consider yourself on call."

Morrie walked out of the cottage, and Chris followed him, not sure what else to do. As they walked into the house, Chris saw Perry in the kitchen, visibly frustrated.

"What's up?" Morrie asked.

Perry clutched his hands into fists and gritted his teeth. "I got a voicemail from a man I've been doing business with. He wants me to become an investor on some new project."

"And?" Morrie asked impatiently.

"I know it's a good opportunity for me, but it would mean going to meetings and parties, and I just don't want to," he whimpered, slumping to the ground, and clutching his head.

Morrie walked over to his boss and yanked him to an upright position. "Look, sometimes you have to do things you don't want to do. When the time comes, you'll just deal with it, and it'll be fine. I know you don't want to lose everything that you worked for, and if you don't make smart business decisions, you'll do just that. Call your financial advisor and talk to him. You gotta pull yourself together."

This pep talk didn't seem to give Perry much relief.

Morrie walked over to the cabinet and pulled a glass out, then filled it with water. Then he opened a drawer in the kitchen and pulled out a prescription bottle, dispensing one tiny pill. "This will get you through it so you can get your work done. Now take it."

Perry reluctantly did as he was ordered.

Chris stood by, feeling uncomfortable with Morrie's method of care. He had seen nurses use this tough-love strategy before, and he found that it wasn't always effective, and it lacked compassion for someone going through a very tough time. From Morrie's perspective, he might see Perry as weak and a problem, but Chris understood that Perry felt as though he were in terrible danger. A former supervisor had once told Chris that if he ever wanted to understand how his anxious patients needed to be treated, to imagine how to talk to someone after being chased by a lion. It would be ridiculous to brush off someone's fear after a frightening experience like that, so he never did that with his own patients.

In time, with chemical intervention, Perry got up to his feet, but he was still shaky and pale.

"Let's go talk to Darryl and see if he can get us something to eat," Morrie said, clapping him on the back. "You need to keep your blood sugar levels regulated."

Chris followed the two down the stairs.

Morrie chatted with Darryl, who put three plates of eggs and toast on the counter. The three men sat on the barstools as Darryl plunked two mismatched mugs of coffee in front of Chris and Morrie, and a glass of orange juice in front of Perry. Perry and Chris ate silently while Darryl and Morrie talked about the Buffalo Bills' chances of making the playoffs. After he finished eating, Morrie gave his compliments to the chef and left unceremoniously. Eventually, Perry went back upstairs, in better shape, but looking sullen.

"Are you feeling better?" Chris whispered as he followed his new boss.

Perry shrugged.

"Do you want me to help you write an email or make a phone call?"

Perry stopped on the stairs and turned around. "Yes, I think that would be very helpful."

"Just page me when you're ready," Chris said, keeping his voice calm and quiet.

Perry didn't say anything, but went back to his study.

Wanting to avoid Morrie, who was taking a walk around the garden, Chris went back to the cottage and sat on the couch. As he flipped through TV channels, Chris hoped he wouldn't have to work too closely with Morrie.

Luckily, after the first day, Chris's and Morrie's paths didn't cross as often. When Morrie was on shift, Chris hung back in the cottage, and when Morrie wasn't there, Chris was as attentive to his boss as he could be. Once a day, he would lead Perry through mindfulness exercises and listen to his worries, validating and helping him come up with solutions for his problems. Some days, he would sit with Perry and help him draft an email or prepare to talk to a business associate. Perry had a tremendous mind but struggled to communicate, which only triggered his panic attacks. With Chris gently assisting him, Perry was able to close more deals, leaving him with more time to spend in his studio with his art. After a few weeks, Chris noticed that the panic attacks decreased in frequency and severity. Perry was in no way cured, but any success felt like a win in Chris's book.

Living at Perry's property was starting to get a little easier, too. While he was no longer treated like a guest of honor and wasn't invited to formal dinner with Perry and his wife, Chris still enjoyed the perks of being an employee of Perry's. He mostly took care of his own breakfast and lunch in his kitchenette, but he had become cordial with Chef Darryl, who would whip up whatever leftovers he had into something special for dinner.

Every two weeks, when the direct deposit dropped into his account and Morrie was on duty, Chris would drive into the nearest town and stock up on supplies. He never wanted to give the impression that he was mooching off his vulnerable and naïve employer, so he only ever took what was offered to him. Bread and sandwich meat was a daily staple, along with coffee and cereal for breakfast. He still picked up a few bottles of cheap vodka on a biweekly basis, but he had made a concerted effort to cut back, and succeeded in avoiding any withdrawal symptoms.

Sleep wasn't coming any easier, though. At night, he lay awake wondering what people back home were doing. He called his sister and gave her a vague overview about his new gig, much to her relief and delight. Laura would never say so, but he knew that she was always half expecting him to be in a ditch. He told her he was busy and wouldn't be able to talk to her often. It was a lie, but he was still at a point where it was hard to talk to anyone about anything deeper than the very surface. At least he knew that if his family or old friends asked about him, Laura could say that he was working in New York and was doing perfectly fine.

He often thought about his ex-wife, whom he had not had any contact with since the divorce went through, and the assets were divided. Looking at the date on his phone, he realized that by now, they would have had a good chance of expecting a baby.

Maddie had given him as much support as she could, even though she knew he had made a terrible mistake. At times it had been hard for her to look across the dinner table at him, but she had stood by him and reminded him that the hospital was at fault for understaffing and not following their own protocols, as well as whoever had put frequently used medications on the wrong shelf.

It was hard to fault Maddie for ending the relationship when he hadn't been present in months and showed no sign of turning things around. She had been pulled into the hell that was contained within his mind, and she couldn't handle it. Eventually, she had decided to make a fresh start. Chris understood that it wasn't fair for her to be tied to a person she didn't like anymore, so he didn't even try to fight it. He'd gathered his few remaining assets and tried to disappear.

He often wondered how Maddie was doing in her new life, but it hurt too much to think about her thriving without him. She, along with all of their future hopes and dreams, haunted Chris on a nightly basis. That was the reason why, even though he was slowly regaining his health, he kept buying vodka. It didn't guarantee restful sleep, but it did take the edge off the loneliness.

Chris hoped that as time went on, just like Perry's improvement with his panic attacks, Chris would find improvement in his longing for his old life.

Until then, he had booze—and stolen glances at his boss's hot wife.

CHRIS WAS startled awake one Friday morning just before seven when the front door of the cottage burst open.

Morrie barged inside. "I need to have a word with you. Now."

Chris grabbed the first pair of pants and shirt he saw on the floor of his room and pulled them on. Morrie stood just inside the front door, it was still ajar, and Chris was sure everyone on the property could hear Morrie.

"What's up?" Chris asked.

"Don't 'what's up' me," he snarled. "Do you have a problem with me?"

Chris's hands defensively went to his chest. "What would make you think that?"

"Well, you're only trying to take my livelihood away from me," he huffed. Morrie breathed loudly, especially when he was angry. His nostrils flared with every inhale.

# 5

"I honestly don't know what you mean," Chris said, getting worried. He wanted nothing to do with this altercation. In general, he avoided confrontation at all costs and especially didn't want to piss off the man who had a lot more pull around here than he did. Plus, Morrie was built like a gorilla. "Who told you that?"

Morrie glared as though he didn't believe Chris. "Then why has Perry suggested that I cut back on my hours? Ever since you came around, he hasn't needed me as much, which is fine until I lose pay. I know I'm old-school and you're new-agey and touchy-feely with Perry, but I was here first. I'm not going to let a little punk replace me. And for what? I'm not going back to working the night shift in some shithole mental institution in Brooklyn."

Out of the corner of his eye, Chris could see Kara storming toward them with a fiery look on her face. His terrified expression must have given it away to Morrie because he turned his thick neck around to catch her seconds before she reached the cottage.

"I swear to god, Morrie," she said. "What are you doing? What could be so terrible that you have to yell like that?"

"I just think it's weird that this guy shows up out of nowhere, and suddenly my hours are cut."

"Talk to Perry about it," Kara said. "I'm willing to bet he only did this because you told him you wanted more free time. You, of all people, should know that everything is black and white with Perry. Don't tell him anything if you don't want him to take you at your word."

She made a good point. In Chris's experience with his boss, he found that Perry struggled to navigate the business world when people tried to save face or beat around the bush. Part of the job, he was finding, was to act as an interpreter from Perry's straightforward mind to the nuanced business world. Oftentimes, he found himself wishing that more people communicated like his boss. At least Chris always knew where he stood with him.

"I'll talk to him," Morrie grunted. "And if you," he said, pointing to Chris, "say anything to him about this conversation, I'm not going to be happy about it. There's something off about you, but I'll let it rest unless you give me a reason to investigate that feeling."

Chris was stunned, but tried not to show it. He didn't know what the legal ramifications were of his work without being licensed in New York. He wasn't doing anything that Kara couldn't do if she wanted to help her husband, or nothing that an assistant wouldn't do for their boss. Still, withholding information wasn't a good look, and he wouldn't be surprised if Perry released him back to the streets if he found out about his past.

"I'm sorry your hours were changed," Chris murmured, "but I promise you that I had nothing to do with that."

"See?" Kara said to Morrie. "Maybe you should check on Perry. I wouldn't be surprised if he heard all of this from the house."

Morrie followed her suggestion, leaving Kara and Chris alone in the cottage.

She closed the door and took a seat on the couch, putting her bare feet on the armrest.

"I don't think I ever had the chance to fill you in on how some things work around here. Have a seat." She playfully kicked her thin, tanned legs onto the couch, pointing her manicured toes toward a chair.

Chris sat down.

"I'm really sorry about how Morrie treated you just now," she said, running her fingers through her blonde, silky hair. "Usually, he's not this terrible, but he's always a grump. To be honest, I wouldn't mind if he decided to leave and it was just you helping Perry."

Chris was honored to hear that he had been doing something right.

"Perry likes you. He says that you know how to talk to him to get him to calm down. And I just like having more handsome men around the house."

Chris was starting to feel uncomfortably warm. It felt inappropriate to accept such comments from the boss's wife. "I enjoy working here. I think Perry's a good guy."

"He is a good guy," she said softly. "Though I do have to admit, it can be hard living with him. When we first met, we would go on the most romantic vacations. These days, he doesn't want to go out and saves all of his energy for business transactions. I try to spend time with my friends, but most of them live in the city. Living here can be isolating, and Perry isn't the warmest person."

"I—" Chris stuttered, unsure how to reply.

"Sorry." She giggled. "I put you in an impossible conversation. You can't talk bad about Perry because he's your boss. Since you're his therapist and you're on the payroll, can I borrow a minute of your time to do a little venting?"

"Sure," Chris said, agreeing with her logic. "But will it remain confidential?"

"Of course. It would be highly unethical if I shared what you say."

"Okay, great," she said, wiggling onto the couch to settle in. "Lately, I've been wondering if I even love my husband. I care about him, but I don't have strong romantic feelings toward him. The sex has never really blown my mind, but there's less of it, and I have needs. I know he's older and doesn't have the same libido as I do, but it's been tough having this desire and not wanting to be with my husband like a wife should."

"Do you think it has to do with his mental state?" Chris asked, trying to analyze the situation.

"Who knows. I look at my friends who live in the city and date and have fun and wonder if I made a terrible mistake. Last night, I was trying to read before bed, and he was talking my ear off, not realizing that I didn't want to chat. Eventually, I told him I wasn't feeling well, so I went to the guest room for a little peace and quiet."

"I don't think there's anything wrong with wanting your own space," Chris said. "How does he handle you sleeping in another room?"

"He'll ask if he did something wrong. If I say no, he'll drop it."

Chris nodded. "What about separate bedrooms? It can be beneficial to couples who don't sleep well together."

She shrugged. "I'll think about it. What if I just came over here to sleep?"

Chris widened his eyes. "I guess, but your guest suites are bigger than this place."

She grinned and tossed her hair around. "I know, but at least I would have someone to keep me company here—someone who won't talk my ear off about any old thing. I really like talking to you. I could talk to you for hours and not get tired of it."

Chris's stomach fluttered. Kara made him feel things that he hadn't felt in a long time. It was an old cliché, but he felt like a teenager talking to her. She was absolutely gorgeous, but more importantly, she liked him. She was always smiling when she greeted him and laughed at all of his jokes. He knew it was taboo, but he was developing feelings for his boss's wife. Of course, he knew it would be wrong to overstep his boundaries as a professional to do anything and get in between Kara and Perry.

"I don't think Perry would like it if you did that," Chris said politely, shutting her down. "Besides, what would the rest of the staff think if they saw you sleeping in here?"

Kara giggled. "You forget how much power I have. If I wanted to get rid of an employee, it would only take a quick conversation with Perry to make it happen. Plus, I'm excellent at keeping secrets. If there was anything you didn't want the staff or Perry to know, your secret would be safe with me."

Chris wasn't sure if she was getting at what he thought she was hinting at, or if she was just flashing her influence in his face. Either way, he was excited and uncomfortable at the same time.

"Have you ever tried couples therapy?" Chris asked. "It

can be helpful to have a space to talk about issues in your relationship."

"No," she said, sounding bored by this turn in the conversation. She looked down at her hands to examine her manicure. "Perry has his own care. I don't think it's something we necessarily need."

"Maybe the two of you need to work out a way to spend more quality time together," he suggested. "You and Perry are always around each other, which can place a strain on a relationship."

Kara sighed and tapped her fingernails on the table. "You are adorable, and it kills me that you're going to make the perfect husband to someone one day."

Chris felt his face flush. "I'm not perfect."

"Whatever you say." Kara smiled. "It was really good to talk to a professional. I can see why Perry finds you so helpful. Do you think it would be okay if we could occasionally meet when I need someone to talk to? I mean, as long as it doesn't conflict with Perry's care, of course."

"Sure," Chris said, an errant chill running down his spine. He was precisely in between wanting to distance himself from Kara and get closer to her. "I'm glad I can help."

Kara peeled herself off the couch and sauntered away.

Once she closed the door behind her, Chris got up from his seat and went to the spot where Kara had been. The smell of her perfume still lingered in the upholstery, leaving a sweet reminder about the kind things she had said to him.

Was he desperate and needy? Perhaps. Then again, he knew there was no use in denying a compliment. After everything he had been through, he thought of it as an act of self-care to soak in the way she made him feel wanted.

It had been a while since he had felt that way.

# 6

Chris's dreams were beginning to change, though the poor quality of sleep had remained unchanged throughout the weeks. When he closed his eyes, he still saw his ex-wife and all of the hopes and dreams they lost, but now he also saw Kara. A lot.

From a medical perspective, he saw this as a good sign that his mental health was improving. Depression killed sexual drive, so just the fact that his thoughts, both conscious and subconscious, were filled with Kara suggested that Chris was on the mend. He still didn't feel entirely like his old self, but he was starting to make peace with the fact that he would never be his old self again.

However, Chris found that he now had the courage to reach out to his sister. It had been some time since he'd talked to her, so on an off-duty afternoon, he gave her a call.

"It's so good to hear from you," Laura gushed.

It made Chris uncomfortable for her to make such a big fuss over a simple phone call, but given the circumstances of his aloofness, he understood where she was coming from.

"How's the family?" Chris asked. "What's new with you?"

She sighed. "Oh, just the same as it always is. I'm exhausted over here, and I'm afraid things will only get more hectic when school gets out and the kids have more things to do."

"Sounds rough." Chris laughed. His niece and nephew were full of energy, but very sweet kids. He missed them. "What's Tony's role in all of this?"

"Ugh," she groaned. "He's joined a golf league and bought a bunch of new clubs. It's for his sanity, he says. Do you know how I deal with the extra responsibilities? I work harder around the house so it doesn't pile up on me."

"Sounds fair," Chris joked. "Do you want to know how the disgustingly wealthy live? I've gotten an inside view of it, and it's just absurd."

"Oh my god, tell me," she gushed. "Actually, wait—is it going to piss me off to hear about this?"

"Probably." He laughed. "Mind you, my boss doesn't have kids, and his wife is younger than me and doesn't work, but they have a chef who cooks all of their meals. They have groundskeepers who take care of all of the yard work, and housekeepers who come around on a daily basis to make sure everything looks like no one lives there."

"What do they do all day?" she asked.

"Well, Perry does spend a ton of time working on his art. Also, he spends several hours a day doing therapy for his various ailments."

"What about his wife?" Laura asked. "If she doesn't work, what does she do?"

"I know she spends at least two hours in the gym every day. She frequently has appointments for her hair and nails.

She hangs out in the city with her friends. Also, she's started to see me for therapy sessions."

"See you?" Laura scoffed. "I'm sorry, but what does someone like that have to go to therapy for?"

"You know I can't tell you that," Chris said. "Admittedly, her problems are small compared to her husband's, but I guess everyone has their own issues." He peeked out the window, as if someone could walk by and hear him talking about Kara's little secret.

"Do you have to fight the urge to slap her when she talks about her so-called problems?" Laura joked.

"No, I actually enjoy talking to her. I wouldn't say that anyone around here is really mean to me, but she's especially friendly to me."

"Well, I'm glad you're making friends. Is he paying you well?"

"It's an arrangement that's hard to beat."

"Good. Would you consider coming back to Nebraska if you saved up enough money to get your own place? You know you can always stay with us if you need to."

Chris exhaled. The thought of returning home made him feel nauseated. Not enough time had passed for people to forget his name. Plus, he had a fear of running into anyone from his old life. Omaha was a sizable city, but still too small for him to avoid people he knew forever.

"I don't know," he said.

"What about Lincoln? You'd be close, but you wouldn't have to worry about running into Maddie."

Chris asked the question he had been wanting to ask since he left home. "Have you heard anything from her?"

There was silence at the other end of the line. He

assumed Laura was trying to decide what to censor for his well-being.

"Is this really something you want to think about?" she asked, with pity in her voice.

Chris thought for a moment. "It might help me get over it faster if I knew what's going on with her. If there was some closure."

Laura sighed. "Maddie took a job in a different district, but is still living in the same house."

"Which district?"

"Bennington," she said reluctantly.

"That's a bit of a drive."

"Yeah, but I think things were awkward in her old district because the girl went to another high school there. I heard that at one point, she had talked about moving to Utah to be closer to her sister."

"I guess that's not too surprising. She loves the mountains."

Laura was quiet for a moment. "If Maddie moved out of state, would that make it easier for you to come back?"

Chris cleared his throat. "That's one too many what-ifs for me to consider at the moment. I could see myself staying here for a year or two. It's quiet. No one really knows me. There are no expectations for me to go out and be social. If I only want to work and hang out in my little cottage, no one is going to say anything about it."

"Won't you get lonely?"

Chris switched the phone to his other ear as he shifted to get comfortable in his seat. "I'm doing fine. Besides, I talk to Perry every day, and I shoot the shit with some of the other employees. And I talk to Kara almost every day."

"You talk to your boss's trophy wife," she said dryly.

"I don't think I've ever mentioned what she looks like," he replied.

"I looked them up," Laura admitted. "He looks like a rich old man, and she looks too young to be married, let alone be married to a man in his sixties. Is their relationship normal?"

"That goes against confidentiality for both parties," Chris said, cutting off that conversation. "Do you want me to be employed or not?"

"Okay, okay," Laura relented. "Hey, I forgot to mention—I ran into Cole at the mall the other day. He asked if it would be okay to call you. I wasn't sure."

Chris's stomach sank. Cole was one of his best friends and one of the few people who had stood by him when he went through the whole ordeal. He hated that his own friends had to walk on eggshells around him.

When Chris had sunk into his depression, he'd essentially lost his social circle. Laura and her family had been good to him, Maddie hung on for as long as she could, and Cole tried to give Chris space while showing that he was still on his side. At the time, Chris didn't feel like he was worth the work. He'd distanced himself from Cole because he thought he was doing him a favor. Now, as the depression fog lifted, Chris wanted his friend back, but felt awkward about how he'd acted.

"I think you should call him," Laura said. "I don't want to sound too harsh, but he was very good to you, and he just wants to hear that you're doing okay."

"I'll call him right now," Chris said. It was time for him to rebuild the relationships he had lost. If he ever went back home, he wouldn't want Cole to be a stranger.

"Good. Would you think about calling me more often? Once a month, just so I know you're alive?"

"You got it," Chris said. "Tell the kids and Tony I said hello."

"I will."

Chris hung up. Feeling nervous about connecting with his old friend, Chris found Cole's number and pressed his name. He heard a familiar voice within two rings.

"Chris, hey, it's good to hear from you, dude."

"My sister just told me that she ran into you," Chris said, his voice slightly trembling as he spoke too quickly. "I thought I should call you to see what you're up to."

Cole said, "I've been wondering the same about you."

Chris filled Cole in on the new job. As he spoke, he found it easier to explain the arrangement he had with Perry, and why he even went north in the first place. For the first time in months, he could talk about his life without feeling ashamed. He was almost proud to hear Cole's astonishment as he described the estate, the employees, and his boss.

"That's insane," Cole kept saying with each new detail. "If the other guy working there ever quits and he needs someone else, you give him my name."

"You think you could switch from working in special education to working with one adult client?" Chris asked.

"I think I'd figure it out." Cole chuckled. "You know I like my job and care about my students, but it's crazy out here. My caseload has grown by six kids this year. There are some days that I think about walking out of the school and never going back. If I could save some money and only have to deal with one person, I'd call that a win. You might just be the luckiest man alive in this economy."

Chris didn't consider himself lucky, but he was starting to realize how good he really had it—all things considered. While his friend was working as a teacher in a city with rapidly increasing rent, he was making decent money and spending almost none of it. He could see why it sounded like a dream job.

"Any romantic pursuits out there?" Cole asked. He was a bit of a player and was always looking for a juicy story. He had been that way for as long as Chris had known him.

"No." Chris laughed. "It's not really possible to date when the only women around are a couple of housekeepers and the boss's wife."

"Ooh, that's rough," Cole said. "Consider my job proposal invalid," he joked.

"But you should see the boss's wife," Chris said, lowering his voice. It felt good to talk about girls with his friend again.

"You got pics?"

"Do you have your computer with you? Search Kara Bryant."

He heard Cole typing for a moment, then a whoop that nearly blew out the speaker on his phone.

"You're kidding!"

"Nope. She even started coming to my cottage for private therapy sessions."

"Does her husband know?"

"Nope." Chris smirked. "And you're going to think I'm insane, but I think she's flirting with me."

"Dude," Cole gasped. "It would make sense. You're a young, good-looking guy who is easy to access. She's hot as hell and way too young to be with that old guy, who, based on your description, sounds like he would be hard to be married to. She's absolutely a gold digger."

"She might be," Chris admitted.

"You're not going to let her seduce you, right?"

Chris thought for a moment. His immediate reaction was

no, but he did find it possible that he could have a relationship without anyone knowing.

"I hope your answer is no." Cole laughed. "Brother, you've hit the jackpot with jobs in your field. Don't you dare mess this up. If you so much as even breathe around this woman, you're going to get yourself into trouble."

"It's not like that," Chris reassured him. "We're friends."

"Keep it that way," Cole said. "Look, man, I have to go. I'll catch you later, all right? It was good talking to you. Glad to hear you're doing well. I mean that."

"Appreciate it, Cole. Talk to ya later."

Chris hung up feeling like a weight had been lifted off his shoulders. It was nice to know that some people still had his back despite everything that had happened.

# 7

Chris stood at the window in the cottage and watched Morrie arrive. Things had been tense between them since Morrie confronted Chris about their working hours. Since then, Chris had done his best to avoid Morrie as much as possible.

A few minutes later, Kara strutted to the cottage in a tight dress and high heels. She carried two paper cups of coffee, like she did most mornings that she visited Chris.

Prepared for her arrival, and somewhat anticipating it with excitement, he opened the door partway and let her in. Technically, there was nothing ethically wrong with them meeting on a regular basis to talk about her feelings, but it still seemed illicit.

"I hope you don't mind, but my friend gave me some yummy liqueur that I thought you might like. There's only a little splash in the coffees."

Chris had stopped drinking in the morning, but he took the drink and enjoyed a sip. "That is good. How was your trip into the city?"

"Oh, it was nice," she said, taking her spot at the table. "It's so good to catch up with old friends. It feels like I'm speaking my native language when I'm around people my age—sometimes Perry doesn't get me like they do. We went out to a new restaurant, shopped, and then hit up our favorite nightclubs."

"You seem like you're in high spirits," he said, taking a gulp of his coffee.

"I am." She smiled. "There is so much life in the city. In a weird way, it's easier for me to breathe there. Meeting new and interesting people gives me life, you know? I like doing new and exciting things. Every day around here is so predictable."

"How long have you been feeling this way?"

She shrugged. "A while, I guess. I see all of my friends living their best lives in the city, and I feel left out. I know I shouldn't feel that way because a lot of them live in tiny apartments and have to work really hard to afford the things I have. Where are you from?" she asked, changing the subject.

"Nebraska," Chris replied.

"So living out here probably feels normal to you," she concluded.

"I'm from a pretty good-sized city, so it's actually been an adjustment coming here."

"Apart from now, have you really seen what life looks like beyond Nebraska?"

"No, not really."

Her face lit up. "There's so much of the world to see. I would love to show you. It would honestly be like therapy to me if we went into the city for a day. You could meet some of my friends, we could get brunch where the celebrities go, and we could stay at a five-star hotel and get room service. What do you think?"

He was considering it until she got to the last suggestion. She was no longer being covertly flirty. She was now dangling bait directly in front of his mouth, waiting for him to bite. Oh, he wanted to bite so badly, but it was wrong.

"I don't know about that," he said politely.

Kara looked Chris straight in the eye. "I'm just going to put all of this on the table. You're a single man. I'm clearly not that happy in my marriage. There's no reason why we should deny ourselves what we really want. What if instead of talk therapy sessions, we took care of our needs together? Perry and I hardly have sex. When we do, I'm always thinking about you."

Feeling uncomfortable, Chris shifted around in his seat. His face felt warm, and there was a thin layer of sweat forming above his top lip.

"Do you find me attractive, Chris?"

Flustered, he tried to come up with some words that got him off the hook and demonstrated that he was merely an employee and not someone to socialize with.

"It's a yes or no question," she teased.

It was a simple question, but a complicated answer. The truth was obvious. The lie was just plain mean.

"Yeah, I guess," Chris said quickly, looking at the table.

"Then I don't see what the big deal is," she said. "Two consenting adults shouldn't have to worry about something like this. It's not like we can't be discreet. If I told Perry that I wanted someone to come to the city with me and it was between the two of you, he'd send you in a heartbeat and wouldn't think twice about it. He's a trusting guy."

"And that's the problem," Chris interrupted. "It's not like

Perry is a scumbag. He's a nice and trusting man who would be devastated beyond repair if he knew that you were fooling around with someone else."

Chris didn't even realize it when he made his argument, but he was considering if it would be worth it to take Kara up on her offer. He wanted her badly, but he also wanted to keep his job and avoid hurting Perry. He couldn't imagine ever talking to his sister ever again if he screwed this up.

"I don't think this is an issue between you and me," he said, returning to his therapist voice. "I think you're bored with your marriage and are looking to go outside of it to get what you need."

She twirled a strand of hair around her finger. "Is there any benefit to doing just that?" she asked innocently. "From a therapist's perspective, of course. I'm in a committed relationship with Perry. I think it would be best for us to stay married. If he isn't able to satisfy my needs, would it be so wrong to take care of myself for my own well-being? If I don't, am I destined to slowly descend into madness because I feel trapped in my current relationship?"

At least she was giving Chris questions he could answer with reasonably sound advice.

"Yes, there are some couples who open their relationship for extramarital affairs. However, Perry needs to be involved in that decision. If you talked to him about going outside the marriage for sex, then it could work out. But the two of you would have to communicate and make clear rules."

Kara rolled her eyes. "I don't think Perry would want to talk about that. Don't you think that what he doesn't know won't hurt him? I walk on eggshells around him all the time because it doesn't take much for him to spiral."

Chris felt some sympathy for Kara and her unfulfilling

relationship, but he couldn't ethically help her cheat on her husband, especially with him—even though he knew he might get away with it for a short while.

"It's just not right," he said simply. "And I'm flattered that you want to be with me, but I'm not the kind of guy who hooks up with married women—especially women who are married to my boss."

"Then what kind of girls do you like to hook up with?" she asked. "If it's role-play you want, I can do that."

Chris blushed. "Unless you could role-play as a woman legally separated from her husband, it's not going to happen," he joked.

"Men are so sentimental," she complained.

"This man knows that he's got a good job and doesn't want to mess that up. I don't need to worry about losing my job, do I?" he asked, trying to ensure that Kara wouldn't do anything crazy to get her way.

"No," she said with a soft smile. "I want you to stick around. You're much more pleasant on the eyes than Morrie."

Kara got up from her seat, then leaned down, resting her elbows on the table to get one last word in. Chris could see all the way down the front of her dress. She wasn't wearing a bra, and it seemed like an intentional choice.

"We don't have to come to a final decision right now," she purred. "You can think of it as an open invitation." She stood back up and walked to the door.

Chris was transfixed on her ass in her tight dress.

"Same time tomorrow?" she flirted.

He could only manage a nod. His mouth was suddenly dry.

"See you then."

Chris waited a beat, then got up and went to watch her from the small window in the door. When he got there, he saw her pass Morrie in the path between the main house and the staff house.

Morrie's eyes immediately locked on Chris's. He had been caught.

# 8

Morrie couldn't prove anything. If he had suspected any unethical relations between Kara and Chris, there was no way to pin anything on him. It was Kara's property as much as it was her husband's, so she could decide where to go and whom to talk to.

Still, Chris had a terrible feeling in his gut when Morrie walked to the cottage and made himself at home. He waddled to the cupboard, took a glass, and filled it with water, gulping loudly while Chris waited for a lecture to begin.

"Perry is having more motor problems than usual," Morrie said, catching his breath. He went to the couch and plopped down.

"Oh," Chris said, not expecting the talk to be about work.

"His hands get a little shaky, especially if he's holding on to something. It's nothing major, but he gets pretty frustrated about it, especially if he feels like it's affecting his work. I scheduled an appointment for him to see his doctor."

"I've started to notice that his perceived health is a trigger for him," Chris replied.

"That's why I always try to downplay any ailment that comes up. He will make a big deal out of a paper cut, so you've got to keep him from panicking about it."

Morrie's approach seemed a little callous, but Chris wasn't going to criticize anything Morrie was doing—not while Morrie knew about Kara visiting Chris.

"I would caution you against coddling him," Morrie continued. "It will make it harder for the two of us to work with him. He needs structure and a reminder about what the real world is like. Otherwise, I think we're setting him up to fail in social settings. Not every client or business partner is going to hold his hand and talk about his feelings."

"Okay," Chris said. He disagreed about their role in Perry's life, but this was not the hill he was going to die on.

"Good," Morrie said. "Now, let's talk about the elephant in the room—or should I say the boss's wife in the room." He seemed pleased with his joke.

Chris felt all of the color drain from his face.

"This was part of the orientation that I didn't want to bring up. Now, it's none of my business what you do with your life outside of work. But if it affects the boss, it affects me, so I'm going to let you in on a little secret. Kara Bryant is bad news."

Chris frowned. Sure, she was a flirt, but it seemed over the line to call her bad. "How so?" he asked innocently.

Morrie smirked. "What was she doing here right before I came in?"

Chris took a deep breath. "It's not really my place to say, but she occasionally stops by to chat about her life. I think she wants the benefit of having a therapist without Perry knowing that she's talking to someone. I see it as being part of an ethical practice. Their money pays my salary, so I should be able to take her on as a client while I'm off duty."

"Is that so? What kinds of things does she tell you?"

"You know I can't say," Chris said firmly.

"Sure, sure," Morrie muttered. "You need to be very careful and decide if letting her vent to you about her nonsense problems are really worth your job and your reputation."

"It's not fair to say that her—"

"Let me tell you a little story," Morrie interrupted. "Once upon a time, there was a young, hunky maintenance guy who worked here when the couple redid their pool area. He would have had the chance to stay on and do other work around the property, but he was caught fooling around with Kara."

Chris's eyes widened in surprise. "What did Perry do when he found out?"

Morrie grunted. "He's the one who caught the two canoodling. Mind you, it wasn't intercourse, but from what I heard, they were scrambling to get dressed and decent when they were caught. Perry was obviously upset, and Kara tried to convince him that he was losing his mind and had hallucinated the whole thing. She did her damndest to convince Perry that the poor guy came on to her and she was trying to push him away."

"Did he buy that?" Chris asked.

It didn't sound like Kara. She was bored and flirty, but she didn't seem devious. In fact, during their sessions, Chris felt sorry for the woman, who clearly didn't make a great choice in getting married to Perry so young.

"Yep. That kid is seriously lucky that Perry didn't try to

press charges. Perry was so nervous about it, and Kara told him to just forget about it and hire someone else. So he did. Perry was a wreck over the whole thing, Kara was sullen, and I had a big mess to clean up."

Chris was having a hard time believing Morrie. It sounded too much like a soap opera to be true, and Morrie seemed like the type to exaggerate a story in order to make someone look bad.

"It wasn't just the pool guy," Morrie said snidely. "She has flirted with everyone here—even some of the girls. She is hypersexualized and made the mistake of marrying the only man I know who doesn't recognize how big a bombshell she is. It's actually pretty ironic. If you want to know how far she goes, get this: she even tried her moves on me." He leaned back with a satisfied smile on his face.

Chris was disgusted at the thought of someone so beautiful and someone so unappealing getting together, but he kept his stony visage. "Yeah?"

"Not long after I started working with Perry, I would occasionally use the pool for therapy after a knee replacement. She would always wait until I went out, parade around in her tiny bikini, and then swim right up to me and get handsy. I told her straight away that I was a happily married old man with kids and that I wasn't going to let some little hussy mess things up for me. She was pouty, but she's left me alone since. If you're wondering why she's so cold to me, that's the reason."

Chris tried not to laugh at Morrie's story. Chris could see Kara flirting with a hot, young pool boy, but to think that she would come on to Morrie was absurd and impossible. No one in their right mind would hit on Morrie, especially one of the hottest women Chris had ever met. He figured the reason Kara was cold to him was because Morrie had an abrupt personality and wasn't very likable.

"Just promise me that you're not going to make my life harder by chasing after her," Morrie pleaded. "If you ignore her, she'll get bored and move on to someone else."

"You don't need to worry about me," Chris said. "This isn't a job I want to lose."

"Oh, and do you know what else would help the both of us out? Convince Kara that she's in a healthy, loving relationship and that it would be stupid to hurt Perry."

Chris bit his lip. "I'm not in the business of putting ideas into people's heads," he said, implying that his counterpart was more apt for that kind of emotional manipulation.

"All right," Morrie relented as he got up from the couch and headed toward the door. "Keep your head on a swivel and don't forget who pays your salary."

"Got it," Chris said, eager to see Morrie to the door. As he left, he spotted Kara going out to her car, now wearing a flowy, yet short, sundress.

Chris had no choice but to take Morrie's warning with a grain of salt. Morrie didn't like Chris, and he was annoyed that his presence affected his work hours and the status quo around the property. Anything he could do to make Chris's life slightly more unpleasant, potentially to the point where he might want to leave, could be in play. Kara might be a flirt, but it was clear that she wasn't flirting with Morrie.

He felt for his employer and his failing marriage. As someone whose marriage had ended in part from poor mental health on his end, he saw how a partner could struggle to deal during difficult times. Perry was a good man, yet he required a lot of care, attention, and gentle handling. Kara's life was too fast-paced for him. Chris didn't entirely understand why they'd ever matched up in the first place.

As much as it felt wrong to be the other man in this scenario, he couldn't help but imagine himself with Kara. She was just too irresistible.

## 9

Chris knew he was in trouble when he found himself thinking about Kara during his sessions with Perry. He had to make a special effort to remain professional, as he had the urge to dig into their marriage and see what things were like on Perry's end. Poor Perry was too focused on his issues with work to even consider that anything was amiss in his marriage.

Chris did glean that Kara was, whether they realized it or not, the impetus for Perry's increasingly aggressive business model. If it were up to Perry, he'd create his art in peace and have an assistant sell it on the internet, completely removing himself from the transactions. He would still be able to earn a fine living, but he wouldn't amass as much wealth as he currently was. It seemed as though it was Kara, along with other business partners, who urged him to meet clients, attend events, and take part in investment strategies to expand his career. This was where much of Perry's anxiety came from.

"I do think about pulling back on my work," Perry

admitted during a session with Chris when he was particularly worried about work. "Though, I do enjoy the fruits of my labor," he said, gesturing to the tall windows in his studio that let in warm sunlight.

Chris often looked out the windows during their sessions, admiring the rich greens and blues in the scenery.

"But I think I could scale back without too much trouble. I've lived in apartments and small cottages and have been just as happy. Kara would never be okay with that, though. I don't think she would ever have given me the time of day if I only ever lived in a three-bedroom cottage. She's not the type of woman to go out and get her own job, so I have to keep doing whatever it takes to support the lifestyle she wants."

"Do you ever feel like you're putting her needs above your own?" Chris asked.

"Oh, sure," Perry said casually. "But at the same time, I need companionship. There have been times when I have been so paralyzed by my own brain that I don't know where I would be if there was no one else around. I don't know if I can ever be alone again. I don't have a lot of family besides my sister, and she has her own life, so I couldn't ask her to take care of me."

Chris twirled a pen with one hand as he listened to his boss. "Yeah, but you've got a pretty extensive staff. I don't think you ever need to worry about not having someone to help you out of a tough spot. Even without them, you'd still have Morrie and me."

He smiled. "Yes, I know I can count on the two of you. You've been invaluable to me, and I would never want to go without someone to help me in this capacity. Kara is able to help me in other ways. I know you're not married, so you might not fully understand this, but there is something very nice about having a beautiful woman at home."

"I think I can understand," Chris said softly, the void of such a presence causing an ache in his gut. His ex was a natural beauty, someone whom he felt proud to have at his side. Until the divorce, he couldn't imagine not having her in his life. Now, his sights were squarely on Kara. It felt uncomfortable to think about the desire for the same beautiful woman as his client.

"Well, our hour is up," Chris said, shifting in his seat. "The next time you go into a meeting, I want you to remember that you can offer something that no one else can. If the work isn't serving you, you can say no and walk away. I'm no accountant, but you have plenty of resources to take care of yourself and your needs. You have to put yourself and your happiness first."

Perry smiled and nodded. "Thank you, Chris, for your perspective. I find myself getting too caught up in this lifestyle, and I forget my passion for the art."

Chris nodded.

"I'm going to go for a short walk. It's too nice a day to stay inside." With that, Perry left without another word.

Chris took some quick notes about their session to keep on file. Then he got out of his chair, stretched, and stole a glance out the tall window in the studio room. He spotted Morrie trudging toward the house for his shift, and he felt glad that he could have a few moments to himself. Chris didn't have much to do, but he was starting to enjoy having leisure time again.

Morrie stopped on his way into the house to talk to Kara.

Chris's stomach dropped. He squinted and pressed his nose up against the window to read lips—expressions—

anything. Chris hoped that Morrie wasn't talking about him and the conversation they had shared about Kara earlier. Grabbing his things, he rushed out of the room and flew down the stairs.

"Hi, Morrie," Chris said breathlessly, trying to interrupt their conversation.

"Everything all right?" Morrie asked, raising an eyebrow.

"Oh, yeah. Had a good session with Perry. I'll share the notes later. What are you up to?"

Morrie shrugged. "Just trying to have an easy day. I'll catch you later. Darryl said he had some new recipes for me to try."

Kara had left without giving any hint as to what she had been talking to Morrie about. Morrie made his way inside without saying anything else to Chris. This left Chris wondering if he was being paranoid as he walked back to the cottage.

He made a snack and watched TV for a few hours to kill time before joining Darryl and the other employees for their family dinner. It was leftover night, which meant that Darryl created an inventive meal using whatever was left from the previous week's menus. Chris enjoyed seeing what the chef could make using ingredients that seemingly didn't go together, so it was one meal that he did not miss. Plus, he knew that he would walk past Kara as she ate her dinner, and he liked getting any benign opportunity to see her.

Normally, Chris dressed casually around the house, as Perry was relaxed about the staff dress code. A pair of khaki shorts and a T-shirt was the daily uniform for most. However, Chris felt like a slob compared to Kara, and he didn't want her to see him in that light. So, he pulled on a pair of chinos and a golf shirt that he thought would accentuate his lean, but muscular figure, but not look so overdressed that he would be out of place. It was more effort than he normally put into his appearance, but if Kara noticed him as she ate her dinner, it would be worth it.

Chris felt nervous as he walked toward the house for dinner. He prided himself on being good at rationalizing his feelings, but he had no control over the sensations going through his body.

Ordinarily, Chris would walk around the dining room so he wouldn't interrupt his boss and his wife as they sat down for supper. However, he decided that this night, he'd walk right along the edge of the room they were in.

"Chris, come here," a sweet voice said before he even made it through the doorway of the dining room. "I have something to show you."

Chris's heart leapt in his chest as he walked toward Kara. Perry was too engrossed in dissecting a piece of chicken breast to even notice that he was in the room.

"I saw this cute video of some golden retriever puppies playing in a sprinkler," she said, flashing the screen toward his face.

Chris had told her about his old golden retriever growing up, and that if he ever had a big place of his own, he would get one.

"They're so cute," he gushed.

"I know." She smiled. "Made me think of you." She put her phone down and returned to her dinner.

Chris walked toward the kitchen, trying to pick apart her words. Was she calling the dogs cute, or was she calling him cute? Either way, she remembered something about him and thought of him when a video caught her eye. Kara wasn't the type to make a connection like that with all of the employees.

Chris felt too giddy to listen to what Darryl's menu was for the evening. The only thing occupying his mind was the fact that Kara thought about him when they weren't together. He absentmindedly drank his "wine blend," which was Darryl's creation that consisted of any undrunk wine in the bottom of old bottles mixed together.

He was almost to the bottom of his drink when he heard the sound of broken glass and a shriek.

## 10

Darryl, Morrie, and Chris jerked their heads toward the door, quickly looked at each other, then hurried up the stairs. Chris's heart pounded as he climbed the stairs two at a time.

They all raced to the dining room to see what the commotion was. Perry and Kara were standing, their body language tense. Morrie, being the one on call that evening, rushed to Perry's side. Perry was standing with open hands in front of his body. His face was turning red, and he was trembling slightly.

Kara stared at her husband, her jaw tense and her hands balled into fists. She shook her head at the broken glass and scoffed.

"What happened?" Morrie asked in his gruff voice.

"He dropped one of the crystal goblets," Kara said, sounding like she was going to cry.

"I told you that my hands have been shaky and weak lately," he snapped back.

"If you knew you couldn't hold on to it, why not use a different glass? You know how special those are to me."

"Then we can buy new ones," Perry retorted, his voice much harsher than Chris had ever heard it. He had never seen Perry be anything but kind with his wife.

"No, we can't," she cried. "These were a wedding gift from a friend. They were handcrafted in Italy just for the wedding. They are one of a kind."

"I'm sure we can find the artist."

"The artist?" she snarled. "The artist is my friend's great-uncle. He died shortly after the wedding. This isn't something you can throw money at and make it better. That was a priceless and perfectly unique set that I can never get back."

Perry scowled and pushed his chair away, taking a step closer to his wife. "There are more important things than material objects!"

Kara shrank back into her seat.

"You're more concerned about some drinking glasses than the fact that my damn hands don't work like they're supposed to," Perry continued. "You're upset that you can't get your precious expensive cups? What's going to happen when I can't work, and you have no money? If I can't use my hands, you can't live in this house and go on vacations and go shopping. What the hell are your little drinking glasses going to do for you then?"

"Stop!" she shouted. "You're being awful. You're the one who broke it. I'm just telling you why I'm upset about it."

"And I'm telling you why you don't get to be upset all the time. You don't care what happens to me as long as you still get the things you want without having to work for any of it. What if I pulled out of all of my business deals and investments? I'd be a much happier man, and I probably wouldn't have to take so many pills. What then? If I lived in a two-bedroom apartment in a small town, would you still want to stay married to me?" He paused to catch his breath.

Kara was silent.

"That's what I thought," he said softly. "Why the hell am I even here if I can't live for myself and enjoy what my hard work has bought?"

"You're being dramatic."

"And you're being a freeloading bitch," he said coldly.

Chris stood in the dining room, absolutely shocked. From what he knew about their marriage, it wasn't particularly warm and loving, but it was civil. He had no idea just how ugly their fights tended to get or how mean Perry could be. What made it worse was that Morrie was supposed to be the first one to respond to Perry, but he stood by and did nothing. In fact, he seemed like he was entertained by the whole spectacle.

Kara burst out crying and stormed out of the house.

Chris glared at Morrie. "Help him," he hissed. He had no doubt in his mind that Perry only said those things because he was dysregulated.

Morrie shrugged and guided their boss away from the table while Darryl sheepishly grabbed a broom and dustpan and cleaned up the mess. That left Chris to chase after Kara.

She hadn't gotten far by the time Chris walked out the back door. In the dim light of the sunset, he could see her briskly walking toward the manmade lake on the outskirts of their property. Her glowing hair was blowing in the wind. It took Chris some effort to close the gap, but he eventually jogged to catch up with her at the boathouse. Because it wasn't boating season yet, the couple's speedboat was in storage, leaving the boathouse and dock empty save for some supplies.

Finally, Kara stopped at the sheltered dock and sat down in a hammock that was suspended from the structure's roof.

"Kara," Chris said softly, testing out the waters. He didn't know how she would react to being followed.

"I don't know how much longer I can do this," she cried, covering her face with her hands.

"I didn't know he could get angry like that," Chris said, feeling guilty for some reason that he couldn't exactly place. He wasn't their marriage counselor, but he felt somewhat responsible for the advice he had given each partner in private.

"Yeah, he can get pretty nasty when things aren't going well." She sighed. "I'm sure you're going to tell me that he only says those things because of his conditions, but it still hurts my feelings."

Chris frowned. "No one gets a free pass to say things like that to someone they love. I understand why his brain would go there. He's scared about a lot of things. Sometimes fear presents itself as anger. It's something he's working on, but it doesn't excuse how he acted. You have the right to feel upset about your priceless items being destroyed."

"It doesn't feel that way." She sniffed. "I sometimes feel like I'm the mother to a spoiled brat. He throws tantrums, and I just have to sit there and take it. I don't have any other options, though."

"Why not?" Chris asked as he looked for a place to sit. The outdoor furniture looked like it hadn't been cleaned since the previous summer, and he didn't want to get his one nice outfit dirty.

"You can sit up here," Kara said, scooting over in the sturdy hammock.

Chris thought about it for a moment before reluctantly joining her. Even though their hips and sides were the only parts touching, it sent a wave of nerves through Chris's body. It didn't seem to affect Kara at all.

"I'm afraid that Perry's right about me," she said dejectedly. "I am a freeloader."

"That's not fair," Chris said.

"I could have had a career. I studied art history in college. The idea of working in the city and running a gallery seemed so romantic. I thought I was going to have this amazing big-city life. I was a little naïve because I graduated college and there wasn't space for someone like me in New York or LA. My friends who planned on being fashion designers are assistants at labels and are basically servants to the big designers. They're still making a living and enjoying the grind of the city, and I'm here. I wanted a certain lifestyle, and this was the only way I could get it."

"By marrying someone with money?"

Kara sighed and pushed a strand of hair off her face. "Yeah," she said softly. "I met Perry through a friend. I wouldn't say that it was love at first sight, but I thought he was interesting. I loved his work, and it revived my dreams of collecting and selling art. He wasn't distributing it like he is now, and I wanted to get in on the potential business. I helped him make a few connections, but once he got big, all of the men working with him shut me out, and I was relegated to girlfriend. At that point, I thought about breaking things off and moving on, but with this new money, he started spending so much on me."

Chris struggled to listen to her story when he was sitting

so close to her. He could smell her sweet perfume whenever she moved. It was so intoxicating that he wanted to bury his face in her neck to take it all in.

"He was already building the house, but the plans started expanding. Once I stayed over, I knew that it would be impossible for me to return to a tiny, shared apartment in the city. When he asked me to marry him, I saw financial security. He was so good to me then, but his anxiety has spiraled since we got married."

Chris looked her in the eye. "Did you ever love him?" This was a question he had for his own curiosity, as the answer could absolve him of guilt for lusting after her.

She shrugged and wiped her eyes on her sleeve. "I don't know. I feel so trapped and suffocated in this marriage."

"What if you left him?" Chris asked.

She slowly shook her head as she gazed out at the gentle waves hitting the dock. "Before we got married, Perry forced a prenup on me. Perry was clueless about it, but his lawyer convinced him that if I really loved him, I would sign it. I didn't have a choice if I wanted to get married. If I leave, I don't get a dime, nor do I get to keep anything in the house, so I would be broke and homeless. It's just not an option for me."

Chris knew exactly what it was like to be divorced, out of his home, and living day to day, not knowing if he'd have enough to eat. For someone who had always lived a modest lifestyle, it was hard. He couldn't imagine Kara living the same life he had when he was living out of his car. She probably had friends who would take her in, but she would struggle without her daily luxuries.

"What if you got a job?" Chris asked, looking for a solution to what seemed like a hopeless problem. "If Perry asks, you can tell him that you're looking for something meaningful to do. It wouldn't have to be anything too labor-intensive or time-consuming. You could work a little and save your own money in a separate bank account. That way, when you're ready, you have a job and some savings to help you out."

Fresh tears came from Kara's eyes. "I don't even know how I would do that. I've never had a real job. I have a degree that people tell me is completely worthless. I've lost a lot of connections because I've been sheltered away with Perry for so long. And I have zero marketable skills and no confidence in my ability to get a job. I am damaged goods. I only know how to be a housewife with staff to do all of the house things. I don't see a way out of this."

She turned to cry on Chris's shoulder. He wrapped his arm around Kara to comfort her. He held her close, stroking her hair as she sobbed. Chris felt sorry for her. She was in a loveless and borderline verbally abusive marriage and didn't have a way out of it.

They sat in the hammock for a few quiet minutes, slowly swaying in the breeze. Night had just fallen, leaving a tiny stripe of sunset at the top of the black horizon. Water trickled onto the sides of the dock, creating a soft soundtrack as Chris held Kara close.

Finally, she raised her head from his dampened shirt and wiped her eyes. "I'm sorry," she said as she regained her composure.

"Don't be," Chris said, mopping a tear track with his index finger.

She stared at him for a moment, then took his face into her hands.

Chris was completely surprised. There wasn't a second

thought in his mind once her lips touched his, though. He found his body softening into hers as he kissed her back. Chris wanted to remain in that perfect moment forever.

"I'm sorry that I've brought you into this," she clarified after finally breaking apart. "I know you work for my husband, but I can't ignore these feelings I have for you. If you want me to leave you alone and never bother you again, just say the word and you won't have to worry about me."

Chris held his breath. What he was doing was entirely unethical, and if he were caught, he'd be back to where he was a few months ago, only with a few more dollars to his name. He would have to tell his sister about what he had done to lose his job. It would ruin him.

But at the same time, he couldn't tell Kara no. He didn't want to. He wanted to stay in the boathouse for as long as he possibly could.

"Do you want me to stop?" Kara whispered as she stroked his chest.

"No," Chris said quietly.

## 11

When Kara propositioned him, Chris didn't stop to think about the fact that he was a quarter mile from the house where his boss was working through a stress reaction, nor that he had been with his boss's wife for upward of thirty minutes in the boathouse. It didn't occur to him that any of the other employees might stumble across them. The only thing that was on his mind from the moment he followed Kara into the boathouse was how desperate he was to be with her.

Chris had never dreamed of getting involved in anyone else's relationship, especially with a married woman. He had always been a rule follower, which included unspoken rules about sex and relationships. He had taken things slow with every woman he had ever dated, never once having a one-night stand, even in his college years.

Though Chris had weighed the ethics of seeing Kara when she stopped by his cottage, he didn't in the boathouse. He was way past the point of making a choice. His mind was made up the second she touched him and made it very clear that her marriage was nothing more than a signed document.

"You don't know how hard it is to go about my day, just knowing that you're always here," Kara breathed as she tugged at the bottom of Chris's shirt. "I've been thinking about how I can get you alone."

"I guess we found a way," Chris murmured, still in disbelief over what was transpiring.

"Do you ever think about me?" Kara asked after kissing his neck.

Chris laughed. "You are all I ever think about."

She looked delighted and untied the back of her sundress, causing the front to fall down and expose her designer undergarments. "So when you're working with Perry?" she asked with a wry smile.

"Thinking about being in a closed room with you," he replied, noticing that she liked to hear these things. They were entirely true, but something that he had been afraid to admit.

Before Chris knew it, both of them were stripped nude, trying to maneuver to a comfortable position in the hammock. They giggled at their clumsy movements until they finally settled with Chris on his back and Kara in full control.

"I've been waiting for this moment for such a long time," she gushed, tracing a long fingernail down Chris's abdomen.

Chris didn't have a single thought in his mind. Pure animal instinct had taken over, blocking him from thinking about any possible consequences. He hadn't had sex in such a long time and had never had sex with such a perfect woman in such illicit circumstances. He was locked in from the moment Kara expressed her intentions, and there was no stopping him from seeking out pleasure.

"You are so beautiful," Chris blurted as he studied Kara's face. He didn't know what he had done to deserve that moment, but he didn't question it.

She kissed him hard and then took control of the situation. Chris couldn't get enough of her body and touched every single inch of her, panting as he tried to keep up with her. He wished the moment could have lasted longer, but was entirely satisfied when she nestled in his side when they were both finished and basking in the afterglow. He ran his fingers down her bare arms, creating tiny goosebumps in his wake, and she wrapped her limbs around him.

The moment was short lived, however. An hour had passed since Chris followed her to the boathouse. Though no one came looking for them, they both knew that if they wanted to avoid getting caught, they had to leave. They devised a plan in which Kara would quietly go back to the house, and Chris would wait a moment longer before returning to his cottage. If asked about their whereabouts, they would both respond that they talked for a short while as they sat by the lake until Kara calmed down, then went their separate ways. Kara would claim that she took more time to walk off her anger, and Chris would claim that he went back to the cottage.

Kara gave Chris one last kiss before they parted. It was evident to Chris that her marriage was virtually over, but he still needed to stay in Perry's good graces in order to keep his job. It would be a one-off love affair under conditions that neither of them ever saw coming, though they had expressed their mutual attraction to each other.

After spending a few minutes on the dock, watching the

gentle flow of water in the lake, Chris got up, dusted off his trousers, and made the trek back to his cottage. He didn't see another soul that night, as most employees had left for the day. Morrie's car was still parked by the garage, but he was nowhere to be seen.

Chris slipped back into his cottage undetected, still riding high from the tryst in the boathouse.

## 12

Once Chris returned to his room, he hopped in the shower to wash away any evidence of the affair. He was still floating after his time in the hammock with Kara. He tried to compare it to the night he lost his virginity, in terms of pure elation, but it was so much better than that. It was as if he had experienced some sort of sexual awakening, it was new and exciting, but both partners knew exactly what they were doing.

Being in a celebratory mood, Chris went to his cupboard and poured himself a healthy portion of whiskey and dropped a few ice cubes into it. He sat on the couch and took a large sip, remembering that his dinner had been interrupted, and he had worked up quite the appetite. He shuffled back into the kitchen and threw together a simple ham sandwich before returning to the couch to watch TV.

Instead of watching the action movie on the screen, he replayed the affair in his head, forcing himself to remember every delicious detail. He would certainly need the memories to sustain him through the lonelier times on the property.

Eventually, the post-coital clarity kicked in, and he was able to rationalize his actions. It had filled a deep need at the time, but it had been irresponsible and unethical. It helped his conscience knowing that Kara and Perry's relationship was on the outs, and seeing that it made Kara happy. It was hard for him to see her so distraught over her life, so he chose to see their affair as a way to bring a very sad woman some joy and comfort. He knew he couldn't do it again, but at that moment, he didn't feel very remorseful. After lounging around for a few hours, he went to bed and had a restful night of sleep.

The next morning, Chris awoke with a nagging feeling in his gut. Perhaps it had been from overindulging in alcohol, but more likely the fact that he had sex with his boss's wife on their property while his boss was having a mental crisis.

After he got ready for the day, he headed toward the main house and was surprised to see that Morrie's car was in the driveway. From what he remembered from the schedule, he was the only one working with Perry that day. When he got to the house, he was unsurprised to see that Morrie was in the kitchen, not with Perry.

"I didn't know you were working today," Chris said to Morrie, feeling uneasy, as if everyone knew what had transpired the previous evening.

"I'm not," he replied plainly. "I'm here to pick up a bottle of wine. Perry offered me a bottle of something nice for my wife's birthday. I swear to god, if anyone pages me for something unnecessary tonight, I'm not going to be happy. Better yet, don't call me unless someone is dead."

"Got it," Chris replied. "What happened last night with Perry?"

Morrie let out a grunt and sat down on a barstool. "He was an absolute headcase for a while. I'm glad he has an appointment scheduled for his hand tremors soon, because he's freaking out about not painting and what that will mean for the rest of his life."

Chris nodded. "He does seem to stress out about money. I've tried to work with him about that."

"You know he mostly does it because he thinks he needs cash to keep his hot wife around," Morrie said matter-of-factly.

"They're not happy."

Morrie glanced at him. "Maybe you're too young to understand this, but if a woman like that has any interest in you, you go with it—even if she's crazy. Their relationship is transactional and is working exactly as designed."

Chris frowned. "He can be pretty awful to Kara. I get that he has a lot of anxiety, and she can inadvertently trigger it, but he can't talk to her that way. Are we really sure that we should be counseling them to stay together?"

Morrie shot Chris a confused look. "What are you talking about?"

Chris shrugged. "When it comes down to it, aren't we here to advise Perry on what is best for his mental health? If their marriage is causing strife for both partners, shouldn't we advise Perry to do what will result in the best mental outcome? If he's so stressed about making enough money to keep Kara happy that he's verbally abusing her, wouldn't it be better to help them work out an agreement that would allow them to separate?"

Morrie shook his head. "Kara knows what she got into,

and I don't think she's really as bothered as she acts. Yeah, Perry can be a prick to her when he's upset, but this is all part of the life she wanted. She can do whatever she wants on Perry's dime. If she has to take a little shit for it—well, it's part of the opportunity costs."

Chris pressed his lips together. Morrie was being unfair to Kara, and he wanted to defend her, but doing so might look suspicious.

"She's not happy," Chris replied. "I don't think their marriage is working out for her. If two people are so unhappy being together, why not help them be happy?"

"You're in over your head on this one," Morrie said. "It's not right to meddle in someone's relationship. Even if he came to me and said that he wanted to get divorced, I wouldn't go out of my way to facilitate it. That isn't why we're here, and it's never been part of the job description. We are here solely for Perry's well-being. He's paying us to help manage his conditions and make everyday life just a little bit better for him."

Chris disagreed, but Morrie wasn't the type of guy who wanted to debate and discuss options. Chris would just have to continue caring for Perry in the way he saw fit.

After Morrie left, Chris had a cup of coffee and a pastry as he read the newspaper in the living room. He nearly choked on his breakfast when he saw Kara strut past him in a short, skintight dress and high heels, car keys in hand.

"Working this morning?" she asked, lowering her voice conspiratorially.

"Yeah." He coughed. "In about ten minutes."

"Not enough time," she muttered. "I'm headed to the city. I'll see you later." She flashed him a smile, then walked out toward the garage.

Chris forced himself to do some mental math in his head to keep his mind wandering from where it should have been. He was busy multiplying numbers by seven when the alarm on his phone went off. Time to go to work.

He dusted the crumbs off his pants and went to Perry's study, where he was waiting for Chris. Perry seemed to be doing better that morning, but the white stubble on his face and dark bags under his eyes made him look tired.

"How are you doing today?" Chris asked as he sat down in his usual chair.

"Fine," he replied nonchalantly. Perry gazed out the window, then examined a sketch he was working on. "How are you?"

Guilt started to trickle in. Just hours earlier, he had had sex with his client's wife while he was in the middle of a mental breakdown. Now he was having a casual chat with the man who fucked his wife, asking how he was doing.

"Not so bad," Chris answered. "Do you want to talk about what happened last night? You seemed very upset."

Perry nodded. "I was. I see now that I was taking my fears out on Kara. I said hurtful things because I felt hurt. I felt like she was putting her things above my health. I shouldn't call her names or assume her intentions, even if I am upset. We talked things through last night and made up."

This surprised Chris. He was ready to hear about how their relationship was falling to pieces. It did explain why Kara looked so cheery that morning. Chris felt a strange feeling of rejection. It was silly to be upset that Kara had made up with her husband so soon after having sex with Chris, but he couldn't shake the hurt he felt, knowing that Kara was no closer to ditching her husband, as he had hoped.

"You talked last night?" Chris asked, trying to keep his voice normal and even and not calculate the time between having sex and working things out with Perry.

"Yes," he said. "Morrie helped me out, and I was able to calm down and get into bed after an hour or so. During that time, Kara was out on a walk to clear her head. By the time she got back, she seemed okay. We talked things over, and I got her a spa package in the city today to make up for the things I said. I think we're on track now."

Chris didn't know how to respond, so he smiled with tight lips. His mind was racing as he listened to his clueless boss be so oblivious about his marriage. At the same time, he was bothered by the fact that Kara was so nonchalant about their hookup. He didn't know exactly how he expected Kara to behave after they had sex, but quickly going to bed and forgiving her husband was not it.

"What exactly did you talk about?" Chris asked. "That is, if you don't mind me asking," he quickly followed up.

"Oh, not much. I just told her that I was sorry for what I said, and I understood that I couldn't replace the glass, but I would do whatever else I could to make it up to her."

"What did she say?"

"That she would try to move past it. Then I gave her a big kiss, and we went to sleep," he said, looking satisfied.

"I'm glad you were able to talk it out," Chris said inauthentically.

"Same here," he said. "It does reassure me to be able to talk about these things with her. I know I'm not the perfect husband, and I don't always think she's the perfect wife, but we're trying, you know?"

"Yeah, I hear you," Chris said absentmindedly.

The guilt was sinking further into his skin. He decided

right then and there that he couldn't be intimate with Kara in any way now. In fact, he would no longer see her privately for therapy sessions. He promised himself that he would be cordial to her when he saw her in passing, but nothing more. It was the right thing to do for his career and his conscience.

Besides, it didn't seem as though Kara had been that moved by their encounter together. At the time, she'd seemed very interested in Chris, but hearing how she'd moved on with her husband immediately afterward slightly soured the memory.

Around midnight, Chris heard a tap on the window in his small room. He ignored it at first, assuming a bug had smacked into the glass, and he continued watching a show on his phone. Then he heard it again, this time too rhythmic to be a fluke. He slowly pulled up the shade to see Kara wearing a floor-length dressing gown. She stood at the window with her arms crossed.

He gawked at her sudden appearance and raced to the front door. Luckily, no one ever stayed at the guesthouse, and no one saw as he pulled open the door and ushered her inside.

"What's going on?" he asked, suddenly feeling awake and alert.

"I was lonely and thought I'd stop by to see you," she responded, walking into his room, and making herself at home as she sat down at the foot of his bed.

Chris let his head hang down in dismay before he followed her into his bedroom. He took a seat at the opposite end, just to leave a few feet of space. "I don't know if it's a good idea to talk to you alone after what happened last night."

She shook her head. "I didn't come here to talk."

"No?"

"If I were bored and wanted a chat, I could call up a friend, silly." She giggled. "I came here to get more of what I had last night."

This got Chris's attention. "I thought you made up with Perry, and everything is fixed."

She laughed. "What makes you think that anything with Perry has changed?"

"I-I talked to him today. You also looked pretty happy when I saw you earlier."

"Because I got a full day at a spa," she replied. "It doesn't mean that I'm in love with Perry. It means that I still have the ability to do what makes me happy. Like it or not, you're part of that now."

Chris was feeling flattered again. He couldn't deny how nice it felt to be wanted. The circumstances of their relationship were not ideal, but it wasn't every day that a beautiful woman wanted him.

"What if we get caught?" he asked, slowly succumbing to her pull.

She leaned in and put a hand on his thigh. "No one else on staff is here, and Perry won't know. I usually go to bed later than him, and it's normal for me to sleep in another bedroom."

"But what about my career here?" he asked as Kara kissed his neck. His hands instinctively reached for her waist, pulling her in closer. Doing so, he realized that she was completely nude under her robe. She had planned for this all along. "What's your endgame?"

Kara playfully rolled her eyes, then kissed Chris on the lips, sliding her tongue into his mouth. "Do I need one? What if I'm just trying to do what feels good at the moment?

Is there anything wrong with wanting to find happiness wherever I can?"

Chris couldn't fault her for that pursuit, as he was in the same boat. Eventually, he was able to turn off his mind and his consciousness and let his body make the decisions.

As it turned out, this night was just as hot as the previous one. The thrill of giving in to temptation for the first time was gone, but the experience only helped Chris find his stride. The pair even went at it for a second round, as there was no rush for Kara to leave.

Exhausted from their exploits, Kara gave Chris a quick kiss before pulling her robe back on. She sauntered toward the front door so casually, Chris had to wonder if he was the first person to hook up with the boss's wife in the cottage.

"I'll see you later for my next appointment," she purred before sneaking back out into the night.

Chris had no time to protest or tell her that it was too risky. He still felt guilty, but not enough not to think about what positions he'd put her in the next time they were alone.

# 13

Kara didn't just permeate Chris's waking thoughts, she seeped deep into his consciousness, visiting him when he was asleep.

The night of her surprise visit, he had a dream that they were in a hotel room together, rolling around plush, white bedding in a sunlit suite. He felt completely safe and comforted and at peace. When he woke up to soft light coming through his window shade, Chris tried to force himself back to sleep.

As he got dressed for work, he revised his plan: he would avoid Kara while there were witnesses around. If he was on the clock, he would be nothing more than cordial and professional to her. However, if the coast was clear and she approached him, he would not refuse her touch. At this point, he wasn't sure if he could live on the property without it.

His first test came when he entered the house for his morning appointment with Perry. Kara was in the kitchen, drinking some sort of green concoction out of a tall glass with a metal straw. She was wearing skintight workout clothes and had her light hair tied into a bun on the top of her head.

"Morning," she said with a smile.

"Morning," Chris replied, trying not to pay attention to her perfect body.

"I'm going to head downstairs for a workout. Wanna join me?"

Chris wasn't sure if it was a serious request, or if she was teasing him. "I've got an appointment with your husband," he reminded her, lifting up his notebook and pen.

"Suit yourself," she said before bouncing down to their home gym.

Chris went to the kitchen and grabbed a glass from the cupboard and poured himself some ice-cold water. He took a few glugs before setting down the glass, wiping his mouth, and walking away. The brain freeze provided some distraction from Kara.

"Spend too much time out in the sun?" Perry asked when Chris came in for his daily check-in.

"I don't think so," Chris said, confused.

"Your face looks a little red," Perry replied. "I thought you might have gotten sunburned."

Chris raised a hand to his cheek. He must have still been flushed from his encounter with Kara. "Oh, maybe. It has been pretty sunny lately."

"I've noticed. My doctors tell me that sunlight is good for my mental health. I think it's been good for Kara, too. She seems happier."

"Yeah?" Chris asked, feeling guilty.

"I know I said some mean things about her intentions with me, but in a way, it comes from a place of truth," Perry said, lowering his voice. "She's actually pretty easy to please. I just have to get her something she wants and most things are forgiven."

"Is that all it takes to be happy?" Chris asked. "You don't think she's looking for companionship? Affection? Love?"

Perry shrugged. "She doesn't always want that from me. There are some days when she doesn't even want me to touch her. I haven't seen her turn down a gift, though."

"Have you ever considered marriage counseling?" Chris blurted.

"No," Perry replied, looking confused. "Why do you ask?"

Chris pursed his lips as he tried to find the right words. "I saw your fight. I wasn't sure how common those were."

"All couples fight," he said dismissively. "Do you think my marriage is bad?"

Remembering Morrie's words, Chris bit his tongue. He also didn't want to put Kara in a bad place by putting ideas into Perry's head.

"I'm not here to make judgments," Chris said, plastering on a smile. "I just want to explore what's going on in your life because we've found stressors that you never realized were below the surface."

"That's true," Perry answered, obviously proud of the progress he had made. "I don't think I've ever looked so hard inside my own mind until you came here. You've been an excellent addition to my medical team."

Chris was flattered by his boss's kindness, but didn't dare share the secret of why he was so fortunate to work with Perry. It was a good gig regardless of his situation, but it reminded him of what was at stake if he messed it up. It was hard to spend time around Perry, who trusted Chris with his life and mental well-being, yet go on to have sex with his wife on more than one occasion. Perry's marriage was on the rocks, and he didn't always treat Kara with respect, but he was trying to make Kara happy in the only way he knew how.

Plus, Perry was so good to Chris, never arguing when Chris told him hard truths—never even raising his voice when he was frustrated with his health. Chris had no doubt that Perry saw him as a friend and confidant, as well as a trusted mental healthcare provider. At times, Chris even saw Perry as a friend, as their sessions often led them to chatting on all sorts of topics. Chris was utterly conflicted as he found his entire personal code of ethics change every time he was in Kara's presence.

"Do you think I'm a burden to people?" Perry asked.

"What do you mean by that?"

"I appreciate Morrie's work with me, but I think he might be annoyed with me. It makes me wonder if other people are annoyed with me, but tolerate me because they need something from me."

"Do you have any evidence to back that up?" Chris asked thoughtfully.

Perry shrugged. "I really can't tell. That's part of what worries me. Reading facial expressions and body language doesn't come naturally for me. I've studied it like a student, but I usually have to accept things at face value. I've learned that people don't always tell the truth or mean what they say. I think I hear frustration in Morrie's voice, but he tells me that everything is fine, and I worry too much."

"Truth be told, Morrie is kind of a grumpy guy," Chris said earnestly. "I think everything annoys him—so don't ever take that personally."

He nodded. "And Kara tells me things are fine after we fight, but is she doing the same thing?"

Chris inhaled deeply. "I don't know her well enough to say," he lied.

"What about you? Are you always straightforward with me? I feel like I can trust you and that every word you say is genuine."

This landed like a punch in Chris's gut. "I tend to be a straightforward guy," he fibbed, trying to choose the right direction for their conversation. "If you're asking if I ever get annoyed with you, the answer is no. You're my client, and it's my responsibility to remain judgment-free and understand what is going through your mind. I would never be upset with you for feeling anxious."

Perry smiled. "Thank you. It's hard to go through life feeling like I'm missing a basic human sense. Can I count on you to help me sort out the lies from the truth?"

Chris sighed. It was a tall task, even for someone who wasn't currently deceiving him. "I'll do what I can. You also have to keep in mind, I'm neurotypical, and I can't always tell the difference."

"That's reassuring," Perry said, seemingly pleased to know that Chris was able to be deceived. "I'm not someone who has a lot of friends. When I was growing up, people thought I was weird because of how my mind works. As I got older, I've found more people who share my differences and others who understand it, but a lot of people never changed their mindset about autism or anxiety disorder. I feel very lucky to have you around because I never have to explain myself. I know I can forget to show gratitude, but I hope you understand how healing it's been to have someone on staff who really accepts me."

Chris wished his boss would stop talking. He was feeling guiltier by the minute. He had to remind himself that Perry's relationship with Kara was in the dumps, whether he knew it or not. It was a conflict of interest, sure, but helping Perry didn't have to prevent him from helping Kara.

And it didn't necessarily mean he couldn't help himself along the way.

Was it so crazy for him to attempt to enjoy what was left in his life?

## 14

After weeks of having an affair, Chris felt like he was in a relationship with Kara. Sometimes he even wondered if it was possible for him to be in love. He certainly felt a deep connection to her. Had their affair turned into something more than a little fling to blow off steam and fulfill biological needs?

Chris still felt guilty, but it seemed as though it lessened on a daily basis. He still worked hard to make his boss happy, but he hardly saw Perry and Kara as a married entity anymore. Instead, he saw Perry as more like a father figure or a sugar daddy to her. His role was merely to ensure that she was taken care of. Chris's job was to give her companionship.

Of course, he knew that Perry would lose his mind if he ever found out about them. At least once a week, Chris would probe into Perry's relationship satisfaction and ask hypothetical questions to judge how committed Perry was to his marriage. Chris couldn't understand why he wanted to remain in a loveless marriage, but he needed a wife like Kara needed Perry's money. Perry had convinced himself that he would be alone forever if she ever left him. Chris tried to convince him that he was worthy of love from others, or that being single wasn't so bad for a guy like him, but Perry remained firm. He took his vows literally and would not give Kara up until the day he died. Even when he fought with Kara, he still maintained that his relationship was essential to continue.

Chris didn't like to see Kara be unjustly criticized in these fights, but he found that their sex was the best on days that the married couple fought. On those days, Kara was super eager and often stayed longer for a second or even a third round of lovemaking. Their conversations were better, too. She would pump him full of compliments about how he was such a great listener, had such good advice, and how physically attractive she found him. His self-esteem had taken a nosedive in the past year, and hearing such nice things from a perfect woman made him feel good.

At times, he wondered if he was in a better place than where he had been before his life went to shit. Sure, he had a fine life in Nebraska with his wife, a stable job, and a handful of friends and family around, but he didn't have the passion and excitement he had now. He had a cushy job, saved just about every dime he made, and got to have the hottest sex imaginable. Things were surprisingly good for someone who had started to think that his life wasn't worth continuing.

"Realistically, how long do you think we can keep this up?" Kara asked one night after a particularly nasty fight with Perry.

"I don't have any plans to stop now," he answered. "Do you?"

"No," she said softly, stroking his bare chest. "That's the thing. The sneaking around has been exciting, but how long can we go on like this? I just want to have a conversation with you during the day, and I can't because there are too many people around. Sometimes, I'm in the mood in the middle of the day, but that's not an option. There are times when I just feel so trapped."

"Even still?" he asked, feeling a little hurt that he wasn't enough to make her feel cared for.

"It's just not enough. It's like having a good partner for one hour a day. I want to be able to freely express myself and not worry about who is watching. I want out of here, Chris. What do you think I should do?"

He saw the hurt in her beautiful eyes and wanted to do whatever he could to take it away. "I know it's not your first choice, but the most obvious thing would be to file for divorce."

"That won't work," she said stubbornly. "I wish it were an option, but it's not. I'm not in a place—we're not in a place where we can make that work for us."

Chris scratched his face. "The only other option I can think of is convincing Perry that he's just as unhappy and put the divorce on his terms. You know that he has a habit of giving you things when you're upset. What if you convinced him to give you some assets and end the marriage?"

"That would take a long time, and who knows if he'd even buy it. I feel like I'm wasting the best years of my life here. Before long, I'll be old, and I won't have the same opportunities that I do now."

Chris racked his brain for another solution. "I don't know, babe. I'm not sure what else we could do."

She was quiet for a few minutes before speaking. "I wish

he weren't in the picture anymore. I wish he would just disappear. I know it sounds harsh, but it's the only way I can keep my belongings and be free from him. I can't take the verbal abuse. I can't pretend to be happy when we're together. I just can't do it anymore."

"Why don't we keep working on Perry?" Chris said, not knowing how to respond to Kara's impossible wish. "I'll continue talking to him about your marriage and his options going forward. We'll make him see that the two of you aren't right for each other."

"And then we can be together all the time." She smiled.

Chris gave her hand a squeeze. "I would really like that."

After Kara left, Chris found himself brainstorming possible new careers that would support him if he left the Bryant home with Kara in tow. He knew he wouldn't be able to give her the things she wanted, but he would try his best to make her happy. He felt bad about meddling in their marriage, but Kara's mere existence made him question everything he ever wanted in life.

It almost made him laugh when he thought about his initial dream, which was to work with patients in a hospital setting and live a very modest, Midwestern life with a nice wife. Now, he craved a glamorous life with a supermodel-esque woman with an element of danger to their relationship. He would have to start planning his gradual exit strategy if he ever wanted to make his new dreams his reality.

The next morning, Morrie and Chris met to exchange notes at the cottage. The pair weren't the best at communicating about their client's condition. Chris reasoned that their break in communication was two-sided: Morrie thought he knew what was best for their boss and felt threatened by Chris's relationship with Perry, and Chris wanted to avoid the miserable old prick.

"Perry's shown some improvement with intrusive thoughts and feelings of panic," Morrie said as he flipped through his notepad. "He's not as agitated as he has been in the past. He reports feeling pretty good about his business endeavors, but has been fighting with his wife more than usual."

Chris nodded. "When we've talked about it, it sounds like his relationship with Kara isn't good, he doesn't have any plans or desires to improve things with her, but he doesn't want to separate. I know you said we don't meddle in his marriage, but at what point is it necessary for him to make a decision with that relationship?"

Morrie put down his notebook and looked at Chris, studying his face.

Chris willed himself not to give off any sort of tell.

"Is there something going on that you want to tell me about?" Morrie asked.

Chris immediately felt bile rise in the back of his throat. "What do you mean?"

"Why is this something you keep bringing up? Why are you so interested in Perry's relationship with Kara?"

Chris shook his head, trying to feign confusion. "Aren't we here to serve our patient? If everything else is going well except for his relationship with his wife, shouldn't we help him with that?"

Morrie stared back, obviously waiting for Chris to slip up.

Chris wasn't going to give him that satisfaction. "What do you think is going on? Just spit it out."

Morrie raised his eyebrows. "I'm just looking out for my

patient. You wouldn't be the first to fall for the woman. I already warned you about her. Have you been spending time with her?"

"I stopped doing counseling sessions with her," Chris said defensively. "Isn't that what you recommended?"

"Yes."

"Then what are you trying to get at? Have you seen me hanging around her?"

"No."

"I don't understand why you're questioning me on this," Chris replied. "Perry is unhappy about something, and it's our job to help him through those things. It's no deeper than that. The only issue would be if Perry thought I wasn't on his side. Has he expressed that to you?"

Morrie sighed. "No, you're his perfect shining star—a little buddy."

Chris frowned at his sarcasm. "Have you ever thought that maybe Perry wants to have someone who is nice to him? We both know that he doesn't have a lot of friends or people in his life who aren't dependent on his talents."

"And you're one of those people who depends on his talents and money," Morrie reminded him. "Remember your part in all of this. I can see how you get your role mixed up when you're here twenty-four seven, but you are not a friend or family member. You're a healthcare provider. You can't forget that."

"I won't," Chris said solemnly. "I haven't."

"Good," Morrie replied. "Have you noticed anything about Perry the past few weeks that I haven't?"

Chris flipped through his notes, scanning for anything pertinent to tell Morrie. It seemed like every interaction with the man went the same way. He was tired of being treated like an idiot, when he really felt like he was a much better therapist than Morrie was, apart from the affair happening on the side.

"The hand tremors come and go. Medication seems to be helping marginally. I think we should schedule another appointment in two weeks if we don't see improvement by then."

"Sounds good," Morrie said with a grunt as he stood. "Then I'll check in on the boss man."

## 15

"There's something I wanted to talk to you about," Chris said as he lay in his bed next to Kara, stroking her hair.

"Yeah?" she replied as she gazed into his eyes.

He melted whenever she looked at him in that particular way, like she was completely infatuated with him.

"I don't think it's anything to be too worried about, but I was talking to Morrie about how Perry was picking fights with you, and he was asking why I was meddling in your marriage. He was asking me as if he suspected that there was something going on."

"Really?" she asked, sitting up a little. "What would make him think that?"

"I don't know. I asked why he was bringing it up, but it didn't seem like he had any evidence. I don't think anyone has seen us together. If his only evidence is that I think your marriage isn't good, then he's got nothing."

"We should be okay, then. Maybe don't talk to Morrie about that. You can talk to Perry and try to convince him that we should come up with an agreement to separate, but don't tell Morrie."

"I usually don't, but we share all of our session notes. Plus, anything that I discuss with Perry can come up in his sessions with Morrie. Perry doesn't know what's going on. I'm pretty confident about that."

Kara sighed. "Do we get rid of Morrie? I can tell Perry that he's being creepy around me. Perry can get pretty jealous."

Chris didn't like that idea very much. Sure, it would get rid of the suspicious party, but lying about something that serious didn't sit right with him. "Morrie is very defensive about his employment here. Remember? If Perry let him go, Morrie would lose it. I'm afraid he'd go scorched earth on us."

"Okay, Morrie stays," Kara said, rolling her eyes. "Now, my next question is: do I stay, or do I go back to the house?"

Chris pulled her in close and smelled the sweet scent of her perfume. "Ten more minutes?"

"Fine." She giggled.

Their moment of bliss was halted when the jarring sound of Chris's work beeper rang. Perry called upon him so infrequently that he nearly jumped out of his skin when he was being summoned.

"Oh my god, he knows," Chris whispered, immediately feeling sick. "What do we do?"

"Go," Kara hissed, shoving his clothes at him. "If he asks, tell him you were sleeping and that's what took you so long to get to him. Once I know that he's occupied, I'll come back to the house."

Chris got dressed as quickly as he could with shaking hands. A minute later, he was out the door. He jogged to the house, punched in the door code, and navigated the dark hallway toward Perry's bedroom. When he knocked and opened the door, he found Perry writhing in bed, clutching his chest.

"I can't breathe," he gasped, still flailing around.

Chris went to his bedside and helped him sit up before coaching him through breathing exercises. It took a few minutes for both men to catch their breaths, but eventually Perry was able to speak.

"What happened?" Chris asked as he prepared Perry's medication under the dim light of a bedside lamp.

"I don't know. I woke up, and I had this bad feeling. Then my airway felt tight, and I couldn't breathe. I was barely able to hit the call button, and I thought I was going to pass out. My chest still feels very tight, and I'm scared I won't be able to breathe again."

After handing Perry his medication, Chris went to his mini fridge and pulled out a small ice pack and placed it in Perry's hand. "Squeeze this. Try to focus on how that feels. While you do that, go through your senses and think about what you're experiencing."

"I feel cold and sweaty," Perry mumbled. "I see dark shadows. I taste the bitter, chalky medicine. I hear your breathing. I smell..." Perry paused for a moment, looking confused. "I smell Kara's perfume."

Chris's stomach dropped. He was on the verge of having his own panic attack.

"Where's Kara?" Perry asked.

"I-I'm guessing she's in the guest room," Chris said nervously. "I didn't see her when I came into the house."

"Then why does it smell like her perfume?" Perry asked, latching onto that particular sensory detail.

Chris scrambled to find an explanation, but could only stutter, "I-I don't—"

"What about my perfume?" Kara asked. She strode into the room, clutching the front of her robe and yawning, as if she had just woken up.

"Oh," Perry said, softening slightly. "I must have smelled your perfume before you even got to the room."

"You have a sharp nose," she said. "What's going on?"

"Panic attack," Chris said, holding his shaking hands behind his back. "I think we've gotten it under control."

"Oh," she said, feigning surprise. "Is there anything I need to do?"

"Go back to bed, dear," Perry said, suddenly looking exhausted instead of manic. "I'm in good hands with Chris."

"Okay," she said, scanning the room for any sign of trouble. "Good night."

Kara was gone, but Chris feared that her scent still lingered. Did Perry really believe that his nose was so strong that he could smell his wife's perfume before she even entered the room? Perry was sedated now, but he wasn't an idiot. He was highly logical and intelligent, yet too trusting of those he thought he could depend upon.

"How are you feeling now?" Chris asked.

"A bit better," Perry said, relaxing back into bed. "What took you so long to get here? I thought I was going to suffocate to death. I thought I was making quite the commotion, but Kara didn't seem to hear me either, even though the guest room is so close."

"I can't speak for your wife, but I was sleeping and must have thought the alarm was part of my dream. It took me a second to get ready."

"You've been quicker in the past," Perry said absentmindedly.

"I apologize," Chris said sheepishly. "I'll try to be quicker."

"It's okay. I should remember that you're not a robot. It is just nice to have someone within arm's reach to help. You're friends with my wife, yes?"

Just when Chris was starting to reassure himself that Perry suspected nothing, dread struck him again.

"Oh, I don't know about friends," Chris said, plastering on a smile. "We don't cross paths often. Why do you ask?"

"Eh, I just wondered if she could learn how to do this stuff," Perry said. "I know she doesn't *like* to do this stuff, but maybe you could convince her to at least sit by my side until you show up. She should have heard me from her room. Honestly, she should be sleeping in the bed with me. Do you think it's weird that my caretaker can be roused from his sleep and make it here faster than my wife can when I'm in need of help?"

Chris shrugged. "I can't speak for your wife. All I know is that I'll bust my ass to get here as soon as you need me when I'm on duty, okay? In the meantime, we can work on strategies for helping yourself out of the panic state so it doesn't seem like such a life-or-death emergency."

"I think that would be good. Also, remind me to talk about my feelings regarding the fact that my wife and I haven't even touched in weeks. I'm not talking strictly about sex—she wouldn't so much as shake my hand if I asked her to. It makes me think something is going on with her."

"We can address that tomorrow," Chris said quickly. "How are you feeling now?"

"Very sleepy."

"Good. I will let you rest. Call me if you need anything else."

Before Perry could respond, he had drifted off to sleep.

Since it was the middle of the night, Chris gave him more sedation than he would if he'd had an attack in the middle of his workday. He typed out a text message to tell Morrie about the incident and to expect Perry to sleep longer than usual in the morning. Then he scheduled the message to be sent after six a.m., when he knew that Morrie would be awake. He hated being woken up if it wasn't an emergency.

"Wait." Perry's soft voice sounded as Chris turned to leave the house. "Can you stay here for a little longer? I'm afraid of having another panic attack alone."

"Sure," Chris gently replied, sinking down onto the couch at the far corner of the room. "I don't know if this will help ease your mind, but the medicine I gave you should make you sleep really well for the rest of the night. If I ever wanted to turn my mind off for a while and get some good rest, that's what I would give myself. In fact, I'm willing to bet that you have a perfectly dreamless eight to ten hours ahead of you. To be honest, I'm a little jealous."

"Really?" Perry asked drowsily. "Is it safe?"

"Of course," Chris replied. "I'm very careful about administering medication. I would never give you anything that I wouldn't take myself. I believe it's better to work on other coping mechanisms than to solely rely on medication, but we're still working on that. Tomorrow, we'll start working on taking the fear out of panic attacks so they don't trigger more attacks. Seeing as you've had so much progress over the past few months, I bet you'll continue on that trajectory with more work."

"Thanks," Perry mumbled. "I hope I can always count on you."

Before long, Perry was fast asleep, and Chris made his silent exit. As he walked out of Perry's room, Chris wondered what Perry meant by that last statement. Perry was always quick to sing Chris's praises as a loyal employee and friend. There was never the implication that he wasn't sure if things would always be that way. In fact, the more Chris analyzed their conversations that night, he had to wonder if Perry suspected that he was being betrayed. He seemed critical of Kara's absence and suspicious of Chris's delay in helping him.

Then again, it could have all been a result of Chris's paranoid mind and a mix of Perry's anxiety and heavy sedation. Chris and Kara had been as careful as they could be while still having an affair on the property.

As he walked outside into the pitch-black night, a chill ran down his spine that had nothing to do with the cool midnight air; he was officially spooked. He tried to convince himself that Perry was still too trusting to suspect anything, and he would be able to convince Perry of anything in their therapy sessions. It was just too coincidental that both Morrie and Perry would voice concerns on the same day.

Chris wished he had the powerful sedatives he had given to his boss at that moment so he could turn his brain off and go to sleep. Even though he was on call, he was confident that Perry wouldn't have any more issues that night, so when he got to the cottage, he poured a small measure of whiskey into a glass and downed it in one go before pouring a little more to sip on. He told himself that he could stop after that glass, as it wasn't good for his career to be wasted on the job, nor was it good for his booze habit, which he was trying to curb.

Next, he slipped off his shoes and went back to bed, waiting for the elixir to lull him to sleep. When he pulled the covers up to his neck, he smelled Kara's perfume—the same perfume Perry had sniffed out on him. It was intoxicating, but damn it—it was trouble. Chris was just starting to feel relaxed when he heard the front door swing open, then close.

"Hello?" he called out, feeling fear rush through his veins. Despite the alcohol, his mind was on high alert, waiting for any sort of danger to occur.

"We need to talk," Kara replied, her voice quiet and low.

She appeared in the doorway of Chris's bedroom, this time wearing sweatpants and a tank top instead of her lacy lingerie. Her eyes weren't soft and coy, but hard and unblinking, and her pouty lips were pressed together tightly.

This was a side of Kara that Chris hadn't seen before. Usually, her presence seemed to make all of his troubles melt away.

Now, he felt more ill at ease.

## 16

"Actually, can I get one of those?" Kara asked, pointing to Chris's drink.

He pulled himself out of bed and walked her to the kitchen, grabbing her a glass and a few ice cubes. He took the bottle from the cabinet and slid it across the table to her.

"Thanks," she said, sloppily pouring a healthy drink. She took a sip, winced, then drank a large gulp.

"Are you sure it's safe to be here?" Chris asked nervously. "Don't you think we should lie low for a while?"

She shrugged, almost as if she was bored by his concern. "Didn't you sedate him?"

Chris blinked. "Yeah."

"Do you think it was enough to knock him out for a while?"

"Yeah, he should sleep for quite a—"

"Then I think it's fine," she interrupted. "I couldn't be alone. I just got a weird feeling that I was being watched, when I know that there's no one else here but us three, and Perry is knocked out. It feels like all of the air is being sucked out of the house. I don't know how much longer I can do this."

"I know," Chris said sadly. "It was so much fun at first, but I think the stress is just starting to catch up with me."

"Same. But I don't feel guilty at all," she said firmly. "You know as well as I do that Perry and I have no business being together, and I can't stop trying to live a happy life because he's stubborn about marriage vows."

"Yeah," Chris agreed, though he wasn't as guilt-free as Kara. "He smelled your perfume on me tonight—way before you got to his room. Do you think he connected the dots?"

She sighed, then took another large gulp of whiskey, shuddering once she got it down. "God, I hope not. Even if he doesn't, what happens if he tells Morrie what he observed and it makes Morrie more suspicious? Morrie doesn't like either of us. He'd have no problem spilling the beans on our little secret."

Chris would have no chance of working in his field again if he were fired, so he would have to find a different career and potentially expose his secret to Kara. If Morrie or Perry researched him further, they would find evidence that could potentially convict Chris of a crime. Then he'd be looking at paying fines with money he had just saved up, or even worse, jail time. He wasn't technically supposed to be providing mental health services, and certainly wasn't supposed to be administering medications since he wasn't licensed in New York.

"Do you know what's worse than me asking for a divorce and losing most of my possessions and money?" Kara continued. "Perry filing divorce, being vindictive, and taking everything I have. I'm going to be out on the street without so much as my Louboutins on my feet. I'm not even exaggerating when I say this: we're absolutely fucked."

He wanted to run away, but didn't know where to run to. If he continued on his previous path, when he was homeless and moving from town to town, his life would surely end along that road. If he hadn't been hired by Perry, he might not have been alive to see that day. His depression had dissolved, and he never wanted to go back to that dark place. If he went back to living in his car, he knew it wouldn't take long before the darkness returned.

Then, there was Nebraska. He didn't want to show his face at home unless he was in a good place and could prove to everyone that he wasn't a complete fuckup. He did like the idea of being close to his sister and her family, and even welcomed the thought of reuniting with a few old friends. He would have to find a job outside of healthcare, but he was willing to part with the profession if it meant another do-over in life. He had enough savings from working with Perry that he could afford a slight pay cut in a new job. It wouldn't be ideal by any means, but with time, the locals would forget his name, and he could forge a new path in a familiar place.

Omaha would be a hard sell for Kara, though. It certainly wasn't New York, but there was an uberwealthy community that might embrace her. Or they could really commit to running away together and head to the West Coast—maybe even leave the country.

When it came down to it, he wanted Kara to go wherever he went. He was falling in love with her and didn't want to break things off. However, if she didn't want to follow him, then he would have no choice but to leave without her. The thought of being sued for practicing without a license or having his name in the papers again for bad healthcare practices scared the hell out of him. Chris didn't know if he could survive another public shaming.

"If I'm going to leave, I want to do it on my own terms," Chris said. "I could graciously thank Perry for my time here and tell him that I've decided to move back home to be closer to family. That's something that he could understand. He'd be disappointed, but he wouldn't bother me too much about it. That way, he wouldn't ever have to find out the truth. And if he did, I'd be long gone, and he wouldn't be able to fire me."

"What about me?" Kara asked with tears in her eyes.

His heart broke to see her so upset. He held her hand between his. "You could wait a little, then leave him. Tell him you're going to the city to stay with friends and that you don't want him following you. Then come find me. I have some money saved up, and I can find work somewhere else. I can make things work out for us—maybe then you can try working, too."

She shook her head. "I've told you before—it's impossible. There's no way I can just leave and ask Perry not to look for me. He would blow his money on a private investigator to keep tabs on me so he can beg me to come back. He'd just bother me relentlessly until I broke down. There's no escaping him when he gets obsessive."

Chris could see where she was coming from. Perry had the inclination to obsess over his personal interests. It was a trait that made him an excellent artist, as he could spend days agonizing about tiny details that made his work so impressive. But it wasn't always a positive personality trait when it came to interpersonal relationships. In some ways, Kara was one of Perry's shiny possessions, and Perry liked things to be in their proper place. He wouldn't let Kara go without a fight. Chris didn't understand why Perry wanted to hold on to a wife who didn't love him, but then again, Chris didn't understand a lot of things that Perry thought.

"I think it's worth a try," Chris said gently. "I think you know that things would be really hard for me if I got fired, but I don't think you understand just how bad it would be. I made a choice, and while I would never say that it was a mistake getting to know you, I have to live with the consequences of that choice. We're in different positions here. If he finds out about us, I'm gone and my life is basically over. Your life won't change that much."

Kara let out a frustrated sigh. "So what you're saying is that you'd abandon me here."

Chris shook his head, though the more he thought about it, that was pretty much exactly what would happen if she was unwilling to leave without her half of Perry's fortune. He could only be responsible for so much. He could leave and figure out how to support the two of them. If Kara didn't want to follow, there was nothing he could do about that.

He wanted to do everything in his power to be with Kara, but he was worried that she wouldn't put in the same commitment for him. He was willing to take a big risk to continue their relationship, but she didn't seem ready yet.

"Can I ask you something?"

"Sure," she replied.

"Do you want to be with me, or do you just want to be free from Perry?"

Her eyes widened, and she blinked a few times. "I-I want to be with you," she sputtered. "But we've found that it's not so easy to be together when Perry keeps getting in the way. I think you're able to run away on your own. I'm not as lucky. You're trying to protect your livelihood, which I understand. But I'm trying to preserve the last bit of my young life that I have. Perry's sixty years old and could very well live for another thirty. In thirty years, I'll be nearly his age now. I can't start over again at sixty—I hardly have a chance now, while I'm still in my twenties. If you leave to go back home, you're effectively sealing my fate."

Chris was taken aback by this comment. It was a serious claim to make and made him feel extremely guilty if his departure made her feel like her life was over. He didn't know a lot about the fashion and art scene, but he could see how age made a big difference, especially to such a young and beautiful woman. It was bad enough that she felt trapped in her current life, but now all of the pressure was on him. If she never got to live as a free woman, then it was all his fault. He didn't know if he could live with himself if he went back to Omaha and tended bar while the woman he cared about was trapped with an old guy who treated her like shit.

"I don't know what else to do," Chris said desperately. "Honestly, I'll do whatever I possibly can to help you out, but you're making it sound like an impossible scenario. You refuse to leave Perry, and Perry refuses to give you up. What else can be done when both of you have made up your minds?"

Kara squeezed Chris's hand and looked him in the eyes. "Babe," she said, melting his heart with her use of the pet name, "I had a thought that I want you to listen to—don't make up your mind just yet without hearing me out."

"Okay," he replied, putty in her hands once again.

"How many people know that Perry has a mental illness that is treated with sedatives?"

Chris didn't know where she was going with this train of thought, but answered anyway. "I'd say just about anyone who has spent time with Perry."

"And what would happen if he took a few too many pills?"

Chris narrowed his eyes, even more confused. "Well, it's not good to take more than prescribed. You could damage vital organs, go into a coma, or even die."

She pursed her lips. "What if Perry accidentally took too many pills, then?"

Chris frowned. "I'm not following."

She tucked a strand of hair behind her ear and took a deep breath. "Let's say that—hypothetically—he overdoses on his prescribed medication and passes away. Maybe he's feeling suicidal over his poor health, or maybe he's freaking out and misreads the label. In that event, I would get the money and the house and everything. I could keep you on as my personal mental health professional, and we could live here and be happy. I could hire a whole new staff who wouldn't blink an eye at us being together. Or we could learn how to cook, clean, and take care of the grounds ourselves. I'd be willing to give it a try if it meant that we could be alone."

"Kara," Chris said softly, not fully processing her suggestion.

"Or," she said, getting more frantic, "we could ditch this place for good. We could go anywhere in the world and just live the lives we want to live. Or if you don't want to be with me all the time, I could buy you your own place. And if you ever decide that you want to be on your own for good, I'd share the money with you. I know what it feels like to be stuck with someone for financial reasons, and I would never want you to feel like you have to be that way with me."

For some reason, Chris felt like his brain was moving in slow motion. He heard everything Kara said, but it was taking him a long time to understand what she was telling him.

"What do you think, baby?" she asked, clutching both of his hands in hers.

Chris sat still, his body unable to move until his brain finally caught up. "Are—are you asking me if it would be okay for you to kill your husband—to kill Perry—in order for us to be together?"

"Um," she replied, looking toward the ground. "I'm asking—hypothetically, of course—if you would be willing or able to help me be free of him. I've thought about it, and it's the only possible solution for escaping his abuse. There's no other way."

Chris immediately felt ill. She was suggesting murder. It was bad enough for her to want her husband dead, but even worse for her to request that he do the job. Perry was a bad husband and treated Kara like shit. Chris could also understand why Kara would want to live her own life instead of being tied to someone who wasn't right for her. But even if Perry was physically abusive, Chris couldn't comprehend killing someone. Especially Perry. Perry wasn't good for Kara, but Chris otherwise liked the guy. He had his flaws, but he got along with Chris, and they had nice chats during their sessions together.

For a single moment, Kara almost had Chris sold on a perfect out. He wouldn't have to worry about getting fired, providing for the woman he cared about, or dealing with moving back home. He'd live a very comfortable life alongside the sexiest woman he had ever known. Life would be incredibly easy.

But it would all come at a tremendous price.

## 17

"Kara," Chris said softly, finding that his voice was trembling. "No. I-I just can't."

Once again, her eyes filled with tears. "I had a feeling you'd say that. I get it. You don't want to take that risk for me. I'm just not worth the trouble."

"That's not it," he said hesitantly. "I want you to be separated from Perry just as much as you do, but what you're suggesting is just too much. I don't think I could live with myself if I were responsible for his death."

She let out an exasperated laugh and dropped his hands, pushing her hair out of her face with her slender fingers. "You think I'm a terrible person."

"No, I think you're feeling desperate," he said, reaching for her hands again. He wanted to provide her some comfort, as she was clearly reaching her limit.

"Do you know that Perry has been suicidal before?" she asked. "When he's doing really bad, he rants about how he wishes he wasn't around."

Chris knew about the ideations because Morrie had

filled him in on absolutely everything regarding their client's mental health. He had even heard Perry express these thoughts from time to time when he was very low, but it wasn't often or serious enough to even increase his prescription doses. Perry had his struggles, but Chris had seen improvement.

"I can't really talk about his health," Chris said, though he saw the irony in refusing to discuss something as trivial as mental health when his wife was kicking around ideas to end his life.

"Honestly, I think that it wouldn't be the worst for him."

"To die?" Chris asked.

"To not have to worry about the torturous life he is living," she responded. "There have been times when I just hoped he'd be put out of his misery. Early in our marriage, I wanted to help him—I really did. He'd scream at me and tell me how pathetic I was for getting upset at me, and I just wanted to see him be at peace. No one would be that shocked if he decided to take his own life. I think it would be guiltless."

It was clear to Chris that Kara had no experience with death. He knew firsthand that guilt was the primary emotion in that situation. Though time had passed and he was now in a good place, Chris thought about the young woman he'd accidentally killed on a daily basis. He didn't feel as much grief as he had in the months after the accident, but her life and the potential it held sat in the corner of his brain, and he wasn't sure if she would ever leave him.

He could reason that the girl was in a bad place mentally. Oftentimes young people who were hospitalized would go on to have suicide attempts in the future or live with depression. While many people were helped and went on to lead normal lives, he could have convinced himself that she would be right back in that ward another day.

That rationale never worked, though, because it wasn't his decision to make. Her family and friends wanted her to make it. Her teachers had worked very hard to make sure she was okay. Her coaches, pastors, and coworkers had wanted the best for her. Hell, even she didn't have the chance to express how much she wanted to live before it was too late. Many people who attempted suicide reported being thankful that they had failed.

Chris had a very hard time wrapping his head around the idea that putting Perry out of his misery would be a kind thing to do. It would be different if Perry had a painful terminal illness, but he didn't. He lived an unconventional life, but it was still a good one. An early death would be completely unjust.

"I think you would feel terrible guilt, and there would be nothing to help it go away," Chris said. A chill ran down his spine as he spoke, and he involuntarily shuddered.

"I'm not so sure about that," she said before biting her lip. "Have you ever heard of battered woman syndrome?"

"I've heard of it. It's often used as a defense for women who kill their abusers."

"Well," she said, raising her eyebrows, as if to prove a point, "that's kind of what I'm going through."

Chris pursed his lips. While he could see that Perry had the ability to be very unkind to his wife, he wasn't seeing the sort of psychological damage that she was implying. To his knowledge, Perry had never laid a hand on Kara. He didn't want to discount her personal experience with Perry, but he also didn't see the emergency she was talking about.

"And just think of what life could be like," she said.

"You're not his friend; you're his therapist. You owe him absolutely nothing. Without him in the picture, we could live our dream life together. Can you at least consider what I'm asking, and promise not to say a word of it to anyone?"

"Yeah, I can do that."

"Good." Kara smiled as she leaned closer to Chris. She placed her hands on his shoulders and gave him a peck on the lips. Then she slid her hands down his torso until they rested on his lap. "I should be going," she breathed in his ear.

Chris's mind melted again, and he wanted to make love to her, but before he could grab her, she had already turned on her heel and was halfway out the door.

"Wait," Chris called out to her. "Stay."

"I can't," she replied. "But you know what to do if you ever want to ensure that we never have to part again."

Chris slumped down onto his bed after she left the cottage. He felt like he was a character in a Shakespearean tragedy. The idea of being with Kara, completely unbothered and with riches beyond his wildest dreams, was more than he could have ever asked for. Unfortunately, he agreed with Kara that her plan was the only way it would work. Chris didn't want to cause harm to anyone, but he wanted to be with Kara more than every other night for an hour. He wanted to wake up in the middle of the night and feel her body pressed against his. He wanted to make her breakfast in the morning. He wanted to go on long car rides with her in the passenger's seat, heading toward some new adventure. He wanted a full life with Kara and still held out hope that it was possible.

After a night of fitful sleep, he awoke later than usual and had to rush to get ready for his day. It was technically his morning to work, but Morrie's car was parked in the driveway when he closed up the cottage.

"Grab your breakfast and come up to the boss's office," Morrie greeted him the moment he stepped into the main house.

Chris was startled by his presence. It was as if Morrie had been waiting for him to arrive.

"I didn't mean for you to get here so early," Chris said, remembering the text he had scheduled to send Morrie early that morning. "I just wanted to let you know what was going on, and I didn't want to wake you."

Morrie shook his head. "Don't worry about that. Grab your food, and let's go."

Chris had been considering taking whatever Darryl had prepared that morning, but suddenly lost his appetite. He poured himself a mug of coffee and trudged up the stairs, wondering what was going on.

When he got back upstairs, Morrie was still waiting for him, as if he needed to be escorted.

"He was in rough shape last night," Chris muttered as they walked together.

"We can talk about it together," Morrie said casually. "I think the boss wants us to be candid with him."

When they got to Perry's office, the two caretakers sat on a love seat near Perry's desk. Chris scooted to the far end of his side so his legs weren't touching Morrie's, as he had his knees wide apart. Perry sat in his desk chair, looking remarkably alert for the amount of sedation he had gone under not long before. Chris touched his lips to his mug, it was too hot to drink, but he found that he could excuse himself from speaking if it looked as if he were drinking.

"Given the circumstances of late last night, it might seem ironic to ask you this, Chris, but how are you doing?"

Chris looked up from the edge of his coffee mug and glanced back and forth between the two other men in the room. "Fine," he replied, then paused. "Why?"

"Morrie says it's important to check in with the employees every now and again. I was thinking about things this morning. You seemed unlike your normal self last night."

"What do you mean?" Chris asked. He felt his stomach clench, and beads of sweat were forming on his lip and brow.

"You're usually very calm, but upbeat. Last night, you seemed very stressed. Even in my state, I could see that."

Chris shrugged. "I was concerned about helping you."

"I can appreciate that, but it doesn't change the fact that you haven't been yourself lately. Even in our sessions, it seems like you're getting frustrated with me and some of the decisions I've made regarding my marriage."

Chris shot a glance at Morrie, who was pretending not to notice.

"That's how therapy sessions work, Perry," Chris said defensively. "It's my job to work through any stressors you may have. You've been fighting with your wife, and it's affecting your mental health. It's no different than you being stressed about investment meetings or gallery events. It's all part of your life."

"And you seem mad at me right now for talking about my concerns," Perry said.

With every word, Chris became more and more stressed. He put so much effort into suppressing his fears about being caught for his misdeeds that it was giving him a splitting headache. He cautiously weighed every word and every facial expression to ensure that he didn't give his secret away. It was exhausting.

"You've worked here for a while now without taking much time off," Morrie interjected. "I recommend taking time off."

"I'm fine," Chris insisted.

"I've taken vacations when I've been under stress, and it works," Morrie said calmly. "You need to take a step back so you can perform your job."

"I'll think about it," Chris murmured. "With all due respect, I think both of you are wrong about this. There's nothing going on with me."

Morrie and Perry exchanged a glance. Morrie nodded his head slightly, and Perry sighed and looked out the window.

"I think there is something going on with you," Perry replied. "Morrie, will you let me speak to Chris privately?"

Morrie looked surprised and a bit irritated, but got up with a grunt and followed his boss's orders.

Chris's stomach dropped. Perry continued speaking, but Chris's brain had placed him in survival mode. Instead of hearing every word, he heard a high-pitched ringing sound that lasted for a few minutes.

Eventually, Morrie returned, and Chris was dismissed from Perry's office with the recommendation to take a few days off. Morrie clapped him on the shoulder with his giant palm when Chris got up to leave. Perry remained in his seat as Chris closed the door behind him. He was in a trance as he mindlessly walked downstairs so he could leave the main house and take refuge in his cottage. He didn't want to see or speak to anyone.

Before he made it outside, a hand grabbed his arm and yanked him aside.

"What was that about?" Kara hissed, looking over her shoulder to ensure that no one was watching them.

Chris shook his head. "It's nothing."

"Tell me," she demanded. "Something is up. Babe, you look like you've seen a ghost."

Chris did feel like he was about to faint or throw up, but he held himself together in Kara's presence. "Can we go out in the garden and talk?"

Kara followed Chris to the garden. The couple stood between tall trellises that would soon support tomato plants. After looking to make sure no one was around to eavesdrop, Chris spoke.

"It's not good, Kara. I think they're onto us."

Her face fell. "Do they have any hard evidence?"

"Do they need to? If anyone sees us together, we're done for. Perry thinks that I'm distracted and I need to take time off. I want to keep my job, so I'm going to go away."

"Where?"

"I don't know yet."

"Will you keep me updated? I want to know everything that Perry and Morrie say. I want to know where you'll be at all times."

"Yeah, I'll keep you updated. I think it would be best if we didn't see each other for a while—at least until after I get back from my vacation."

Tears welled up in her eyes. "I don't want you to go."

"I don't want to go either, but I don't have a choice. Perry is onto me, and I can't give him a reason to be suspicious."

"I wish he weren't here," she said, her voice breaking.

"I know," Chris said in a low voice. "I wish he weren't, either. We'll talk after I get back. We'll figure this out."

He leaned forward and gave her a kiss before he walked back to his cottage, leaving her sniffling in the garden. Chris knew in that moment that trouble had finally caught up to him. He had tried to escape to a new state and a new job, but he was foolish to think that things could be better.

Back at the cottage, he crawled underneath his covers, wishing there could be some other way to resolve his problem.

Unfortunately, the plan had already been laid out for him. He just had to figure out how he was going to pull it off.

## 18

A few years back, Chris and his now ex-wife had gone on a vacation to the Pacific Northwest to celebrate their wedding anniversary. It had been a lovely time spent driving long distances while listening to audiobooks and classic rock, hiking in the most beautiful landscapes that either of them had ever seen, and relaxing for once in their busy lives.

It was the last true vacation that Chris had taken. There had been a few short trips for friends' weddings, and Chris had also done his fair share of camping once his divorce was finalized and he had nowhere to go. Until Perry's suggestion to take a few days off, Chris had spent years without putting things on pause to take time for himself.

His vacation was no anniversary trip to one of the more beautiful corners of the country, though. He had searched for affordable hotels in the area and came up with a Holiday Inn about fifty miles from the Bryant estate. It was situated on the outskirts of a town that boasted an outlet mall off the interstate exit and a small lake a little farther down the way. It would have to do.

After much internal conflict and lots of pouting from Kara, he whispered the location of the hotel and the dates he would be staying there, promising that he would only be gone for a few days, and that it wasn't wise for her to leave home, as Perry might suspect that she had gone to meet up with him. Furthermore, he made her promise that she not breathe a word of her plot to anyone else in case it was foiled. He didn't know what the typical sentence was for conspiracy to commit murder, but it was more time than he wanted to pay.

On the day of his departure, Chris tossed his duffel bag into the back of his car while Morrie watched from the garden. He didn't speak to his coworker, but Morrie gave him a solemn nod as he drove away. Since that fateful day that Perry hired him, Chris hadn't spent more than twenty minutes in a car and found himself oddly comforted by the solitude. He scanned through radio stations until he found the seventies rock that he liked and hummed along to the hits that came before his time.

After the half-hour mark, Chris's mind drifted to Kara, who occupied most of his thoughts those days. Instead of thinking about the trouble they were in, he let himself fall into a daydream about her. He imagined that they were a real couple and that he no longer worked for a millionaire, but ran his own private practice. Kara, his longtime partner, was going to meet him at a resort for a romantic getaway after a very important meeting with art collectors who frequented her store.

Deep in the fantasy, Chris imagined that they would go for a couple's massage, then get all dressed up for a fancy dinner. They would sip champagne and eat expertly crafted meals until they were almost too full to move. Tipsy, they would go on a moonlit walk along the shore, arms draped around each other. When she was least expecting it, Chris would pull out a sparkly diamond ring and make their relationship official. After she said yes, they would go back to their hotel and make love on silky sheets until the sun came up.

This daydream was a far cry from anything he had ever experienced in real life. Most dates he had been on consisted of very affordable restaurants before going to the movies or checking out a new brewery. Most of his spare time with his wife had been spent on the couch, watching TV. He had never thought of himself as particularly romantic until meeting Kara. Since they got together, he felt like he was the main character in a romantic film and prayed that their story would have a happy ending.

The fantasy dissolved as he pulled off the highway and checked into his hotel room. It was a decent room by his standards: clean, smelled faintly of disinfectant, and came with a flat-screen TV, microwave, and mini fridge. After dropping his bag on the desk, he flopped on top of the bed, resting his hands behind his head. Save for the hum of the cars on the road and the buzz of the air conditioner, it was silent. He wasn't sure what to do with his time away but chose from the fifty channels offered by the hotel chain.

He chuckled to himself as he thought of how much Kara would hate the vacation he'd thrown together. His hotel had little more than a few treadmills in the fitness center, a pool filled with splashing children, and a continental breakfast, where everything served had been in a freezer at some point. There was no one to make her green juice or lead her through her yoga routine. The closest salon was a budget hair salon in the outlet mall, and all of the designer shops there were beneath Kara's threshold of fashion. When they whispered to each other at night about how they wanted to have a getaway, this wasn't what Kara had in mind. Luckily for her, she hadn't been invited on this trip.

After a short nap, Chris put on his running shoes and went for a stroll around the lake. As he walked on the paved path, he watched happy families walk by, and it gave him a strange pang of longing. He felt so isolated in this town. Apart from his sister and Cole, whom he rarely called anyway, there was no one for him to talk to. Kara was off-limits for obvious reasons, and once he had some distance from the estate, he understood that no one else there was an actual friend.

The distance was good, though, because it finally gave Chris a little space to think about his options. Away from the house, everything felt less urgent. He wasn't under pressure from anyone to make a hasty move. And while Kara's idea to kill Perry to solve their problems was extreme and scared Chris, he couldn't help but think about the end result of her plan. Once guilt was pushed aside, they would have all of the time and money in the world.

Whenever the lottery reached a record-breaking jackpot and all news stations reported on it, Chris would imagine what life would be like if he had multiple millions of dollars at his disposal. He couldn't fathom the freedom it would buy him. He could do whatever he wanted to do, wherever he wanted to be. In a way, Kara's plan would yield the same results. He wouldn't have to work if he didn't want to, and Kara wouldn't be tied to a husband she didn't love. It would be the only way, apart from a tragic accident, that he could be with Kara.

It frightened Chris that he could even consider her plot. Somewhere along the way to New York, Chris had lost his morals. He imagined walking through their mansion, picking any item that he wanted. That thousand-dollar espresso machine? His. The extensive wine collection? He'd sample each bottle with Kara. Everything that he had given up on years ago when he chose his career path could now be his. It was an idea too enticing to completely wipe from his brain.

Though at the end of the day, he knew that killing someone to make his life easier was wrong. Kara cried about how mean Perry was to her, but she had never been in real danger. She would have to make the choice to be miserable and rich or happy and poor. It was out of Chris's hands. He started to feel at peace as he walked back to the hotel with a takeaway pizza and a six-pack of beer.

Chris was eager to turn down the AC as low as possible, find a good movie on TV, and eat as much of his supreme pizza as he possibly could. He looked forward to steadily finishing his six-pack by the time midnight rolled around so he could drift off to sleep in the king-sized bed with the soft glow and low volume of old sitcoms lulling him to sleep.

All of these plans were dashed when he opened the door of his hotel room and saw Kara sitting on the edge of his bed, waiting for him.

## 19

Chris nearly dropped his dinner on the carpet. "What are you doing here?" he breathed. His heart was pounding out of his chest, and his fingertips were tingling. Chris set the pizza and beer on the desk before his legs gave out from underneath him. It took him a few moments to calm down.

Kara jumped up from the bed and put her hands on his hips, bringing him back to reality. "I know I wasn't supposed to come here, but I didn't know where else to go." Tears were forming in her eyes and threatened to spill out.

"Where did you tell Perry you were going?" Chris asked, a feeling of dread coursing through his veins. "If he suspects you're here, we don't stand a chance."

"I don't know where he thinks I am right now, and I don't think he even cares. Look what he did to me." She took two steps back and unzipped her leather jacket. Underneath, she wore a white tank top. On her thin, tanned arms were welts and bruises. Several oblong bruises lined her biceps, as if someone had grabbed her arms with significant force. She pulled her long hair back, showing purple bruises on the sides of her face. Kara took the bottom of Chris's sleeve and wiped at her eye and neck, showing more bruising that was covered in makeup.

Chris was shocked that Perry would hurt her. "Sit down," he told Kara as he placed a handful of half-melted ice cubes from his ice bucket into a plastic bag and twisted the top. He delicately placed the ice up against her cheek, then sat on the bed next to her.

"I don't know what to do," she said hoarsely. "I don't want to go home."

"Tell me exactly what happened," Chris said seriously, wrapping one arm around her waist to comfort her.

"We were fighting again. I said I wanted to go to a runway show in the city. Perry got snippy and said that I'm spending all of his money to go into the city, which was not true because I was planning on staying with a friend. I told him that he was being unfair, and that was when he grabbed me. He shook me and screamed in my face, then started pushing me around. I fell to the ground and hit my head. He picked me back up and kept shoving me until he got so worked up that he started hyperventilating. Perry went to get his medication, and that was when I quickly packed a bag. When I got in my car, he was still yelling at me. I drove here because it was the only place I felt safe."

Chris leaned in and planted a soft kiss on the top of her head. "You're safe here. Did you call the police and report it?"

She shook her head. "I can't. Perry basically funds the police force. He has donated tens of thousands of dollars to the department."

"You have the bruises to prove it," Chris said.

"Perry has suspicions that we're together," she countered. "It's more likely that he will convince the police that you beat me up instead. And you know as well as I do that he looks like he couldn't hurt a fly."

She made a good point. Chris wasn't just worried about his athletic physique making him more likely to use force on another person. If the police looked into him, they would see that he had accidentally killed a young woman and was essentially a drifter without a license to practice in this state. It seemed way more believable that this young interloper, having been faced with suspicions about the affair with the boss's wife, beat the hell out of her for whatever reason.

"What do you want to do, then?" Chris reached toward the six-pack and pulled two sweaty bottles from the cardboard. He popped the top off and handed one to Kara and opened the other one for himself.

"It was one thing when he was being emotionally abusive. Now, he's being physical. I'm afraid to go home when you're not around to save me. I just need someone to save me. Please," she said, looking into his eyes.

He took a deep breath and weighed his options. "Look, I'm here for a few more days. It would be suspicious if I came back early with you. You can stay here tonight while you find another place to go. Go to the city and stay with friends if you have to. When we get back to the house, you have to act like you never came to see me, understand? You can call me if things get bad at home, and I'll come up with an excuse to come inside. Does that work for you?"

She looked disappointed by this answer, but Chris didn't know what else to do for her while also protecting himself.

"It's all we can do right now," he said, "unless you want to report the abuse to the authorities."

She took a sip of her beer without looking up at Chris. "Okay."

THE NIGHT at the hotel wasn't something that Chris could have ever imagined, though he thought about meeting up with Kara outside of the house on an almost daily basis. After talking about what their plan was moving forward, Chris offered part of his pizza to Kara, who took a few bites and complained that it was too unhealthy to continue eating.

Chris finished his slice, then went on an expedition to find the healthiest food along the highway exit, which was a feat in itself. He returned with a prepackaged fruit cup and Caesar salad, which Kara picked at, then stuck the majority of it in the fridge. She was more interested in the bottle of dry white wine he'd scavenged from a bottle shop in the mall.

Chris was surprised to find that intimacy with Kara didn't come as automatically as it used to. He didn't know if it was the circumstances of her visit, the age and comfortability of their relationship, or something else, but their secret reunion was not the pornography-level experience that he had imagined. After some beer, wine, and a long shower together, the two took to the bleach-scented sheets, just like they had many times before. The sex was still good, but seemed to lack a certain spark that Chris had come to crave. Afterward, Kara turned on her side, facing away from Chris. This time was usually spent with soft praise from each of them, telling the other how sexy they were and how they loved being together. Now, Chris was wide awake as he spooned her, while soft snores came from her mouth just a few minutes later.

He chalked that up to a long and traumatic day. After all, she was covered with bruises, which must have been difficult for someone who worked so hard to keep up her appearance. The only time he had ever seen her bruised was after she'd gotten fillers injected into her face and one time after a particularly heated session in the boathouse, when her hip bones had accidentally hit the hard planked flooring.

In the morning, Chris went downstairs to have breakfast in the hotel while Kara made phone calls to arrange for a stay in the city until Chris got back to the estate, at least. Once he finished his waffle and eggs, he brought two cups of drip coffee back to the room, handing one to Kara. Her face was stony, unlike her normal sultry face she put on in Chris's presence.

"What's up?" he asked.

"I'm going to a yoga retreat upstate," she said as she put her makeup case in her bag. Chris noticed that her bruises were expertly covered. "I plan to get back after you do. That should give you enough time to prepare for it."

"For what?" he asked, feeling the sense of dread return.

"You know," she said darkly. "You'll figure out how much medication to give him and when you're going to do it. I think I need to be there and put on a show of how upset I am when it happens so no one thinks that it's a money grab. Also, you have to promise me that you won't mention any of this to Perry. I will text him and let him know that I went to a yoga retreat, but I won't say where. If you talk about the abuse to him, he'll know that I saw you."

"Oh, right," Chris said. "I won't say a word."

"Good. I want to thank you for being good to me. I'm looking forward to all of this being over so we can have a normal life."

"Same." Chris sighed. "I'll see you back at the house."

"See you then," she said, leaning in to give him a kiss. Then she grabbed her overnight bag, slipped on her sunglasses, and walked out the door.

Chris went to the window and watched as she got in her car and drove away.

"Christ," Chris muttered to himself as he slumped down in the chair next to the window.

The plot was getting more complicated by the day, and he was exhausted. He wanted advice, but was in no place to tell anyone what was going on. He didn't know what his future held, but he didn't want to spend the rest of his days sneaking and planning. It had been exciting at first, but it was getting old.

Having nothing else to do to pass the time, Chris called his sister. He called so infrequently that Laura always sounded concerned when she answered the phone, probably fearing the worst.

"What's up?" she asked. "Working today?"

"Actually, no." He chuckled. "I'm taking my first vacation—if you can call an affordable hotel next to an outlet mall a vacation."

"Good for you," she said. "You really haven't taken a day off since you got there. I'm sure you deserve it."

Chris couldn't respond to that statement, as he didn't feel like he deserved anything from Perry after what Kara had convinced him to do. He so badly wanted to ask Laura if a chance at love and millions of dollars was worth doing something bad, but he knew he couldn't.

"So how has the job been treating you lately?" she asked. "It's been a while since we last talked."

"I don't know," he said honestly, finding himself getting

emotional. "It's a good gig on paper, but after a while, living in someone else's house in the middle of the country gets weird. It's not like I can leave work at work because I'm eating most of the meals in the house and seeing Perry on a daily basis, sometimes multiple times a day. The only people I socialize with are the people who work there, and I'd hardly call that socializing. Then I have to be on call and help Perry through whatever is going on with him. I think I'm starting to have a bad attitude about working there."

That was an understatement, but Chris didn't know how else to express how he was feeling.

"Is it time to move on?" Laura asked. "Sometimes that's the best sign that you should start looking for another job before you really start hating it."

"Maybe, but I don't know what I'd do," he said, rubbing his forehead. Chris sat on the bed and kicked his feet up. "I can do something that I'm good at here, but I can't do it anywhere else. I would hate to leave and never get that back."

"I get that," she said. "You could always go back to school."

He laughed. "I'm thirty-four. I'm not going to go to a 101 college class with a bunch of eighteen-year-olds."

"There are online classes these days," she replied. "You could complete a whole degree without having to set foot inside a classroom. Besides, you know it's not only young kids in college these days. I'm sure with all the money you've saved working there, you could take some time off and work on a new career."

"I don't know," he said. "Sounds like a lot of work for something I'm not really interested in."

"There are a lot of jobs that don't need a degree," Laura

replied. "You could use this as your chance to do something you never thought you would do before. For example, if I were younger and didn't have kids, I think I would try working at a high-end cocktail bar."

"Why?" Chris laughed. "You hate staying up past ten."

"Yeah, but think of the tips," she answered. "It would be kind of fun. What's something that you could have some fun with? You like being outside. Maybe you could work for a state park. Or get into farming or ranching."

"I don't know, Laura. I'll think about it. I'm also just not sure where I'd even go at this point."

"Come back home, obviously," she said, as if it were silly for him to even question living anywhere besides Omaha. "I can't tell you what to do, but I think it would be good for you to stay with us for a while. You don't have to go out and see anyone you don't want to see. It's a big enough city that I think you'll be just fine."

He hated that she knew his anxieties that he tried to keep to himself. Perhaps the best thing about working for Perry was that he had the chance to be himself—or at least a different version of himself. He didn't have to look at the floor every time he went to pick up groceries because he was afraid of being recognized as the psych hospital killer. He didn't have to go out of his way to avoid people because there was no one to avoid there. His chances of running into his ex were virtually nonexistent in New York. He felt free.

Except he didn't because he was trapped in between his boss and his boss's wife. The feelings of relief that he once had were fading fast.

"I'll take it into consideration," Chris said earnestly. "Thanks for the offer."

"Anytime."

"So if I were to make a decision in the next week or so, you'd have room for me?"

"Of course," she said.

Chris could hear excitement in her voice. "It's not a sure thing," he added quickly. "Just wanting to keep my options open in case I decide the time is right."

"I get it," Laura said. "Just know that a room is ready for you whenever you're ready."

When Chris got off the phone with his sister, he felt somewhat comforted that he had options, even though they weren't great. As it stood at that moment, he could either stay and deal with the paranoia and awkwardness, get rid of Perry and live like a king, or give it all up. If he left, he could wander the highways like he used to, or face his fears and go back to Nebraska.

He wasn't happy about where he was at the moment, but he had a little more confidence in his ability to make something good out of a shitty situation. With that spirit, he logged back on to his job search profile and started browsing anything that sounded remotely interesting in the Omaha metro area. Wages for entry-level jobs weren't great when he considered housing costs, but he had found that it was easy for him to live a very simple, modest life.

With his remaining vacation time, Chris went on long walks, caught up on sleep, and tried to avoid eating and drinking his feelings.

He didn't hear anything from Kara until she called the night before he checked out.

"What's wrong?" Chris instinctively asked, knowing that she was at a retreat and likely wouldn't have phone access.

"Nothing," she said quietly. "I wanted to ask you if you want to extend your vacation a little longer. We could do something fun. Or we could just hang out at your hotel room."

He sighed. "I can't afford taking that much time off, and it would seem suspicious if I randomly decided to take more time off. Plus, I think Morrie would be pissed if I messed up the schedule."

"But it would be so much easier to see you outside of the house," she whined. "We'd just have to go back to sneaking around the cottage."

He needed to make a good decision for once in his life, but was having a hard time finding the words. Finally, he just spat it out. "Kara, we can't be together right now," he said, as much as it pained him to do it.

"You're breaking up with me?" she said incredulously.

"No, no, I wouldn't say that," he said quickly. "We just need to put things on pause right now. It's in both of our best interests if we practice the most caution, which means that we can't see each other right now."

"This sucks," she said flatly. "God, is this what it feels like to be dumped? I hate it."

"No, sweetie," Chris said, trying to sound gentle. "You know I'd do anything to be with you. Now just isn't the right time."

"Do you mean that? You'd do anything?"

It was a poor choice of words on his part. Now he was trapped. He heard the pain in her voice and hated that he caused it. He needed to make things better. "Yes, I mean it."

"Good. I'll see you back at the house."

She hung up, leaving Chris to think about what he had promised her as he packed up his room in preparation to return to work the next morning.

## 20

"How was your vacation?" Perry asked casually as he reclined in his desk chair.

Chris had been nervous to return and face Perry after things had been so uncomfortable the last time they were in a room together. "It was fine. How were things around here?"

"Quiet," Perry replied. "Kara went to a yoga retreat, so I decided to give the staff a couple of days off—except for Morrie; he was here. Actually, I got a lot of work done on a new project." He pulled a heavy piece of white paper from his desk and showed it to Chris.

At first, it looked like squiggles, but upon closer inspection, Chris saw an intricate map. "Wow," he breathed. "What is it?"

"I had a very active imagination as a kid. I used to read fantasy books and think about the settings in a two-dimensional scope. I even dreamed up my own imaginary land. I had forgotten all about it until something triggered the memory. I sat down and realized that it came back to me when I put pen to paper. I only started it because it was in my head, but once I sat down, I just kept going. It felt really nice to get all of it out of my head. Very comforting."

"What do you think brought back this memory?" Chris asked.

Perry stared off beyond Chris's head, toward the door. "I'm not sure. I guess I was just contemplating the direction my life has gone over the past decade. There are some people who have known me for a while who thought I was capable of big things. I think there were far more people who thought I was really going to struggle in life, and that I'd be lucky to hold down any sort of job and live alone. I've realized that I've exceeded expectations. I get to practice my craft and have a lot to show for it. I have a wife, and I haven't been completely alone in this house since I built it."

In some ways, Chris lived the opposite. Chris was poor, divorced, had been run out of town, and did the only job he knew how to do.

"Do you ever feel like you were motivated to prove people wrong?" Chris asked.

"Not really," Perry replied, as if it were a strange question to ask. "I just did what I knew I was capable of, and the rest worked out. I don't feel like some sort of success story. If anything, I think I remembered my old fantasy land because that is the place I want to be the most. Some people like to live a complicated life. Kara, for instance, loves things like glamor, action, and drama. I like things to be comfortable, controlled, and predictable. Drawing this map has brought me so much peace because that's what I desire the most. My life led me in a certain direction, and it's brought me a lot of things, but now I just wish I could have a little less, you know?"

This was a sentiment that Chris could understand. While he knew Perry was capable of having erratic thoughts, he had never sounded so wise to Chris. He found himself wanting to tell Perry everything that had happened before their chance meeting on the side of the road, and ask him for advice moving forward. He wanted to get everything off his chest because there was so much that he couldn't say without outing himself as a terrible person. He desired some reassurance that he would have no problem getting his life back on track after everything that had happened over the past year and everything that was about to happen. He was terrified of what was to come. What if things didn't work out? What if their plan went wrong? Still, he carried on with the conversation as though everything were normal. It was the plan, and it was the only way forward now.

"You could have that if you wanted," Chris said, going back to what Perry had been saying and finding himself slightly annoyed by his boss's dissatisfaction when he had enough resources to do whatever he wanted in life. "What's stopping you from living with less?"

Perry sighed and gave Chris a look that suggested that Chris was too young to understand, but it seemed he'd given this a lot of thought. "It's harder for me if I make choices and things go poorly. Let's say that I divorced my wife, fired all of my staff, and moved to a cabin in the woods. It might be what I want at this moment, but what if I regret that choice? What if I miss my estate and all of the luxuries? What if my employees face hardship after being unemployed? What if my wife completely flounders on her own? There are too many what-ifs. I can't live with that."

Chris found this reasoning extremely frustrating, but he

knew he would never change his mind. Perry would always do whatever Perry's brain told him to do.

They spoke for a little while longer, and then Perry announced, "I'm feeling a little on edge."

His words had Chris choking. A million thoughts flashed through his mind. Should he do it now? He thought he'd have a little longer. "Anything I can do?"

"I don't know," he replied, as if he hadn't given it much thought. "It's just one of those feelings, you know? Anyway, I think I'd like to keep working now."

"That's fine," Chris said, finding the humor in Perry's abrupt conversations and feeling a little relieved that it wasn't time to enact the plan yet. "You know how to reach me if you need me."

Chris went back to his lodging just in time to see Kara walk out of the house. He lingered outside for a moment, though he knew it was safer to go inside and pretend he wasn't there.

"Is it done?" she whispered, a glimmer of hope in her voice.

"I just went in for a session," he whispered back, eyes darting toward the house. "He's working in his office, so no, I haven't given him any meds yet. I'd try to avoid that part of the house if I were you."

"Fine," she groaned, stomping her way to the house.

Chris checked his surroundings one more time before retreating into the house.

Less than an hour later, Chris's pager went off, startling him from his seat at the kitchen table. He jumped up and ran toward the house. It was time. It was a quiet day at the property, the employees who tended to the home had already left, Darryl was out buying groceries, and Morrie wasn't coming in until later. To his knowledge, the only other person on the property was Kara.

As he jogged up the stairs, he heard a door slam at the end of the hall. He found Perry in his bedroom, scanning the labels of his pill bottles all lined up on his nightstand like chess pieces.

"What's up?" Chris asked, feeling keyed up.

Perry shook his head. "Can't talk to Kara without some dramatic act," he wheezed. "I told you I wasn't feeling right today, and now I think I'm having a panic attack."

"Here," Chris said nervously, guiding his boss to his bed. If there was ever a good time to do something terrible, it was then, but Perry trusted him. "I'll prepare your medicine for you. Just lie back and work on your breathing exercises. Have you taken your morning medications yet?"

"Not yet," he murmured, pressing his palm to his forehead, as if a headache was coming on. Eyes closed, he held out his hand and allowed Chris to pour a small handful of pills into it. He opened his eyes and stared at Chris. Giving him a nod, he clutched them in his grasp, then popped them all in his mouth and took several gulps from a water bottle to get them down.

"Are you going to stay with me?" Perry asked sleepily, his eyes darting toward the door.

Chris swallowed hard. This was the most difficult part of the plan. Getting out the words he needed to say. "I-I think I left the stove on in the cottage," he said, his voice quivering because he was terrified something was going to go wrong. He needed to stay calm, normal. "I'll run and turn that off, and then I'll come back to check on you. How are you feeling right now? Relaxed enough?"

"I think so."

"I'll be right back," he said before striding from the room, then running down the stairs to the cottage. He heard a door creak as he went, but he didn't look back.

Chris was out of breath by the time he got to his kitchen, glancing at the clock on the stove, which hadn't been used in days. He would wait a few minutes, then walk around the front of the house, where there was a camera. That would provide him with a time stamp, an alibi. It was normal for him to check in with Perry a few times a day; this would be when he found Perry in his state.

Then he would call Morrie, who would be coming in very soon. If he timed it right, Morrie would be the one to call an ambulance. It needed to be Morrie who called. Then the rest of the plan would naturally play out.

Chris was desperate to have a swig from the whiskey bottle in the cupboard, but the smell of booze on his breath would make him a target. Well, a bigger target at any rate. Instead, he tried to steady his breath as he looked out the window for signs that anyone was coming—anyone who could mess up the plan.

When he saw a car cruising down the dirt road, Chris's stomach leapt into his throat. Morrie was ahead of schedule.

Chris left his quarters immediately and walked toward the front door before continuing around to the back. If Morrie saw him walking through the front door instead of the usual side door, he'd look suspicious. He slipped in through the door as Morrie parked. Nervous, he slowly made his way through the kitchen, praying that he could pull the plot off. He wasn't an actor, but he was attempting to pull off an Academy Award performance.

He was at the bottom of the stairs when a scream rang

out upstairs. It was so loud that he was positive that anyone on the property could hear.

"Dammit," he hissed under his breath.

"What happened?" Morrie's gruff voice sounded from the doorway.

"On my way up," Chris called back. He hustled into Perry's bedroom and found Kara collapsed at the foot of their bed in hysterics.

"He's not waking up," Kara cried.

By then, Morrie had stormed upstairs, sweaty and out of breath. Morrie surged forward, nearly pushing Chris out of the way. He eyed the pill bottles by the bedside. They were scattered with the tops missing, some on the floor. Connecting the dots, he whipped out his phone and called an ambulance.

Chris went into the medical kit that was stored in the hall closet and pulled out a stethoscope. He listened to his boss's vitals while Morrie told the dispatcher that their client might have overdosed and needed to go to the hospital where his psychiatrist worked. "He's still breathing," Chris murmured.

"Perry!" Kara screamed. "What happened to him?"

"Take a few steps back," Morrie said firmly.

She scowled at Morrie, but listened. Morrie had the ability to make anyone in the room follow his orders. Chris didn't like him talking to anyone like that, but he had to admit, Kara was laying it on too thick.

"Breathing is shallow," Chris said. "Pulse is forty-eight."

"Damn it," Morrie cursed. "And we have no idea what he took?"

"I-I don't know," Chris stammered, knowing he needed

to lie since it was part of the plan, but he wasn't the best actor. "I didn't administer anything to him today."

"Did you see your husband take anything?" Morrie asked Kara.

She shook her head and held a hand to her trembling mouth. "I don't know what he took."

"You should know; he's your damn husband," Morrie said under his breath. "He needs to get his stomach pumped for good measure and be flushed with saline until toxicology comes back—if he makes it that long. Did he not say anything to you about feeling poorly today?"

"No—nothing," Chris said. "We had a session earlier today, and he said he was a little on edge, but otherwise feeling good."

"He didn't page you?"

"No."

Morrie sighed. "Something must have triggered him, and he took matters into his own hands."

"What would cause him to do that?" Kara cried.

Morrie looked back at her with squinting eyes, as if he were trying to see through her. He went to Perry's bedside table, shook a pill out of a bottle, and handed it to her, along with a glass of water. "Take this," he said, his voice dripping with exasperation.

She looked over at Chris, then after seeing no reaction from him, she took it and sat down on a couch in the corner.

"I'm going to call his doctor," Chris said, pulling out his phone with shaky hands. "Perry will want her there, and I want her to be there when we arrive. She knows his case better than anyone."

Chris stepped out of the room, just beyond the doorway, to

make the call. The doctor assured him that he was doing everything right and that she would meet them at the emergency bay to personally take Perry into his treatment room. After hanging up, he saw Kara wandering into the hallway with her arms crossed against her chest, looking like she was about to cry.

"This is awful to watch," she complained. "How long until he's gone?"

Chris shrugged, hoping he gave nothing away to anyone watching them. "He's hanging on, but there's a good chance he won't make it."

"I can't watch this any longer. I'm going to go lie down. Please find me when it's over."

"It's not a good look," he warned her.

"I'm sorry, but I can't do this."

Chris parted ways with Kara. Maybe it was because he had dealt with the death of a patient before, but he looked at this situation no differently than he would any other medical case.

"Kara wasn't feeling well, so she went to her room," Chris told Morrie upon returning to Perry's deathbed.

"And I wonder who was the one to upset him," Morrie muttered. "I see lights coming. Go open the front door and show the paramedics in."

Chris did as he was told, reminding the driver where they needed to go. He then quickly filled them in on Perry's condition and how there wasn't much for them to do but drive like hell to the hospital.

Chris insisted on riding in the ambulance, so Morrie drove behind them. It was a tense ten-minute drive to the hospital as he let the paramedics take charge, but he listened closely to them report on his vitals. So far, everything was going according to the plan. Perry had overdosed, and at the moment nobody suspected anything other than that.

When they arrived, Perry's doctor was there at the automatic doors, just like she said she would be. Chris told her all of the information he had, though he had already mentioned it over the phone. She gave him a knowing nod and took hold of the gurney, jogging alongside the other nurses who came to collect him. In the blink of an eye, they disappeared down the hall.

Five minutes later, Morrie pulled into a parking spot and hopped out. He waddled toward Chris, who was standing outside the emergency room, feeling numb.

"What room is he in?" Morrie asked, looking exhausted.

Chris shrugged. "I don't know. The doctor told me that she would call once she had an update. There's nothing we can do for him right now."

"Tell me what happened," Morrie said again, as if he didn't accept the answer Chris had given back at the house.

"I had a session with him in the morning," Chris recited, remembering the lines that he'd practiced, and stuck with the plan. "It went well. We were chatting about a new project he was working on. He seemed excited about it—he was more hopeful than I had seen him in a while. He reported feeling a little on edge, which I thought was strange, given his calm disposition. I told him that I'd be on the property all day if he needed me. I left, went to my room for a while, took a short walk around the grounds, then went back to check up on him, like I normally do. He had been so focused on his new piece that I was going to peek my head in and try not to disturb him. That's when I heard Kara scream. I think you were just a few steps behind me."

Morrie nodded, but didn't respond.

He could tell Morrie was suspicious, and he needed to throw him off. "So tell me what I did wrong," Chris said, trying to keep his irritation with Morrie at bay.

Morrie thought for a long moment. "I don't know, Chris," he said morosely.

"I did exactly what I was hired to do," Chris replied, trying not to sound defensive but matter-of-fact. "If you had been the one on duty, I wouldn't be blaming you. You know just as well as I do that sometimes patients seem like they're doing okay when they're really not. I'm sure you've had patients who died by suicide, and you promised their loved ones that they're not at fault. If you wouldn't look at a friend, family member, or care provider and tell them that it was all their fault, when they've been trying their hardest, then you shouldn't blame me." Every word out of his mouth seemed like a bullet to Chris's ears, but they needed to be said. He had to follow the plan. He couldn't be found guilty. He didn't want to go to jail.

Morrie didn't have any words. In fact, it seemed that he couldn't even look Chris in the face. The two stood in silence, waiting for news.

Thirty minutes later, Perry's doctor peeked her head out to look for the caretakers. She seemed surprised to see them standing outside, completely silent.

"He's still unresponsive, but he's stable," she said, looking at Morrie. "I can keep you updated if anything changes."

Morrie nodded, but didn't move.

Chris wanted to ask him to drive him back to the house so he could check on Kara, but he didn't want to give Morrie a reason to get upset with him.

"I don't see anything changing anytime soon. Go home, rest up, and come back tomorrow. He's in good hands here."

"Okay," Morrie relented. "Thank you, Doctor."

Morrie drove Chris back to the house, still in silence. The sound of talk radio filled the air. Chris knew that Morrie had his suspicions, but had no evidence to back it up, and that was why he was speechless. It made Chris uncomfortable, but it was better than making small talk with Morrie.

When they got back to the house, Chris got out of the car, expecting Morrie to drive away. Instead, Morrie went into the house and headed straight for the basement.

"Wait," Chris called out to him. "What did you give Kara? We should check in with her."

"Enough to shut her up," Morrie scoffed. "You can check on her. I'm going to have a drink."

## 21

"Come here," Kara said as Chris rapped his knuckles on the doorframe and stood at the threshold of her bedroom. Kara had told him that her room was originally the guest suite, but as no one ever visited, she turned it into her own room to get some space from her husband. Over time, it permanently became her bedroom.

Chris sat on the edge of her bed, not knowing what to say. Kara wasn't as devastated as she had seemed when Perry was in the house. Now, she was lying under her covers with a mug of tea on her nightstand and a book on her lap.

"No, come here," she offered, pushing the book aside and draping an arm over the second set of pillows.

"Morrie's still here," he said quietly. He hadn't thought to plan for Morrie sticking around. It made things more awkward than he'd thought. He knew his counterpart was downstairs, but he was still paranoid that someone would show up and see them cuddling in Kara's bed. What if

Morrie suspected they'd caused Perry to overdose? What if he stormed up here and caught them in bed?

"I doubt he'd come up here," she said.

"I'm not willing to take that risk," he replied. "Morrie hates me and has no problem marching around here like he owns the place. We have to give it time. Eventually, he'll spend less time here."

"So you can't even comfort me after seeing what I saw today?"

Chris let out an exhale. He didn't want to downplay her emotions, but she'd essentially seen her husband sleeping. Besides, he knew it was all an act on her part. She didn't care about Perry.

He held out his hand, palm facing upward. She placed her silky hand in his. Chris wanted to pull her in close, if only for his own personal benefit. He was in need of some comfort and reassurance as well. This plan was going to be the death of him. Why had he ever agreed to it? He was going to end up in prison. He should have thought things through more. Hell, if he were honest with himself, what he should really be wishing for was to never have gotten involved with her in the first place. Still, he couldn't help enjoying having her pressed up against him.

"Tell me everything is going to be okay," she whispered.

She looked concerned, but Chris didn't understand why, seeing as she was too eager to stay home while her husband was fighting for his life in the hospital. He knew he needed to continue to give her comfort. She was clearly upset, and he didn't want her saying something to the wrong person because she was mad at him.

"It will be okay," he repeated.

He hoped it was true for himself at least, but he had a

terrible feeling that something would go wrong along the way. The plan wasn't foolproof. It was extremely risky and could go wrong in a million different ways. Especially since so much depended on him and his acting abilities, which weren't all that great.

Kara's bruises looked mostly faded by that point. Faint tinges of yellow-green showed under her cheekbones and were almost imperceptible with her tanned skin. Chris wished that he had taken pictures of her in his hotel room if the need for evidence ever arose.

"I've been thinking about what I'm going to do when this is all over," she said, swirling a fingertip around Chris's palm. "I came up with a few ideas, but I thought I should share them with you before making anything final."

"Oh?"

She smiled at him. "Well, I figured that all of the funeral stuff is really going to suck. I'm thinking about booking a trip to Europe. A yacht cruise in Croatia might be exactly what we need to get back to feeling like ourselves."

"We?" he asked.

"Of course." She laughed. "Do you really think I would repay you by ditching you for a month while I tan on the front of a boat? Babe, who's going to rub the tanning oil on me? Of course we'd go together. I know you're not as comfortable with the club and fashion scene, so I thought we could spend most of our time together on a boat, just hiding out from the rest of the world. After spending time with Perry's acquaintances, I'll be ready to avoid all people for a while."

"You're not going to book this now, are you?"

She furrowed her brow. "I might. Why not?"

Chris could think of several reasons why it was a bad

idea, but there were two that prevailed in his mind. First, it wasn't part of the plan, and second... "If there's a ticket booked in my name before Perry's in the ground, that's going to look really bad. That's proof that's not hard to come by."

Kara rolled her eyes. "We'd fly private, obviously. I've done it before, like when I had my bachelorette party. I know someone with a plane we can borrow, and a pilot we can hire. I don't need to give anyone your name until they ask for the flight log. Even then, that's not widely publicized information. In our world, privacy is one of the most valued possessions a person can have. People use discretion when you're spending a lot of money."

This made Chris feel slightly off-kilter. It felt gross thinking of vacationing while Perry was struggling in the hospital, but the thought of sailing crystal-clear water on a boat that had everything he could ever ask for sounded like heaven, and he could admit that.

"It sounds nice, Kara," he said gently. "I think it would be best to hold off on the planning for a while."

She shrugged. "Fine. I was also thinking about what I would do long term—after the vacation is over. Perry never liked when I posted pictures of myself online, so part of me is itching to try my hand at Instagram modeling. As much as it kills me to think about, I'm getting too old to do runway or print work. What have you been thinking about doing?"

Chris was surprised by this question, as she had alluded to the fact that he would receive a large chunk of their cash and wouldn't have to work if he didn't want to.

"I-I'm not really sure," he stammered, recalling some of their major plans that they'd whispered to each other as they embraced in bed when they had first started all of this.

"I'm going to sell the house," she said decisively. "It's time for a fresh start. I'm looking into buying an apartment in the city that will probably be home base for me. I also like the idea of buying another property in Colorado or Montana. The mountains have become super trendy, and I like the idea of having my own place when I go skiing with the girls." She smiled. "Wow, it feels so good to be single again. It's going to feel like I'm on a never-ending girls' trip."

Chris frowned. He was feeling that she was starting to forget about him, and he was torn by that thought. Even though she asked for his input as they held hands, she talked as though she was restarting her life as an unattached woman. Part of him was glad to see her happy again, but it felt wrong when he wasn't included in every thought, which was a little crazy. There was also the fact that Perry was still alive.

"Are you sure you still want me around?" he asked moodily, playing his part.

She shot him a look as if he was being ridiculous. "Yeah, of course. I wouldn't be able to do this if it weren't for you. You're my hero—my savior. I owe you my life. No matter where things go in our new lives, I'm going to make sure you're taken care of and happy. I'm just ready for us to be able to enjoy our time together without all of the bullshit. Husband was too restrictive for the life I'm meant to have right now. Boyfriend feels so much better."

Chris occasionally thought about the long-term effects of their affair on his life, especially late at night after Kara left him alone. He had been married once, and it had ended terribly for him. He didn't know if he wanted to go through that again, but there were times when he thought he would do whatever it took to have Kara on a permanent basis. Their affair was hot and exciting, but it was never enough for him to have a hookup who went home at the end of the night. Other guys would have killed to be in his position, but he wanted an emotional connection as well. If things had been different, if they'd met before she'd married Perry, perhaps he could have been a good boyfriend for her. He just wasn't sure now if they would work long term.

"Are you sure we can't have a quickie?" she asked coyly.

"We can't," Chris replied, feeling sick. "It wouldn't be right to be intimate while your husband is in the hospital."

She threw up her hands in frustration. "Then what was this all for? We did this so we could be together."

That wasn't entirely true. She'd proposed the idea to get away from her abusive husband and still get his money. Chris was just her means to that end. He was so smitten by her that he almost didn't care. Still, he couldn't do it. It would be too dangerous to have sex with her while there were others around. He needed to keep everyone from getting suspicious.

"We can't wait until he's no longer with us," she said, raising her voice.

Chris reminded her that there were still others in the house. "What choice do we have?" he asked, feeling helpless.

"Go to the hospital and finish the job," she hissed.

Chris let out an incredulous laugh. That was definitely not part of the plan. There were cameras everywhere; he'd be caught in a heartbeat. "How do you expect me to do that?"

"I don't know," she replied, sounding upset. "Slip him some more drugs. Hold a pillow over his face when no one's looking. Can't you inject air into his IV line and no doctor can tell what happened?"

Chris was dumbfounded by her new request. "I'm going

to assume that you haven't spent a lot of time in hospitals before. I'll tell you how it works. First of all, there are people everywhere, all the time. Medical staff are in and out of rooms on a regular basis, without warning. Secondly, there are sign-in sheets for visitors and cameras everywhere. If he died suddenly, they would know that I was there. Or if I jammed pills into his mouth or messed with his IV, it would be very obvious. Suffocation takes a little while, and the heart-rate sensors would go off before he was dead. It would be too risky."

She let out a dramatic sigh. "So you're not going to even try?"

Was she trying to get him arrested? "No," he said immediately. "I'm sorry, but that's crazy."

Kara scowled and sat up in bed, yanking her hand away from Chris. "If he's still alive, I'm still married. I can't be married to him anymore."

"What does it matter at this point?" Chris asked, getting up from the bed. "You can still do whatever you want, and you still have access to the bank accounts. He's not able to hurt you if he's in a coma."

"It's more than that," she yelled, climbing out from under the covers. "I'm still tied to everything related to Perry. You said it yourself—it's a bad look to move on before there's a funeral. Am I just supposed to hide in my room for months and listen to people tell me how sorry they are for my husband's illness? I just want to get it all over with. I don't want to be the pathetic widow. I want to change my last name and begin again. I want freedom. You said you were going to give it to me."

Chris was shocked by her sudden change in disposition. They were both under a ton of stress, manufactured or not, but he didn't think it excused the things she was saying. A minute ago, he was her hero. Now, she yelled at him like she scolded a housekeeper for forgetting to iron her pillowcases. Frustration bit at the corners of his mind. He understood some of where she was coming from, as he wanted it all to be over also, but there were things that needed to happen first before it could. He needed to stick to the plan. It was his mantra, and he was going to follow it, even if it killed him.

"Kara, I did what you asked me to do. I was afraid of what might happen if I went through with it, but I did it anyway because I knew it was what you wanted. You wanted to be free of Perry. I know he's still alive, but he's not able to hurt you now. Today has been unbelievably stressful, and I'm sure you're dealing with some confusing emotions. I'm going to leave the room because this fighting is not helping either of us."

"I don't want to be trapped in his house alone," she growled.

"I get that," he said, talking in his therapist voice. He felt like he was trying to keep a lion from pouncing on him. He took a few steps back, creating more space between them. "It's temporary. After a little time to process this, and a good night's sleep, you'll be ready to face whatever is next. We've got to be smart. If we slip up and get caught now, then it was all for nothing, and neither of us will live the happily ever after that we wanted. Trust me on this. It will all work out as it should in the long run. Please be patient until then, okay?"

Kara rolled her eyes and sat back on her bed, pouting. "I really hoped it would be over soon."

"Just give it time. Things will run their natural course, and then it will all be resolved," he said. Before he left the room, he took her hand and kissed her knuckles before letting it go. "I'll check on you later, but I think a little breathing space would be best right now. Want me to have Chef make you something to eat?"

She shook her head, looking childlike. "I'm not hungry. I'm too upset to eat."

"Well, make sure you have something to eat today. We don't want you to land in the hospital too. You have to take care of yourself."

"I'd rather have you take care of me," she said, her voice turning slightly sweet again.

"Later, dear," he said softly. "I'll be back later."

Chris went back downstairs, feeling like all of the energy had been drained out of him. It was almost dinnertime, but he didn't feel particularly hungry, either. All he wanted was a few stiff drinks. Knowing exactly where to get those, he headed downstairs to the liquor collection. He knew that Morrie was likely still down there, but the promise of getting completely shit-faced was more important than dealing with Morrie's moody silence.

## 22

When he got to the kitchen, Chris saw Darryl wiping down the employees' bar while Morrie sat with both stubby hands wrapped around a glass. Hesitantly, Chris tiptoed down the stairs, desperate for a drink.

"Hey, man," Darryl said welcomingly, with pity in his eyes. "Can I make you something to eat?"

"Thanks, but I'm not really hungry."

"Thirsty?"

Chris nodded.

"I'll pour you something. What's your poison?"

"Vodka," Chris said after much deliberation. He figured a clear liquor would make it so he was sharp enough to function the next day if he overdid it. "And anything you have to mix it with. If you could make it a double, that would be great."

"You got it, champ," Darryl said, retreating to his fridge to gather ingredients.

Chris awkwardly waited for his drink. He turned to

Morrie. "Kara's shaken up, but I think she'll be fine. It might be best if we give her some space for a few days."

"Sure," Morrie grunted before taking a sip. "Might as well give her some of Perry's downers. He's not going to use them."

Thankfully, Darryl came back with a drink in a highball glass, garnished with a lemon. "It's cucumber and melon mineral water with a squeeze of lemon and a heavy pour of vodka. Try that on for size."

The cocktail was exactly what Chris needed. He softened in his chair and gave the chef a smile. "It's perfect, thank you."

"No problem, man. If you want another one, the water is in the big pitcher. Lemons are in the glass container, and vodka's on the shelf. If you want anything to eat, we've got tons of leftovers in the fridge."

"Are you not staying?" Chris asked.

Darryl looked at Morrie, who didn't respond, and shrugged. "I'm going to head home early. I'm not making dinner, and Kara will only eat rabbit food anyway. I've made her juices and shakes already. I'll come back tomorrow and see what she wants. It sounds like I won't spend a lot of time here this week."

"No use," Morrie said. "You should take it easy while payroll is still going out."

Darryl nodded and wiped his hand on a towel. "I'll see you guys later. Be well."

The two sat in silence once again as Darryl walked up the stairs and out of the house. By then, Chris had slurped down his drink and went behind the bar to make another one.

"How many patients of yours have killed themselves?" Morrie broke the silence to ask Chris.

Chris was a little taken aback by the question, but in his slightly inebriated state, considered it carefully. "I know of a few, only because their families let us know or someone saw an obituary in the paper. How about you?"

"The same," Morrie answered. "But it was never a total surprise. I've been trained to see the warning signs. I never saw anything like that with Perry."

"No?" Chris asked nervously.

"Not recently, anyway. He had been doing so much better, to the point where I was starting to wonder what I would do if he never needed my services again. I rarely saw him upset unless his wife was egging him on."

"She doesn't egg him on," Chris said defensively.

"Then you must be living under a rock or just not paying attention. I don't meddle in relationships, but I'm sure he could have found a nice woman who saw his quirks as endearing. I've never seen a married couple despise one another like they do. Kara more so than Perry. If I were married to her, I guess that might make me off myself."

"Hey," Chris said, warning him. "That's fucked up. You were the one who scoffed at me when I said we should counsel him on his relationship. If you really think Kara made Perry overdose and we could have convinced them to separate, then you can take the blame for this."

Morrie gritted his teeth. "I won't, because I'm still not convinced that Perry did it."

Chris frowned. He hadn't considered Morrie and his suspicions when planning all of this. Could he mess things up for them? He hoped not. "Why not? How else did he end up in a coma?"

Morrie raised an eyebrow. "That's what I've been trying to figure out. When Perry has a panic attack and needs to be sedated, how many pills do you give him?"

"One," Chris responded quickly. "I give him one pill and work on non-pharmaceutical coping strategies. My goal was to get him using a lower dose."

"And if he doesn't calm down?"

"Maybe another half a pill, but I'd wait at least twenty minutes before giving it."

Morrie pursed his lips and nodded, as if he was trying to catch Chris making a mistake. "I don't think Perry would have any idea what acceptable doses are. As smart as the man is, he was never good about taking medication. Trusting, too. You could hand him enough medication to knock out an elephant, and he'd gulp it down because you were the caretaker."

Chris took another drink. He was starting to wonder if Morrie had hidden cameras around the house. Otherwise, how were all of his hunches about Chris correct? He was so careful, yet Morrie seemed to have him figured out at every turn. It had him very worried. What if Morrie went to the cops with his suspicions? The idea of going to jail terrified him.

"I've gone over everything in my head for hours now," Morrie said as he poured another drink from the crystal whiskey decanter. "But I can't make any sense of this."

"I don't see what there is to make sense of," Chris said, getting agitated. "Perry got upset—or was secretly planning to harm himself—and took way too much of his medication. Maybe it was an accident, and maybe it wasn't. It's not our job to speculate. It's our job to be there for our client."

"It's my job to speculate if negligence was involved," Morrie said. "I used to work at a psychiatric hospital. I found that there was always a handful of the most incompetent people on the floor. They made careless errors that resulted in serious injuries and death. When Perry found you on the side of the road, I had my concerns. I let Perry know them, too. I thought it was really odd that he would come across a psychiatric nurse who would be so far from home and have no job. It was crazy to hire someone to move into his house and provide medical care without checking credentials or references. But Perry trusted you, so there was nothing more I could say."

"You just thought I was there to steal your job," Chris said in a low voice.

Morrie scoffed. "Among other things. I've been working for Perry for a while. He has reason to trust me. You may say I'm old-school, but I'm a straight shooter and conservative with medication. That's because I've seen what happens when you're too soft with a patient and they rely on your comfort and drugs. I wanted Perry to toughen up to the world because I didn't want to see him getting taken advantage of. He will trust anyone who appears kind to him. Someone with that much money is a target for scammers and swindlers."

"And you think I'm a swindler, too?" Chris asked. "Want me to get out a copy of my diploma to prove that I have the knowledge to do the job?"

Morrie shook his head. "Like I said, I've seen plenty of screwups made by idiots who somehow managed to get through the required training. It doesn't make you good at what you do."

Chris's face burned. He felt as though Morrie knew his secret and was using it to hurt him. Emboldened by the drink, he turned to face Morrie. "Here's a theory: maybe Perry overdosed because he knew that you would berate him for being weak, and then hold out on his prescribed medication when he needed it. Maybe he took it to escape you." It was a low blow, and Chris knew it.

Morrie grabbed Chris by the collar, yanking him so they were face-to-face. "Listen here, you little shit. This happened on your watch. If it had happened while I was on call, I would have owned up to it. Because of you, I'm out of a job. I have to go home tonight and tell my wife and family that there won't be any vacations or extras of any kind because my boss is brain-dead. I'm going to have to go back to working in shitty hospitals on shitty shifts so I can pay my mortgage. I had a good thing going. Then you showed up and fucked everything up."

"Get your hands off me," Chris yelled, shoving Morrie back.

Morrie took a swing at Chris, knocking him on the side of the face.

Stunned, Chris took a step back, but was now feeling rage coursing through his veins. He normally internalized all of his feelings, but once they started to bubble to the surface, he couldn't stop them. He gave Morrie a hard shove, but the old man was sturdy and hardly moved. This gave Morrie a chance to smack Chris across the face with the back of his hand.

"You've been a jerk to me this whole time, and I never did anything to you," Chris raged. "There were so many times that I wanted to call you out on your bullshit, but I didn't say anything to keep the peace. There were even times where I just wished that Perry would fire you so no one would have to deal with your bad attitude anymore."

Chris took a swing at Morrie and managed to hit him in the ribs, causing Morrie to double over momentarily. It only incited more violence, though, as Morrie fought back like an angry warthog. He rushed Chris, hitting him just below the sternum. Winded, Chris fought to take deep breaths as Morrie caught his breath.

They drunkenly scrapped for a few more minutes, each landing hits that would certainly leave a mark. A few glasses were broken, and chairs were knocked down in the fight. Eventually, the two were too tired and battered to continue, and stood facing each other, several feet of space between them.

"I've had enough of this shit," Morrie panted. "Since this is the last time I'm ever going to see you, I'll let you know that no one will ever convince me that this wasn't your fault. You killed a man, and now you're responsible for a bunch of good, hardworking people who will be out of a job around here. If we die from getting back in the rat race, then that'll be on you, too."

"Perry isn't dead," Chris said exasperatedly. This fight, this outcome, wasn't part of the plan. He hoped he could fix it and keep Morrie from going to the cops. "You're not going to at least stick around for a little while to see how he's doing? You're not going to be here if he wakes up and needs medical care?"

Morrie shook his head. "I don't have the time for that. If he's not awake, I'm not getting paid. I have a family to think about. I have a retirement to work toward. I can't sit on my thumb and eat Kara's leftovers for an indefinite amount of time. It's over. If you had any brains in that head of yours, you'd look for another job, too."

"Suit yourself," Chris said with frustration, picking up a barstool. "When he wakes up, I'll tell him that you're not coming back."

"That's fine," Morrie said coolly. "Just so you know, you won't last long freeloading here. Kara will get tired of you eventually. I know for a fact that she'll move on to the next new thing. If there's anything I regret about leaving this place, it's that I won't be able to see what becomes of you."

A chill ran down Chris's spine. It felt like Morrie was making some sort of prophecy, in addition to being as hurtful as he could. It was scary how right Morrie was about a lot of things happening around the house, even though there was no way of knowing—unless Chris hadn't been as discreet as he thought he had.

"Goodbye, Morrie," Chris said stonily.

Morrie shot Chris one last glare before limping up the stairs and out of the house.

Chris held his breath and listened for the back door to open and close before he moved again. When he heard the car pull around the driveway, Chris let out a sigh of relief. He lowered his shoulders, realizing that just about every muscle in his body was clenched.

It was eerie to be in the basement of an empty home save for Kara, whom Chris didn't feel like seeing at the moment. Feeling guilty for making a mess in a home so meticulously kept by good, hardworking people, Chris picked up the fallen furniture and located a broom and dustpan to clean up the glass.

When everything looked as it had when he went down

there, he poured himself a final drink—this time a single—and sipped it as he rested his elbows on the bar. Out of seemingly nowhere, his eyes filled up with tears, and he blinked out a few drops onto the top of the bar as he sat there alone.

## 23

That night, Chris slept on the small couch in the sitting room between the home gym and the kitchen and employee bar. He did this because he was very drunk after ingesting several cocktails in quick succession without eating, and it made him feel uneasy to be so alone. For some reason, Perry's absence made him uncomfortable, which was unusual because he had spent so much time fantasizing about what it would be like to have Kara all to himself. Finally, they were alone and had a very low risk of being caught, but he had no urge to be by her side. Was it because of what she'd asked him to do? What he'd actually done because of her? It wasn't lost on him that she hadn't come looking for him once that evening, even though he had been in the basement.

Chris woke up the next morning much earlier than he would have liked. He felt like hell for multiple reasons. For starters, he was hungover. His skin was peppered with bruises from his fight with Morrie. And he ached from shivering on a too small couch all night.

He peeled himself off the couch and scoured the fridge in search of relief. He found a can of ginger ale and held it to his throbbing cheek before cracking it open and carefully sipping. He also scavenged some oyster crackers and took them back to the couch. He wished that it was later in the morning and that Darryl was there to cook up something greasy to soothe his nausea.

He checked his phone and saw a missed call from Dr. Hansen, but noticed that she'd left a voicemail. She said that it didn't seem like there was any serious damage to his stomach and liver, as he had feared, but they would run a few tests over the next few days and encouraged him to come visit. Chris looked up the hospital's visiting hours on his phone and counted the hours until he could go in. Seeing as it would be a while and he was in no shape to present himself as a caretaker, he went into his employer's home gym, swapped his clothes for a towel, and sat in the sauna.

Perry had given Chris permission to use the gym, but he always felt uncomfortable barging in on Kara's sacred space. Now, he couldn't care less about that. Besides, he knew that Kara wouldn't be up for a while.

As he sweated out the alcohol, Chris started feeling guilty for how quickly the estate was going into decline. By Morrie's account, the Bryant home had been the picture of peace and harmony before Chris arrived. He couldn't help but blame himself for how things had gone. He knew that Morrie didn't have the whole story, but a lot of the words lingered around him like a swarm of bees, threatening to sting if he let his guard down. Most of all, he felt sorry that Perry was lying in a hospital bed, alone. He felt guilty about the affair and about his part in everything that was going on.

Chris knew that he would have to do some serious good to make up for the trouble he'd caused.

Light-headed, Chris took a few wobbly steps from the sauna to the kitchen and grabbed a bottle of water. He sat on a barstool in his towel and drank the painfully cold water, feeling it move down his parched esophagus. When he was finished, he slipped back into his day-old clothes and finally returned to his quarters to shower and change.

By the time he emerged from his cottage, Darryl was pushing a small cart of groceries into the house. Chris jogged to catch up with him and helped him load the paper bags into the service elevator.

"I've been thinking," Darryl said as he put away groceries. "I was hired because Perry was particular about his meals, but Perry was always working, and Kara didn't cook. Without Perry—and a full staff to share leftovers with—I'm basically working at a smoothie shop, which was never what I wanted to do with my life. I'm already planning on spending less time here because I hate sitting around and doing nothing."

He glanced at Chris and then went right back to his work, as if he was embarrassed. The two had never spoken this much before.

"I'm just thinking out loud," Darryl said. "I don't know what to do—that's all."

Chris nodded and put the final bag of produce in an industrial-sized fridge. He needed to do what he could to keep Darryl around, not just because it would look suspicious if all the staff left or were let go, but also because he liked Darryl and enjoyed his food. "Personally, I would stay on for a little longer—a month or so. Use that time to enjoy a slower pace. I'm not planning on leaving yet—not while

Perry's still at the hospital. I just hate the thought of giving up on him, you know?"

Darryl nodded. "Perry's a good guy. I'm still in shock about it all."

"Yeah," Chris said softly. "I'm going to visit him today. I'll send your regards."

Chris gave Darryl a parting nod, then silently walked upstairs to Kara's room. He tapped on the door and peeked his head in. She was sitting up in bed, looking at something on her phone.

"Hey, Kara," Chris said softly. "Can I come in?"

"Oh, hey," she said warmly, clearly in a much better mood from the previous day. "I was just looking at apartments in the city. Look at this one. What do you think?"

Chris sat on the bed beside her and took her phone. She waited eagerly as he scrolled through photos of a high-rise apartment that was bigger than his childhood home. There were multiple bedrooms, a huge kitchen, and two separate living rooms. At the bottom of the page, it showed small photos of the building's state-of-the-art gym, outdoor pool, greenspace, and an underground garage. Chris didn't even scroll back up to look at the asking price.

"It looks really nice," he said unenthusiastically. "Hey, I wanted to check in on you to see if you needed anything."

She thought for a moment before shaking her head. "Nope, I think I'm content at the moment."

"Chef is planning on stocking the fridge with things you like, but I'm sure he'd make you something special if you want it."

"Nah, I'm good."

Chris had another question for her and wasn't sure if she would respond like he hoped. "I'm planning on going to the hospital soon to see Perry. Do you want to go with me?"

She scrunched up her nose. "No, I don't think so. Not today."

"Why not?"

She sighed and put down her phone. "I hate hospitals. Why would I want to go somewhere so morbid if I could just stay home?"

Chris pursed his lips and rephrased his request. "I've worked in hospitals. If a married man were to be taken by ambulance, his spouse would be there in an instant. Most spouses don't leave their partner's side. The only instance in which a spouse isn't there a lot is if they have small kids or a job that wouldn't allow for time off. You have neither of those things keeping you from visiting. It's important for you to go. It would look really bad if you didn't show your face there."

Kara pouted. "I'll go, just not right now. I'm not ready yet. Tell the doctors I'm not well and can't risk getting Perry or the other patients sick."

She looked like she was getting ready to cry, so Chris didn't press it. A lot of people disliked going to hospitals, but Chris was surprised to see that Kara had some sort of phobia surrounding her husband's state.

"Okay," he said, trying to be gentle with her. "I think I'll go now. Call me if you need anything."

Chris looked back before he walked out the door. Kara was back to looking for her next home. He just hoped that she would hold off on firing staff until things played out as they hoped. He didn't want anyone losing their job before it was necessary.

. . .

THE NURSES at the hospital were very kind and understanding when Chris explained that he wanted to visit Perry Bryant even though he wasn't family. One of the nurses was on her way to check on him and said that he was on the accepted list of visitors, so she walked alongside Chris. The halls were lit with natural sunlight, soft classical music was playing, and there was no crowding or commotion. The nurses he passed smiled at him, as though they weren't completely exhausted and generally fed up with their jobs. He felt a longing as he considered putting in an application, and then realized that working at such a facility would never be in the cards for him.

Perry's room was a spacious suite with a wide window, just like the one in his study. Soft light trickled in through the partially opened blinds, falling on the cream cashmere blanket. Perry was perfectly still in the middle of the bed, his arms tight at his sides. Chris had never seen his boss look so well rested, no purple bags lay under his eyes, and his skin looked clear and smooth.

"Hey, Perry," Chris said sheepishly. It felt wrong to visit him like an old friend, but it would have been worse for him to stay home with Kara.

A nurse brought in medical supplies, cleaning and packing up used items. He wondered if she had been sent in to act busy while he was there.

"I know you can't respond to me right now, so I'll just talk," Chris said, feeling uncomfortable. "Morrie left, and I don't think he's coming back. He's never really liked me, and I tried to tell him to wait around for a little bit, but he blew up at me and stormed off. Darryl brought groceries this morning, and he said that he's feeling unsure about his employment. I told him to stick around for Kara for the next few weeks, and I think he's going to. I tried to get Kara to come with me today, but she seemed really upset at the thought of seeing you in a hospital bed. She said she would visit later, though. She hasn't left her room since you got here. She doesn't want anything to do with anyone right now. I think everyone's going to give her space."

He looked at Perry's face and watched his chest rise and fall. He should never have ended up in the hospital. They should be back at the mansion, chatting about Perry's mental state and whatever other thoughts came up between them.

"I'm sorry this happened, and I'm sorry for not being a proper friend," Chris whispered. He sat down in a chair near Perry's head, not knowing what to do. There wasn't anything left to say that he hadn't already said, and there wasn't anything he could do to help his boss in this situation now. He was just going to have to endure this part of the plan until the end.

Chris sat with Perry for a while, occasionally thinking of a conversation they had shared, desperate for any topic to talk about. Once or twice, he reminded Perry that the labs done on his liver and kidneys looked clean and that he shouldn't worry about any side effects from the pills, well, other than what was happening to him right now with the coma and all. Mostly, he sat in uncomfortable silence.

He was about to call it a day when Dr. Hansen stopped by to talk to the nurse. They exchanged a few quiet words, and the nurse took her supplies and departed.

"We're moving him to a hospice tomorrow," she shared with a smile. "There's nothing else we can do for him here, as you know. Our facilities are right next to this building, so it's an easy move. He will be very comfortable there. The staff is excellent, and he'll have his own private space. Just call ahead and let us know that you're coming to visit and if his wife will be visiting as well."

Chris was glad to hear it. He'd wondered about how this would all work, but Perry's doctor was a smart woman and had prepared things for his care. "Gotcha," he replied. "Thanks for everything. This has been a nightmare."

"I'm hoping things work out," she said, looking down at Perry. "I've known Perry for a while, so it's tough to see him go through this. I wish we'd caught on that something was wrong sooner. Maybe we could have prevented this." With a wave, the doctor left the room.

Chris followed her a few minutes later. He felt guilty for so many reasons, and at the moment he felt bad about leaving Perry alone, but there wasn't any reason to stay longer. "Be back soon," Chris said quietly as he went.

IT TOOK a couple of days of convincing, but eventually Kara came around to the idea of visiting her husband. The point that struck a chord with her was the fact that she would get absolutely nothing if she was investigated and found guilty of harming her husband. Chris hinted at the fact that he would not take full responsibility if they were caught, but he wasn't sure why he bothered because Kara seemed oblivious to it.

Kara dressed the part of the mourning widow-to-be in a black lace dress and large sunglasses. Her heels clicked down the halls of the hospice center as she followed Chris and a nurse to the room at the back of the building.

"I don't know if I can do this," Kara said as she saw Perry in bed, covered in a web of wires and tubes. He looked just as peaceful as he did in the hospital, but now a thin layer of stubble had grown around his mouth.

"Talk to him," the nurse urged. "I know it looks like he can't hear you, but I'm sure he can and would like to hear your voice."

Kara looked at Chris and let out a sigh before turning back to the nurse. "Could we please have a little privacy? It's hard enough to see him like this."

"Sure," the nurse said kindly before backing out of the room and closing the door behind her. It remained a tiny crack ajar, but Chris could see there was no one within earshot.

"So people just come here to die?" Kara asked quietly, her voice squeaking.

Chris had noticed that her hands remained clutched to her purse, as if she were afraid to touch anything in the facility.

"People receive comfort care in places like this. They have their symptoms managed, but yeah, it's generally for people who have not had luck with other treatments."

"So they're just waiting for Perry to die?" she asked.

Chris pursed his lips and looked at Perry. "Not necessarily. At the moment, there's nothing the hospital can do for him. It's rare, but it's possible for the brain to heal to the point where he regains consciousness. They're going to keep him here and watch him while they see if anything changes."

She looked crestfallen at this explanation. She started pacing around in small circles, picking at her fingernails.

"So you're saying that I'm going to have to keep coming back here until something changes?" she asked, her voice cracking as though she was about to have a meltdown. "And what if something changes and his brain gets better, and he wakes up? Can't I tell these people that I want them to pull the plug?"

Chris reached for a chart on the bedside table that the nurse forgot to put away. He opened it to a particular page and turned it toward Kara.

"They have to follow his advance directives," he explained. "At some point prior to all of this, Perry completed paperwork with the healthcare system that said if he were ever in this situation, he wanted doctors to take any lifesaving measures necessary for ninety days. If no positive changes in his condition occurred, then he would be fine with 'pulling the plug.'"

"Three months," she said under her breath.

"It's really not that long," Chris said.

"I don't care that much about the wait. The thing that terrifies me is that it gives him enough time to recover. Then it's back to the fighting, yelling, and beatings." Kara pulled a tissue from a box beside the windowsill and dabbed at her eyes.

"It'll be okay," Chris said, a part of him wanting to put his arm around her to comfort her, but he knew that was a bad idea, especially since Perry was right there and any one of the staff could come in and see them. They might get suspicious and call the cops. He wanted to avoid that.

"Let's just finish it," she pleaded. "Look, there's no one here. I can even go in the hall and be a diversion if we need to. There's got to be a way to silence any alarms and just pull out some of those tubes and disconnect wires for a few minutes."

"No, Kara," Chris said, knowing that she was going to keep pushing. He just hoped he'd be able to talk her down.

He wasn't going to do anything further that would tempt his fate. What he'd done already was bad enough.

"There's an extra pillow at the foot of the bed," Kara said manically, pointing. "Just hold it over his face. Or, I think I have some pills in my bag," she said, rummaging through her Birkin bag. "Pour a few down his throat, and it might just put him over the edge."

"That won't work. I'm sorry, but even talking about doing that here is madness. It's so risky, and there's so little payoff because it might not even work. I'm begging you to stop asking me to do anything to harm him while he's under a doctor's care. I'm not going to change my mind on this."

"Then what's changed since you caused him to overdose in the first place?" she muttered under her breath.

"It's different," he muttered back. "If it makes you feel any better, the chances of someone who loses consciousness like that coming around are pretty damn low. I'd say that it's best for you to keep your cool for three months, and then you can do whatever you want." He really needed her to back off and let things play out because he wasn't going to go to jail. Not by himself at any rate.

This seemed to appease her enough, so they said goodbye to the staff and headed back to the house. They didn't speak much on the way, as Kara seemed utterly disappointed with the outcome of that visit, and Chris was unsettled by Kara's callousness. He couldn't be too horrified by the things she'd suggested, as he had briefly entertained the idea of killing his boss when she'd first mentioned it, and now he just needed to stick to the plan.

He prayed that Perry hadn't heard how conflicted he was when he was with Kara. He was sure if Perry was conscious, he'd probably heard her plotting. She wasn't exactly quiet about it, but she wasn't loud enough for the nurses in the other room to hear. How much could a person in a coma comprehend? Chris wondered. His thoughts turned to how long it was going to be before the next part of the plan took effect, and if he was going to be prepared for it.

Somehow, he didn't think he was.

## 24

On days that Chris didn't visit Perry, he spent most of his time hiding away in his cottage, trying to keep himself occupied.

Over the past year, Chris had learned that spare time was not good for his mental well-being. If there was no task to focus on, there was nothing to keep his mind from wandering to scenes that he wanted to leave in the past. He'd visit his old workplace and watch nurses sprint through the halls to his late patient's room to try to revive her; he'd stop by his old house in the middle of a fight or, worse, silence with his wife; and he'd watch himself decide if he really wanted to continue living while he poured the last drops of a vodka nip into his mouth at a day-use campsite. Sometimes, he'd even time-travel to happier times, like his nursing school graduation or a tender moment in bed with his wife while they talked about their life goals. This was sometimes more painful, given how things turned out. Now, he also included the memories of the nights he'd had sex with his boss's wife, convinced the poor bastard that they should break up, and then plotted to kill him with said wife. In those moments, he tried to remind himself that there was a plan, and it would get better. It had to. He couldn't go to jail.

Time spent ruminating on any of those failures would typically result in a period of depression that could last anywhere from an hour to a week. It brought him back to how he felt at the time, which was so painful that he could hardly stand to be sober. This was the reason why Chris never stopped buying booze at the estate, though he had found it easier to drink moderately.

These days, he forced himself to slip on his dusty running shoes and hit the country roads, running in one direction until he got tired, then making the long walk back to the estate. There was something about the physical exhaustion that quieted his racing mind so he could think without feeling terrible about everything that had happened. It allowed him to return to his temporary home with a clearer head. The running, along with the stress and the leftover diet food that Chris ate, caused the pounds to drop off in a relatively short time.

At this point, his looks made little difference to him. Kara was no longer infatuated with him, at least not like she had been before Perry went to the hospital, and he was mostly happy about that. There had been moments early on when she wanted him close—perhaps too close—for the present situation, but now she focused all of her attention on moving on from Perry, as if he were already buried.

He went back to his cottage to get cleaned up. After he showered, he put on a T-shirt and a pair of jeans, noticing how his clothes were already starting to fit differently. Before he walked out the door, he spritzed himself with a cologne that his ex-wife had bought him for their wedding day. The bottle only contained a few sprays left, as he had only ever used it for special occasions. He liked it well enough, but the sight of the glass bottle on his dresser made him think of her, so he was eager for it to run out so he could ditch it.

Chris had done his best to give Kara her space, as her mood seemed to be all over the place. At times, she was agitated and angry, and at other times, she was oddly elated and optimistic. Plus, there were a few staff members milling about the place, and Chris didn't want to give them any reason to spread rumors about their interactions or, god forbid, go to the authorities about it. They would chat on occasion, usually when Chris wanted her to go to the hospice center with him, which she begrudgingly agreed to do. On the drives there, she was sullen and pouty, but would brighten up on the way back.

Chris let himself in through the back door and found Kara in Perry's bedroom, neatly folding clothes from his closet and placing them on his bed. Open boxes and storage containers lay scattered around the room.

"What are you up to today?" Chris asked.

"Oh, just a little spring cleaning," she said casually, placing her hands on her hips as she looked around the room.

Perry was a neat person, but he had a ton of personal possessions. Every piece of furniture and shelf was covered in papers or awards or trinkets. The closet was filled with suits and designer clothing, even though Perry wore the same baggy button-up shirt and trousers every day.

"I figured I could donate Perry's clothes and things to charity. I bet there are tons of people who would be ecstatic to wear these suits."

"I'm sure," Chris replied, thinking about the only suit he

owned, which was likely in a storage space in Omaha. "What if Perry gets better and wants to know where all of his stuff is?"

She shot him a look, as if to ask him if he was stupid. "Even if that did happen, I don't know why he would be mad. He doesn't even wear these clothes. I've been stressed for days thinking about what I'm going to do with all of his things."

"So you're still planning on selling the place?"

She shrugged. "Not immediately. The more I think about it, the more I like the idea of doing a renovation and hosting events here. I've lived with stick-in-the-mud Perry for so long that I totally forgot how much I enjoyed hosting events. What if I turned this house into a venue that I could rent out and make arrangements for clients? It could be the perfect hobby for me. You've been telling me that it would be a good idea to find a way to make money."

"Yeah, but that was so you could divorce Perry," he said.

"It's still a good idea," she said, stroking his upper arm. "I'm thinking it would be the perfect location for a wedding. You could set up seating in the backyard for an outdoor ceremony and then open up the house for a reception. The bedrooms would be great for the family, and this room could be remodeled to be the newlywed suite. I could also see it being a rental for Hollywood types who want a little countryside escape."

"I guess it would be a good way to retain your staff," Chris said.

"What?"

"Your staff," he reminded her. "The people Perry—and you—employ to keep this place looking how it does. Have you spoken with anyone about their jobs? I think they might be concerned about making a paycheck with all of this uncertainty."

"I haven't really thought about that yet," she said. "Why would they be worried?"

Chris gestured around the room at the boxes. "It looks like you're packing everything up. It might be a good idea to let everyone know that they're still going to be paid."

She crinkled up her nose. "Yeah, fine. I think that money just automatically comes out of the account. I don't want to give anyone false hope that I'll get rentals here and it will be enough money to keep them on for good. I would have to talk to an interior designer and hotel manager and maybe an accountant to see what it would take to make it happen." She smiled softly. "I'm getting ahead of myself again. I need to get this place cleaned out before I can even make those calls. Think I can just hire a moving service to take everything I don't want to a thrift store?"

Looking tired, as if she had worked a full day of manual labor, she draped her arms around Chris's shoulders. "I'm sorry I haven't been very attentive to you," she said as she hung on him. She closed her eyes and rested her head on his chest.

His stiff body loosened beneath her, and he let his head hang to the point where his face brushed the top of her head. "You don't have to worry about me. I think the most important thing is that we get through the next few weeks without trouble from anyone. If someone tries to talk to you about Perry, act sad. If someone talks to you about something unrelated to Perry, try to keep your emotions in check. Looking too cheery would send the wrong message, even if you're feeling good. People expect you to be in mourning or worried sick."

"I know," she murmured. "It's just so hard to act upset when I feel relief. I want to move on."

"Not yet," he said softly, stroking her hair.

Chris wished he could feel relief. Instead, he felt this lingering feeling of dread at all times. He checked the windows fifty times a day, waiting for a police car to cruise up the long driveway to take him away. Some nights, he slept fully dressed in case he was yanked from his slumber to go to the police station and didn't have time to choose an outfit before he left. He was always on edge and prayed that no one noticed or thought about him. At times, he wanted to pack his things and leave forever, but there was a plan in place, and he was honor bound to follow it. Besides, leaving would make him look guilty.

"You haven't been around much," she said, slowly swaying in Chris's embrace. "I've started to wonder if it's because you're not into me anymore."

"It's not that," Chris said, not pausing to truly consider his feelings. Things were different between them, but he chalked it up to stress. "When I thought about us being together, it wasn't like this. I liked to imagine us being in our own place, not Perry's bedroom with all of his stuff."

"I know, but it's the best we've got," she said. "What if you came up to the house tonight? No one will be here but us. It might be nice to do it in the house for once on a proper bed. Or we could go to the steam shower or the hot tub."

Chris peeled her away, still holding on to her arms. "I-I don't know," he said, looking her in the eye. "I'm still feeling very on edge."

She leaned in and gave him a long, yet soft kiss. "Think about it, okay?"

Kara went back to her cleaning. She pulled shirts and

jackets from their hangers, placing them in a storage bin until it was full. Nudging it aside, she grabbed another one and repeated the process, this time with sweaters from a dresser.

Chris wasn't in the mood to help her get rid of his boss's things, so he went downstairs to get a bite to eat. On his way, he ran into one of the cleaning ladies, Marie.

"Did she tell you to pack your things, too?" she asked, putting her hands on her hips.

"What?"

"Mrs. Bryant. She told me that there's no point in me coming in tomorrow or the next day because she was cleaning out the closets and packing up. Do you think I'm going to get paid, or should I thank her for the day off? I don't want to find out when I get my paycheck."

"I wouldn't worry about it," Chris said, feeling uncomfortable being the middleman, but he knew he needed to try to get her to stay. If the staff left, that would just make Kara—and him because he was staying on—look more suspicious. "I would just enjoy your day off."

She pursed her lips and nodded. "If you don't mind me asking, why are you still here? You work just for Perry, and Perry isn't here. Why isn't she telling you to take off like Morrie did?"

Chris drew in a deep breath. This was what he feared. People questioning why he was still there when he was supposed to be Perry's caregiver and was no longer needed. It didn't matter that he had nowhere else to go, or that leaving might make him look guilty. Staying was doing the same, it seemed. He tried to come up with a reasonable explanation. "I'm here to take care of Perry's medical things. I take Kara to the hospital and work with his medical team.

She really doesn't like hospitals and all of the medical jargon, so I go with her and explain everything to her."

"Oh," Marie replied. "I guess that's good for you. Sounds like there isn't much to that job, and she still needs you to stay the night here. I wish she took my livelihood that seriously."

Marie gave him a nod and left the house, leaving Chris feeling uneasy. Was she in a bad mood about the uncertainty around the house, or was she subtly hinting to Chris that she knew that he was there for more than a ride to the hospital? Had she guessed at the plan? Had anyone? he fretted.

No longer feeling hungry, Chris rerouted and went back to his cottage to watch TV. It was about all he had to take his mind off Kara and Perry.

THAT NIGHT, Chris considered going to the main house, but managed to convince himself that it was a bad idea. It was a silent night at the house, and despite his slowly waning feelings for Kara, he still needed companionship. His boss, whom he had considered a friend, was in the hospital. Darryl, who had always been kind to him, didn't spend much time at the house those days. Even Morrie's absence made life around the mansion a little duller. He didn't always enjoy conversing with his coworker, but they had some cordial moments when they discussed Perry's care. Now, there were fewer people in his social circle.

While the thought of holding Kara in his arms sounded nice, he had a hard time being in the house without picturing Perry lying in that hospital bed. He could only replay the conversations he'd had with Perry about Kara over the past month and wondered what Perry was really thinking during those sessions. If he was capable of keeping secrets, Perry might have kept some suspicions to himself. Had he known about the affair? He'd not given Chris an indication that he had. Still... he had to wonder.

Instead of seeing Kara, Chris turned on the TV and watched syndicated sitcoms as the sun set. He laughed to himself as he thought about the fact that not so long ago, he'd imagined that he would be enjoying romantic dinners at sunset with Kara. Now, when he had the chance, he forced himself to stay away.

Headlights illuminated the grassy prairie as a car made its way up the drive.

Chris got up from his seat on the couch and peered out the window to get a closer look. When he saw the familiar shape of the white cruiser making its way to the house, his blood ran cold.

He knew this moment would eventually come. The police were here.

## 25

Immediately damp with sweat, Chris reached for his phone to call Kara to warn her. It was a reflex, but before he touched her contact information, he changed his mind. If the police saw his phone, they'd certainly wonder why he'd called her. He shoved his phone back in his pocket and sat back down on the couch, waiting to be called up.

He watched from the tiny sliver of visible window as two uniformed officers got out of the car and strolled to the house. They knocked, then folded their arms and chatted while they waited.

Kara opened the door, first looking shocked, then furious.

Chris didn't trust her to act cool with the cops and had an intense need to know what she was saying to them, so he sprang from his seat and walked briskly to the front of the house, trying to act as though he were confused by the police's presence.

"I saw a car drive up," he said innocently. "What's up?"

"They want in the house," Kara said, tightening the tie on her silk dressing gown. "But I don't want anyone here right now."

"It's regarding Mr. Bryant," the older of the two officers said. "It's protocol if someone is hospitalized for a drug overdose."

"A suicide attempt?" Kara grumbled. "I'm not trying to be rude or to tell you how to do your job, but I don't see what's so mysterious about that. Perry has a severe mental illness. Is it so crazy to understand that people can die of mental illnesses?"

"No, we understand that, ma'am. It's just something we want to check up on. Just so we have all of the facts."

"Here's a fact," Kara said snidely. "I personally know the chief of police."

"I understand, Mrs. Bryant. He's the one who asked us to come here tonight."

This shut Kara up. Obviously, she now realized that Perry's allies did her no good if Perry wasn't around.

"I still don't want anyone in the house," she said, removing some edge from her voice. "Things have been really hard, and the place is a huge mess. Plus, I'm not even dressed, and I feel uncomfortable having men in the house without Perry here."

Chris cringed at this remark. The officers wanted to take a look around the house, not at her. If Perry had been suffering from a self-inflicted illness, there wouldn't have been any reason to keep the cops out, especially ones who were friends of the family. The longer Kara made them wait on the stoop, the more suspicious she looked.

"I think you should let them check things out." Chris finally spoke up. He understood how suicides and accidental overdoses occurred and knew how the scene should look. He doubted the average small-town cop would think anything of it, which would cause them to leave quickly.

"Fine," Kara groaned. "Come in." She waved them in and shuffled inside.

Chris turned to go back to his quarters, but the younger of the two officers called out to him.

"Why don't you come inside so we can ask you some questions?"

Feeling like a kid being called to the principal's office, Chris nervously followed the crowd into the foyer of the mansion.

"You're Chris, right?" the younger police officer said.

"That's right," Chris said, feeling nervous. He looked toward Kara, who was pouring herself a glass of white wine. She lingered around the living room.

"Mind if we sit down and I ask you a few questions?" the cop asked Chris.

"Sure, Officer—"

"Detective Johnson." He ushered Chris into the living room, where they sat down on opposite couches. "Our police chief said that your employer spoke highly of you."

"I didn't know that he spoke of me at all," Chris said, surprised to hear that anyone knew he existed outside of that home.

"You're not originally from here, right?"

"I'm originally from Nebraska."

"That's quite the distance," Detective Johnson said, pulling out his notebook. "What brought you here?"

"A change of scene," Chris answered dryly. "I got a divorce, and I didn't want to see my ex-wife at the grocery store, you know?"

"I can understand that. So, what kinds of services did you perform for Mr. Bryant?"

Chris shifted in his seat, watching Kara eavesdrop from the room over, and knew he needed to keep his wits about him. "General mental health services. He likes to have an employee on call in case he has a panic attack. I also conduct regular therapy sessions under the guidance of his doctor, and I help schedule appointments for him."

"What do you do if he's having a panic attack? I've never heard of anyone having a doctor on call for that."

"Most people don't have the luxury of having a personal nurse," Chris said with a shrug. "Most of the time, he needs someone to remind him to breathe or drink water. If it's really bad, I remind him to take the dosage of sedative prescribed by his doctor."

The detective paused and gave him a curious look. "Did Mr. Bryant know of your prior work history?"

Chris swallowed hard. "Perry hired me because I found him on the side of the road, having a panic attack. He trusted me, and if he were here right now, I think he would agree that I was always very careful with his health."

Kara went back to the refrigerator for a second pour. She looked in and made eye contact with Chris. He had never seen her so nervous before. She was always cool and collected, even when they were sneaking around her husband's house.

The other detective came back downstairs with a camera. Chris wasn't worried about the pictures he'd taken. However, he was worried about his current conversation, even though he knew there was nothing for him to worry about. He was telling them everything he had practiced.

"Do you think that he would have qualms about hiring

you if he knew that you lost your job in Nebraska? I don't know about the legality of what you're doing, as you're not licensed to provide health services here in New York."

Chris shifted his glance to the corner of the room, where Kara was now standing, looking utterly confused. He knew things were bad when there were secrets that would shock Kara.

"My ex-wife used to give me neck massages, but she's not a licensed masseuse," he said, his voice low. "I talk to a man, who has become a friend of mine, about his problems and try to give him advice from a neutral source. I comfort him when he's upset and remind him to take his medication when he's not in a state to remember it himself. If Kara were doing these things, you'd say she's a kind and doting wife, not someone committing medical malpractice."

A tiny smirk came across the detective's face. Chris didn't know if it was because he'd done a good job making his case, or a terrible job, and the cop was trying not to laugh in his face.

"I could see that if you were a family member, but he doesn't know your history, and I'm sure he paid you generously for your work. If I were you, I'd be praying every day that he makes a full recovery."

"I do hope he makes a full recovery," Chris said, getting agitated with the cop's insinuations. He'd known this line of questioning was coming, but it didn't make it any less uncomfortable for him, and his guilt over everything was adding to his stress. He just hoped they couldn't see it.

Detective Johnson got up from the couch. "I read the files on the case in Omaha, and I'm surprised you weren't charged with negligent homicide. I can't see you being lucky again, given your history."

Chris pursed his lips, anger bubbling inside him, but he stayed silent.

The detectives gave half-hearted well-wishes and went back outside.

Chris didn't say another word to Kara, who looked like she expected him to stick around and give an explanation. Admittedly, he owed Perry the truth about why he'd met him on the road that day. But as far as Kara was concerned, she was the reason that local cops were reading his file.

He'd left his old life behind in Nebraska—he didn't want to talk about it in New York.

## 26

Chris didn't sleep the night the police interviewed him. He knew the wheels of justice turned slowly, but he still worried about the police coming back in the middle of the night to drag him out of bed. Technically, he didn't have a criminal record, but as far as the police department was concerned, Chris was responsible for the death of his patient once, and his next patient was in hospice care. He tried so hard to run away from his past, but clearly, that was impossible. He could leave town, but the cops would track him down in an instant. There was no running away, not from the police.

Running away from Kara was another story. The next morning, he went to the house to convince Kara to go to the hospice center with him. It was part of their daily routine, he'd tell her they needed to make an appearance, and she would complain and try to talk him out of it.

This morning, she called him over to the couch to sit with her as she watched TV. "Last night was weird," she said.

Chris was having a hard time looking her in the eye, so he watched the reality show that was on the screen.

Kara reached for the remote and muted her program. "What were the cops talking to you about?"

He shrugged, trying to think of an excuse that would align with what she might have overheard. "I think he was trying to get under my skin. Sometimes they do that if they think they can get a confession out of you."

"But what did he mean about you losing your job?"

Chris shook his head. "Back when I worked at a psychiatric hospital, there was a patient who died. I was part of the medical team who treated her. That's part of the reason why I moved up here. I couldn't go back to that place after that happened."

"Oh, I'm so sorry," she said, rubbing his shoulder. "That must have been hard."

"It was," he said, letting out an exhale. He felt a small weight being lifted off his shoulders. "I was in a pretty bad place after it happened. Everything in my life fell apart after that."

"Your divorce?"

He nodded. "That's why I packed up my car and left. There was nothing for me back home. I stopped talking to my family and friends. I don't blame them for letting me drift out of their lives."

Kara put an arm around his shoulder. "You've got me."

"Yeah," he said softly, letting himself rest on her arm, even knowing he shouldn't.

They sat in silence for a few minutes. Chris desperately wanted to close his eyes and fall asleep with Kara by his side. She had caught him in a vulnerable moment, and even though he knew he shouldn't be in contact with Kara, he felt comforted by her touch. He needed to put an end to it. Them being together right then would just make them look more suspicious to anyone who saw them.

"We should see Perry," Chris said, sitting up from his relaxed state on the couch.

"Can it wait?" Kara asked in a small voice. She wrapped her slender arms around Chris's neck and pulled him in closer.

He stared at her glossy, pink lips, feeling a magnetic pull toward them. "We can't," he murmured, frozen in place. "If anyone saw us, the police would find out. That would be the end of us both."

"Then what was all of this for?" she complained. "Why did we put ourselves at risk if you didn't want to be with me? You know that I have physical needs. Perry couldn't fulfill them. That's why things were so good between us. I just have this appetite for it, and I'm absolutely ravenous right now. Please, Chris, no one would know."

"We can't," he said, pulling away from her.

"Are you not into me, or are you not into having sex anymore?" she asked moodily.

Chris groaned in frustration. "You know that's not it. This is not the time or the place. We have a standing appointment at the hospice center, and it's important that we keep up appearances. We should have already left. Darryl will be here to prepare food for the day. We can't be in this room together right now."

"Fine," she huffed. "Let me change my clothes, and then we can go."

In a clear attempt to entice Chris, Kara promptly

stripped down, revealing lingerie that was not meant for the average weekday morning. She strutted to her closet and pulled out a pair of jeans and a sweater, making a big scene out of bending over to put on the pants and tugging her sweater over her breasts. There had not been enough time for Chris to leave the room. Knowing there was no one there to catch them at that split second, he decided to stay at the doorway and wait for Kara to finish getting ready.

The two drove in silence, punctuated by questions from Kara about their plan.

"How long will we be there?" Kara asked. "I have movers stopping by later."

"Moving what?" he asked, looking over to her.

She shrugged, looking casual. "Just some things I boxed up. They're cluttering up the house. I needed someone to put some boxes in a truck and take them to a storage rental. Don't worry, I'm not moving everything out of there."

Chris didn't want to respond but couldn't help himself. "Yeah, and get more witnesses," he grumbled under his breath.

"What do you mean?"

He turned off the highway and entered town, past the coffee shops and fast-food restaurants he patronized during his visits to Perry. "You're going to allow some strangers into the house to load up boxes of things belonging to your dying husband so they can stuff them in a storage container away from the house. If the cops know that people are at the house, they may ask them questions. It doesn't look good for you."

"They're just college kids looking to make some extra cash," Kara said defensively. "I can pay them a little more to keep quiet about it."

Chris rolled his eyes. "That's not suspicious at all," he said sarcastically as they pulled into the hospice parking lot. Part of him wondered if he should just let it go, but then it was Perry's things they were talking about, and he was pretty sure Perry wouldn't be happy about it if he heard what she was doing.

When the pair entered Perry's room, a nurse was giving Perry a sponge bath. Chris felt uncomfortable seeing his boss partially disrobed. However, Kara seemed far more disturbed by this sight, which made no sense to Chris, as she had obviously seen her husband in the nude before. She immediately made an about-face and headed toward the lobby, where she made a beeline toward the coin-operated coffee machine. She dug in her purse and pulled out a few quarters as Chris followed her.

"What?" he asked her, trying to hide the exasperation in his voice.

"I don't know," she said shortly as coffee trickled into a paper cup. "He looks gross. Like a corpse."

"Isn't that what you wanted?" Chris whispered as he peered around the room to ensure no one overheard him.

Kara shot him a dirty look and snatched her steaming cup. "Stop. Can we go now? We made our appearance."

"Hardly. I'm going to talk to the nurse and cover for you."

Chris went back into the room to find the nurse covering Perry with his blanket. He asked about Perry's condition and then explained that Kara was having a hard time seeing her husband moved around like a puppet.

The nurse was sympathetic and offered to let Kara bathe him herself, as some relatives preferred to help their loved ones. Chris thanked her for the offer, not disclosing that

Kara was likely to jump out of her skin if she had to touch her husband's body.

After the nurse left, he managed to coax Kara into the room for a half hour before she begged him to take her home. He agreed, as she had fulfilled her duty. As they walked out of the center, he recognized a few visitors who were always there. That was how Kara was supposed to behave, though she didn't want to hear it.

Her mood lifted the moment they crossed onto their property line. It was as if she became possessed every time she had to deal with Perry, then instantly cured the moment she was free of responsibility.

Chris went toward his cottage after parking the car and was surprised to see Kara following him when he looked over his shoulder. "What are you doing?" he asked as he opened the door.

"What? We can't hang out?" she said cheerily as she pushed her way inside. Before Chris could kick off his shoes, Kara plopped herself down on the couch. "Come here," she beckoned, patting the cushion next to him.

"Didn't you say you had movers coming?" Chris asked, filling a glass of water at the sink, wishing she would leave him alone. His guilty conscience was eating away at him and his feelings for her. "You shouldn't be here when they come. I'll probably hide out here so they never see us in the same building."

She checked her diamond-studded watch. "They won't be here for another thirty minutes. That's more than enough time."

"For what?"

Kara's smile instantly fell, then turned into a snarl. "This morning, you said we couldn't have sex because we had to visit Perry. We already visited Perry, and there's time before anyone will be here."

Chris was too tired to deal with Kara's badgering. He needed to process the police visit from the previous day and desperately wanted to take a nap. His head hurt, and his eyelids were unbelievably heavy. He had yet to eat anything that day because he had been too busy taking Kara to see Perry to keep up appearances, and she'd hardly cooperated with that.

"Is this all a joke to you?" he snapped. "I haven't slept well in weeks because I'm scared to death of going to jail for the rest of my life. We are not even close to being out of the woods yet. If you get busted for murder, you can't throw money at the judge and get away with it. You need to take this seriously." He wasn't even sure why he was bothering or what he was hoping to achieve anymore when he spoke to her about her behavior. All he wanted was for this to be over and for him to have survived the aftermath of it all without going to jail.

She stood up abruptly and balled her hands into fists. "It sounds like you have a history with the police, and you didn't tell me about it before. If the cops come for you, you'll just have to confess and leave me out of it. If you cared about me at all, you'd never speak my name to them. If you get busted, it's your fault."

"I'm the one being careful," he said, his anger rising to new heights. "You just have to chill out and act normal for a few weeks, and you can't even do that. Be fucking normal for once."

She stormed out of the cottage and slammed the door behind her.

Chris paced around the small kitchen, waiting for his

heartbeat to return to normal. He had been irritated with Kara on occasion, but this was the first big fight they'd ever had. It felt bad to fight with her, but he wasn't sorry about what he said. She deserved to hear so much more. All of this was driving him insane. "Just follow the plan," he muttered to himself. "Follow the plan and stay out of jail."

Without thinking, he went to the refrigerator and poured a splash of soda into a glass, then dumped a healthy measure of whiskey into it. He took a long drink before refilling his glass. It didn't take long for the booze to kick in, which amplified the drowsiness he was already feeling. Before he passed out, he saw a trio of young, muscled men in matching orange T-shirts make their way to the front door. Chris threw himself into his bed and was out without another thought.

By the time he woke up, the sun cast a pink glow in his bedroom. He felt absolutely awful and stumbled to the fridge in search of something to ease his aching head and bubbling gut. There was nothing.

Chris slipped on his shoes and walked to the house, shielding his eyes from the setting sun. The house was dark and quiet. He thought about checking on Kara to see if she was still upset with him, but he didn't have the energy. Instead, he raided Darryl's fridge for a ginger ale and a pint of leftover chicken noodle soup. He heated up a bowl, ate a serving, then grabbed a package of crackers from the pantry for later. He still felt like shit and planned on spending the rest of his night on the couch, watching TV until he fell back asleep. He'd talk to Kara in the morning and figure out a way to mend their disintegrating relationship.

Hearing footsteps as he made his way back upstairs, he held back in the doorway, not ready to speak to anyone.

Instead of seeing Kara or one of his coworkers, he saw one of the movers pulling his orange T-shirt over his tanned torso. Even in the dim light, Chris could make out ten red streaks on his back, Kara's calling card.

## 27

Hangover days were reserved for Chris to take stock of his life, purge toxins from his body, and feel a deep shame for everything that had transpired since the last time he swore he'd cut down on his drinking.

Luckily, Kara was not using the gym when he went downstairs to grab a snack and a cool drink. Using the empty space to his advantage, he hopped on the stationary bike. Out of all of the cardio equipment, he was less likely to get dizzy and fall off it. He pedaled until he felt like throwing up, then sat at the bar and snacked on crackers and some fancy sports drink that Kara kept in her gym. Then he lounged in the sauna, followed by a quick dip in the ice tub. It did wonders for his physical state, but his mental wellness needed much work.

Both Laura and Cole had contacted him earlier in the week, but he ignored them. It was hard enough to keep up with people from home, but it was especially difficult when his boss was in the hospital and the police suspected that he was the one who put him there.

Back in his cottage, he turned on the TV, muted it, then called his sister.

"What's up?" she asked.

Chris could hear children's television on in the background. He couldn't imagine dealing with a hangover with that noise going on all the time.

"It's probably a good sign that when you call now, I don't worry about something being wrong," she joked.

"Interesting that you say that." He laughed weakly. "Actually, things are pretty bad at work right now."

"Oh," she said, sounding crestfallen. "What's going on?"

"My boss is in the hospital," Chris said, letting the words spill from him. "He was on a ton of different medications for all of his mental and neurological conditions, and we think that he overdosed. He's in a hospice center because he's been in a coma for a few days now."

"Oh my god," she breathed. "That's horrible. I don't mean to sound insensitive, but if he's in the hospital, what do you do during the day?"

Chris knew she was trying to find a delicate way to ask if he was still bringing in a paycheck. "Not a lot, honestly," he said, kicking his feet up on the couch. "Most of the time, I'm trying to convince his wife to visit him in the hospital. Sometimes, I just go without her."

"Do you remember when Great-Grandma had cancer and she basically lived in the hospital for a month? Mom used to bring food to the hospital and visited her. You were pretty young."

"I remember," he said. He could still imagine the antiseptic and mothball smell from the rural hospital that his relative stayed in. He and his sister had visited at least once—it had been Chris's first experience with death. It hadn't been highly traumatic, as he didn't know the woman well, but he remembered being sad to see so many of his family members cry at her funeral.

"So why doesn't his wife want to see him?"

He sighed. "She says it's because she doesn't like hospitals. It has more to do with her not liking her husband."

"Seriously?"

"I know their marriage was in a bad place before this happened, but she doesn't even know how to make appearances," he said, letting out his frustrations with Kara. "I drive her all the way to the hospice center. Mind you, I plead with her to just get in the car and go. Once we get there, she hardly looks at Perry. I talk to the medical staff, and she has nothing to say. She'll do whatever she can to avoid being in the room. Then, after about ten minutes, she begs me to leave. We spend far more time in the car than we do with her husband."

"Is he—do things look pretty bad for him?" she asked.

Chris felt a slight tinge of nausea return, as he knew what he had to say. "The doctors say that there are currently no signs of him recovering. Kara's acting like he's already dead. She's packing up all of his things to put in storage. She's probably going to lay off staff soon. I keep telling her to keep people on payroll. Perry's still alive, and these are people he hired. I know he'd want them taken care of."

"You have that much say around there? I would have figured that others have been working there longer than you have."

He wasn't going to get into his relationship with Kara, not

with Laura. She would be so disappointed to know that he had been sleeping with his boss's wife.

"Kara trusts me. I don't think she's ever gotten to know anyone else on the staff. She doesn't know what it's like to need a job. She sees people hanging around her house that she doesn't want to live in for much longer. She doesn't realize they've grown accustomed to having a relatively cushy job and will now have to find a new gig. I know it's not the worst thing in the world, and people have to look for other jobs all the time, but I think the staff feel like Perry's family. He's odd and can be difficult sometimes, but he is a genuine guy. I feel absolutely terrible about how everything has worked out."

"It's tragic," Laura said. "Even if my marriage were on the rocks—I can't imagine not visiting my husband in the hospital. I mean, wouldn't you?"

"Yeah," he said, not wanting to bring his ex into the conversation. She was right, though. If he heard his ex was in poor health, he'd at least show some concern.

Besides, while he avoided seeing his ex like the plague, he had no real ill will toward her. She'd tried her best under the shitty circumstances of having a husband who turned into a ghost for months at a time. Some might regard her as a saint for trying to break through to him for so long.

"I don't know the lady, so I don't want to speak out of turn, but is there something wrong with her?"

"What do you mean? If you're asking if she's neurodivergent like her husband, she's not."

"No, not that," she replied. "Is she not a nice person? Does she have some sort of personality disorder? You're the expert in these things."

His job wasn't to diagnose, but he did often speak with

doctors when he noticed something no one had caught before. On occasion, he had tipped doctors off on observations that caused them to make a formal diagnosis that got the patients the proper treatment they needed. That didn't mean he spent a lot of time diagnosing people he encountered in daily life. He hadn't spent much time thinking about Kara's mental state, apart from when he would talk to her about her unhappy marriage.

The more he thought about it, the more he wondered if his sister, someone not trained in psychology, was onto something. He knew that Kara and Perry's relationship was rocky and honestly shouldn't have occurred in the first place, but to show no remorse or concern toward Perry wasn't normal.

"Who knows?" Chris said dismissively.

"I don't mean to sound like a broken record, but you should probably pack up and move on if you think he isn't going to make it. Sounds like his wife is heartless and is cleaning house. I'd really hate for you to get caught off guard because you put your hope in the wrong person. If she doesn't understand what employment means to a person, she might give you the boot without warning."

"I know." He sighed, knowing he couldn't leave even if Kara tried to fire him. "I can't tell you what the future holds for me here, but I'm thinking about trying to hold out until my role is clearer. I would bounce, but you know that I had a really good thing going here. It's going to be really hard if I have to go."

"I understand," she said. "I wish it were easier for you. Take care of yourself, okay? You're not drinking, are you?"

"Not really," Chris fibbed. Overall, he was drinking less than he had been at rock bottom. Still, the way his stomach turned when she brought up booze was not a good sign that he was handling the stress well.

"Good. You know, I would stay away from your boss's wife. She sounds like trouble."

"I have to take her to visit her husband," he fired back. "I don't really have a choice."

"Oh," Laura said. "Well, make sure you're careful around her. I know I'm a bad feminist for even saying this, but there are some women out there who are just plain manipulative and will eat a nice guy like you alive."

"I'm fine," he groaned, knowing she was right and trying not to laugh at her sincerity. She wasn't that much older than him, but she spoke to him like a mother would. "Mind if I let you go? I missed a call from Cole earlier, and I was going to call him back."

"Oh, yeah, no problem," she said cheerily, likely relieved that Chris had at least one friend whom he still kept in contact with. "Please update me on your situation. I don't know your boss, but it's really sad what's going on with him."

"It is," he said, knowing that Laura would be devastated if she knew the full truth. "And I will."

He hung up the phone and grabbed a sports drink from the fridge, then poured it over crushed ice. He texted Cole to see if he was free while he crunched on the ice, slowly rehydrating the body he continuously punished. Cole called immediately, and Chris picked it up on the third ring.

His conversation with Cole was similar to his talk with his sister. It was impossible not to tell Cole about his trouble with Perry when Cole asked how work was going. The only difference was that Cole remembered his work details differently than his sister did.

"Kara's the hot one, right?" Cole asked. "I remember you

talking about someone who was the hottest girl you'd ever seen."

"Yeah, that would be her," Chris grunted. "Unfortunately, her weirdness has overtaken her good looks as of late."

"A shame," Cole replied. "Do you think she knows she's hot, and that's why she can get away with being a dick?"

"I don't know." Chris sighed. "She wasn't happy with their marriage to begin with. She would do therapy sessions with me and tell me about all of the mean shit Perry would say to her. I thought they should get divorced, but neither of them wanted that, so there wasn't much I could do to help the situation."

"A sexually frustrated housewife with too much time and money on her hands?" Cole joked.

"Actually, yeah," Chris said.

Cole didn't say anything for a moment, but then the words burst from his mouth. "Dude, did you hook up with her?"

Chris tried to lie for a moment before finally coming clean. He didn't feel good about any of it, but Cole seemed delighted to hear his tales.

"I'm not proud of it," Chris said, lowering his voice even though no one was around.

"Honestly, I'm impressed. No offense, but after your divorce, I didn't think you'd ever get back out there. I was worried that you'd never get laid again and become some sexually repressed weirdo."

"Really?" Chris responded, mildly offended.

"I'm kidding, but yeah, I was just worried about you. I know the boss's wife is not a great match, but if you're taking care of your needs and their marriage sucks, I guess there's no harm done there."

"We're not hooking up anymore," Chris admitted. "We haven't for a while. It seemed wrong with Perry in the hospital. Plus, it doesn't seem right anyways. I really thought she was great, but something has changed, and she doesn't seem like the same person I was interested in to begin with."

"I think that's a good thing," Cole said. "She sounds a little crazy. You don't need to get dragged into that. Trust me. Remember that girl I dated that first year after college?"

"I remember," Chris said. "We all hated her, and we didn't hear from you for weeks."

"Because she was crazy and didn't want me to pay attention to anyone but her. She was mad hot, but I was miserable when we weren't having sex. I think it's best if you stay as far away from her as possible."

"I'm doing my best. I still have to take her to see her husband in the hospice center."

"Oh," he said, his voice falling. "So things are looking pretty bad for him?"

"Yep," Chris said. "He's still unresponsive."

"Because he took too much of his medication?" Cole questioned. "If you don't mind me asking, how would that have happened if he had around-the-clock medical care?"

Cole's tone had changed. He sounded as if he were walking on eggshells, which was something that Chris had experienced and hated.

"What are you asking?" Chris asked, his voice flat. He should have expected it, but to have Cole ask that threw him off.

"Nothing," Cole said abruptly. "I was just curious about what happened."

Chris explained, trying to keep his voice even. He hated having to talk about this, as it brought up all the unpleasantness from his past. "Perry overdosed, either on purpose or by accident. I wasn't there. I'm not with him every moment of the day."

"Of course you aren't," Cole said desperately. "I just—"

"You just thought that I had fucked up again."

There was silence from the other end of the line.

Chris immediately regretted getting upset but didn't want to apologize for snapping just yet.

"I wasn't saying that," Cole said, sounding sullen.

"Okay," Chris said, sounding resigned. "I'm sure everyone thinks it, but doesn't want to say it. I get that. I found out that the police still have the incident on their records, even though I was never tried for anything. It makes sense that everyone thinks I would have something to do with this."

"Hey, man—" Cole started.

Chris cut him off. "I gotta go. I'll talk to you later."

"Okay. Let me know how things go."

"I will," Chris said, knowing that he probably wouldn't. It was too hard with as many lies as he was telling.

"Take care," Cole said before Chris hung up.

Chris felt unbelievably lousy. It was just another reminder that no matter what he did, his troubles would always follow. It didn't matter what good he did in the world if there was always a record that people would point to whenever something went wrong. He could leave New York altogether and dedicate his life to helping the mentally ill, but it wouldn't make a bit of difference.

Chris tossed his phone across the living room and buried his head in a throw pillow. Life was turning into a series of colossal mistakes, and he couldn't seem to keep himself out of trouble.

## 28

"Mrs. Bryant," the sweet hospice nurse said, placing a hand on Kara's shoulder, "do you want me to tell the detectives to come back at a different time?"

The nurse was an older, motherly type who was always so gentle with Kara and her moods. When Kara would leave Perry's room to sulk, the nurse would sigh and remark to Chris about how hard this whole thing must be on the poor young woman. Chris always nodded along, though he knew that Kara didn't deserve that kind of sympathy.

Kara didn't respond to the hospice nurse immediately, but instead looked to Chris for the answer.

"You should probably see what they have to say," Chris urged.

Kara nodded, and the nurse left the room.

"Just stick to the story and act normal," Chris hissed under his breath, regaining composure just as the two detectives who had shown up at the house returned for more interrogation. Chris's heart fluttered in his chest, and he had to force himself to take steady breaths. He gave the detectives a cordial nod, but did not extend himself any further than that.

Detective Johnson gave him a smug smile, then focused his attention on Kara.

"Is there somewhere that we can speak privately?" the older detective asked Kara.

Chris squinted to read his name tag. Matthews.

"He doesn't care," Kara said flippantly. "Anything you can say in front of me, you can say in front of him."

Chris didn't know if she was referring to him or her unconscious husband.

"We would prefer to speak in a separate room, if you don't mind," Detective Matthews said patiently.

"There's a family lounge next door," Chris proffered. "I didn't see anyone in there earlier. I'm sure the staff wouldn't mind if you took up that space."

Detective Matthews held out his hand, gesturing for Kara to lead the way.

Once they were out of sight, Chris rushed to Perry's side. He slid the chair back as far against the wall as he could, and pressed his ear up against the wall. He knew from previous experience that that particular wall was paper thin, as he had heard other families have conversations while he was sitting with Perry. As a bonus, the windows were cracked open in Perry's room and the lounge, making it possible to hear a conversation next door.

"How's your husband doing?" Detective Matthews asked Kara.

"No change," she said morosely. "Every day feels worse, though. I'm trying to hold out a little hope, but it's hard when he's in a place like this. People come here to die. My entire life is on hold, and it's so hard to take the uncertainty of it all. I really don't know how much more of this I can take." She sniffled for effect.

So far, Chris thought she was doing a fine job playing the role of the grieving wife. He rolled his eyes and glanced over at Perry. He looked as though he was just peacefully sleeping, but he was hooked up to several tubes, and Chris couldn't help but feel his guilt return tenfold.

"Can you tell us a little about the state of your husband's mental health?" Matthews asked.

"I know his brain isn't like yours or mine. It's not necessarily a bad thing—he's just different. He also needed to take medication for his anxiety and some other conditions."

"What medications did he take? Can you give us a list?"

"I don't have any idea. It always made sense to have more qualified people take care of his health. It would be crazy for him to depend on me for his mental healthcare, right?"

"Sure," Matthews said understandingly. "So you don't know much about his mental health?"

"Not really," she replied, sounding almost proud of that fact.

"We know that Perry had too much of his prescribed medication in his system when he was brought to the hospital," Matthews said. "How do you think that happened?"

"He took too many pills," she scoffed. "What kind of a question is that?"

Chris could hear frustration in her voice. He silently hoped that she could keep it together long enough to make it through the interrogation. He mentally pleaded with her to keep her cool in exchange for a trip to the nearest clothing boutique on the way home.

"How positive are you?" Matthews asked carefully. "Did you see him do it?"

"No."

"So how can you be positive that he overdosed? Was it done accidentally, or did he do it on purpose?"

"On purpose," she spat. "He had a mental illness. He struggled every day. People kill themselves all the time. Why is it so crazy to think that someone who battled with it their entire life would decide that it's too hard to keep going? People who are suicidal aren't able to make sound decisions in that moment. If you think about it, it's like being in the wrong place at the wrong time. He was having a low moment, and he was by himself with a bunch of pills by his side. If any factor in that situation had been different, he'd be at home. It's just really unfortunate."

Chris was impressed with how Kara was doing. She was sticking to a story that minimized blame on anyone but Perry. He had to admit it was a smart move.

"It's been a nightmare," Kara blubbered on. "I saw him passed out in bed and then stretchered away. Now, it's been hell to see him in a hospice center. We have a bit of an age difference, so I've had to face the harsh truth that I would likely outlive him, but I thought we had much more time. The doctors say that even if he pulls through and regains consciousness, he could have serious brain damage. I don't know what that means for us. I have been in hell since this happened."

Kara was laying it on thick. She was not always a sympathetic character, so if she could convince the cops that she was innocent, they might dismiss their suspicions. Chris wasn't sure how he felt about that. If they dismissed their suspicions about her, would they move on to thinking it was just him?

"What more do you want to know?" Kara cried. "I wish I could tell you something that could make this all better, but I can't. Every time you people question me about this, it feels like someone digging around in a wound. It makes me feel like I am an inadequate wife and that there was something I could have done to make sure this didn't happen—to make him happy so he didn't suffer from depression. How much longer will it be before you can let me be?"

"Not much longer, we hope," Matthews said empathetically. "Can we ask you about Chris Abrams?"

Chris tensed up on the other side of the wall. He wondered what she would say about him. Would she do what he expected, or would she put his head on a platter for them?

"What about him?" she asked, sounding as if she didn't care about Chris at all.

"We understand that Perry had one of his medical attendants on call at all times. Was Chris on call when Perry overdosed?"

"Yeah. If Perry would have paged him, he would have come to the house. That was how it worked. If they weren't doing a session or if Chris didn't stop in to check on Perry, he would stay at his housing."

"Is that what Morrie did when he was on call?"

"Morrie would hang out in the kitchen and drink and scavenge food that our private chef made," she said with disdain. "But yeah, if Perry was feeling upset, he would page Morrie, just the same as he would page Chris. Both guys would check in on Perry on occasion throughout the day, but Perry liked to stay in his office and work. He didn't want to be bothered, and it wasn't necessary until—" Her voice dropped off.

"Do you think there was anything Chris could have done in this situation?"

"I don't think so," she said.

"Even though he was hired to provide around-the-clock mental care for your husband?"

Chris gritted his teeth. He didn't like the implication that he was bad at his job. Apart from the one incident in Omaha, he was proud of his work. He had made great progress with Perry in his short time with him. But then again, Perry was lying there in a hospice instead of back at home where he should be, and that was pretty much Chris's fault. Well, his and Kara's.

"Perry has a mind of his own," she explained. "If a person feels the strong urge to kill themselves and they have the means to do it, there isn't a lot that can be done. If he meant it, he wouldn't call for help because Chris would have stopped him, right?"

"That's what we're wondering," Detective Johnson said. "Do you think Chris had the expertise and care to prevent this from happening?"

"Well, he is new on the job. I don't know if Morrie would have done anything differently, though. I don't blame Chris. I'm not upset with him in the slightest. I'm shocked that Perry has done this, but I'm not even that angry at him. I'm just emotionally drained right now. I don't want to spend the rest of my life waiting in this place, wondering what is going to become of my husband and our life together."

"I understand," Matthews said. "Does it change your mind to know that Chris was fired from his last job for accidentally causing a patient of his to overdose?"

"No, it doesn't," she said sharply, surprising Chris. "He's also having a hard time. He had a good working relationship with my husband. I would like it if we didn't have another conversation like this. I am not at fault for my husband's overdose, and neither is Chris. These kinds of interrogations are upsetting for both of us."

"We don't mean to cause you any distress," Matthews said diplomatically. "We'll be leaving shortly."

"No," she said with a huff. "Stay all you want. I'm going home now. I'm not feeling well, and this added stress is not helping in the slightest."

Chris heard her get up, which was his cue to move from his spot against the wall. He silently leapt from his seat and scurried into another chair on the opposite side of the room, where he casually read aloud from a newspaper to Perry.

Kara walked in and, in an uncharacteristic move, placed her hand on top of her husband's.

The two detectives watched from the doorway.

"I need to go home now," she said weakly.

"I'm just reading to Perry. I know we don't know if he can hear us, but if he can, I'm sure he appreciates it."

"I need to go home now," Kara repeated firmly, turning toward Chris.

"Oh—okay," Chris replied hesitantly, slowly getting up from his seat.

The detectives parted so the couple could move through the doorway. Kara marched out of the building, and Chris followed, using the windows of the entrance as a mirror to watch the police. The two men stood still, just watching Chris as they headed toward the car.

"I think we should have stayed there for a little longer," Chris said once he started the car. "Holding Perry's hand was a nice touch, but we could have done more to show the police that we aren't just making appearances. They are bound to talk to the staff if they haven't already. They're going to hear that we're only ever there for ten minutes, and that you're in a terrible mood whenever we're there."

She shot Chris a glare. "My husband is in a hospice. Why would I be in a good mood?"

"You know what I mean." He sighed. "What if they thought we ran off because they were there?"

"I don't care," she groaned. "I did exactly what you wanted me to. I'm holding up my end of the bargain."

"Hardly," Chris said under his breath.

They rode the rest of the way home in silence. When they got back to the house, Kara was quick to jump out of the car and strut toward the house, where she was preparing for her masseur to arrive for an appointment.

"Kara," Chris said as he followed her, "we need to talk."

"When I'm done?" she asked. "Do you want to stop by the house after the chef leaves for the evening?"

Chris had an idea on the drive back that he wasn't sure about going through with. He needed to break up with her. He needed to just end things, a clean cut. He should have done it before all of this started, but he'd been a coward. Now, he felt more confident in his decision. "How about the boathouse, for old times' sake? Eight o'clock?"

A coy smile appeared on Kara's face. "It's a date."

## 29

Chris stepped out of his cottage and felt a chill in the air. Before leaving for his evening stroll, he reached back inside for a sweatshirt, throwing it on over his T-shirt. He shivered, but didn't know if it was from the cold or from the dread that hung over him like a storm cloud.

He had learned to brace himself at all times, as something bad was always just around the corner. The second he felt good in his position in life, disaster would strike. Life had been good in Nebraska, and he had never felt so comfortable until the accident happened. Life at the estate was easy and exciting once Kara came into the picture. The constant threat of getting arrested was the universe's justice for thinking he could run away with the boss's wife, live off her wealth, and live happily forever with a hot woman with an insatiable appetite for sex. He had flown too close to the sun, and he could feel his wax wings melting.

As he walked across the grounds, the reality that he

wouldn't be there much longer lingered in the back of his mind.

Like his time at the estate, his relationship with Kara was coming to a close. In the beginning of their tryst, she had been cool and fun. He liked talking to her almost as much as he enjoyed sneaking around with her. She had taken an interest in him, a literal nobody and staff member employed by her husband. When she felt the need to take care of her sexual needs, she could have chosen any man in the entire world, yet she chose him. It felt unbelievably good to be wanted at a time in his life when he couldn't have felt any more alone and rejected. When they were together, life felt worth it. When they were apart, he couldn't think about anything other than seeing her again, by whatever means necessary. He imagined them going on getaways. He thought about creating a future where they could be together. It wasn't just the idea of sex and money that fueled these daydreams—he truly wanted her companionship.

But something had changed. She was no longer cool and fun, but cold and manipulative. She was demanding and careless. His entire future was on the line, and he didn't trust her to look out for his best interests. He desperately wanted the old Kara to come back, but he feared she was gone forever. Probably never really existed. That was why he wanted to talk to her at the boathouse.

She was sitting in their hammock when Chris arrived. She was wearing a matching sweatsuit, and her jacket was unzipped far enough to see that she wasn't wearing any undergarments. She flashed a bright smile at Chris and quickly invited him up to sit with her.

"I wanted to talk to you," he said gravely.

She frowned. "We talk all the time in the car. I thought tonight was going to be special—like old times."

Chris sighed. "But it doesn't feel that way, does it? After everything that's happened with Perry, I don't think I feel like I used to. I don't really know what's changed, but there isn't the same spark between us."

"You're exhausted and scared," she explained. "We're both under a ton of stress right now. Things didn't go according to plan, and we just have to work through it. Eventually, I do think that we'll have our resolution. When Perry isn't haunting us, we'll go back to our old selves. I'm sure of it."

Chris shook his head. "I'm not so sure. I'm mentally packing my bags. The police are all over the place, and I want to be here for Perry—and you—but my future is on the line, and I don't want any trouble."

Kara's lower jaw dropped open. "You're leaving?"

"I can't stay here forever," he said dejectedly. He hated doing this, having this conversation. "If Perry dies, there's no point in me being here."

"What about us?" she complained. She hopped out of the hammock and confronted Chris. "Don't you want me anymore?"

He placed a hand on her shoulder to comfort her and keep her at an arm's length. "I don't know if we're right for each other. We come from completely different worlds. At first, I thought we were attracted to each other because we were different and embodied something that the other didn't have. Now, I think that you'd be happier with someone who understands your life, and I would be happier…"

He didn't know if he should tell her that he'd be happier alone, as he couldn't see himself entering into a successful relationship ever again. He was damaged goods, and he was certain that his curse would continue to follow him.

"You don't know what you want," she sputtered. "You're out of your mind if you came here and didn't want to hook up. We're the only people here. We could be having sex on every surface of my home if you wanted to. You don't know how many guys wish they were in your position. You're getting paid to live here, which could mean that you're getting paid to fuck me. And you're telling me you don't want to? You don't know what you want. Let's just move past whatever it is that you think you're feeling about this Perry situation and take our clothes off."

"I'm really not in the mood," he responded, taking a step back. "It doesn't feel right with Perry in the hospital. Things haven't felt right since that night."

"Fuck your moral high ground," she snapped.

Chris threw up his hands in exasperation. "I don't like getting pushed around. Things used to be so easy between us. You were sweet. Now, you're getting mad at me because I don't want to have sex with you on your husband's property while he's in hospice care because we tried to kill him and it didn't work? It seems like every day there are new demands. I have to drive you to the hospice center and leave when you want to leave. I had to give Perry the pills because you didn't want to do the dirty work. Now, I have to have sex with you because you're in the mood, even when I'm not. Have I always just been a pawn for you? Do you see me as a person or just someone you can manipulate?"

Kara scowled and stamped her foot on the plank below them. "Are you kidding me? You think I'm manipulating you because I want to spend time with you? You're mad at me because I was hoping we'd have sex?"

They were both shouting now. Chris realized that even though they were alone, the cameras around the property were still on, and anyone could come up the driveway at any point and hear them screaming at each other about everything they had been up to. Maybe that would be a good thing? He sighed. *Stick to the plan,* he thought. *Need to keep going.*

"We can't talk like this," Chris said, feeling resigned. He hated arguing and knew that it wasn't good if they couldn't get along. "For better or worse, we went through with this plan, and we have to make peace with whatever the outcome is." He knew he was saying what she wanted to hear.

She nodded and placed a hand on his hip, trying to pull him in closer. "I don't want to fight. I'm just so stressed, and I want everything to work out. You know that I'm a passionate person. I'm the type of girl who sees what I want and does everything I can to get it. It's why I know that we can get through this."

"We need to be careful," he said softly, very aware of his surroundings. "We need to be a united front until all of this passes."

She nodded. "I think I just needed to hear that from you. You still have my back, and you care about me. That's all I needed. I'm a little disappointed, and I feel embarrassed that I thought we'd be intimate again, but I think being emotionally close is just as important as being physically close."

Kara continued on about how they would soon reach the end of their journey and other plans for the future, but Chris was only half listening. She was clearly more invested in the relationship than he was.

"We should go back to our places," Chris suggested. "At this point, I don't feel like we're ever going to be completely alone here. We don't know when the police will show up to ask us more questions." And he knew without a doubt that they would. "We shouldn't be seen together like this. It's too suspicious."

She bit her lip and dropped her hand from Chris's waist. "Yeah, I suppose. I'm going to think about you tonight when I'm in bed."

"Me too," he said weakly. He turned to walk back to his cottage, but not before Kara planted a quick kiss on his cheek. He gave her a half-hearted smile and walked across the lawn.

He would think of her that night, but not in the way that she hoped.

## 30

In the following days, Kara had made it painfully clear that she was not finished with Chris. When he went into the house to grab food from the fridge, she had left a trail of lingerie along the gym floor. It seemed as though she had picked every piece of strappy lace undergarment that she had ever worn when they were together and dropped them where she knew he would see them. In the afternoon, when the sun was shining, she set out a deck chair in the driveway and tanned in her skimpiest bikini. At one point, she took off her top and dropped it to the side of the chair. Chris almost locked eyes with her from his bedroom, but ducked in time so she wouldn't catch him looking. He pulled the blinds after that episode.

When she wasn't getting the response she had hoped for, she escalated things. Chris wondered if she had made it her full-time job to seduce him, because it just so happened that every time he went into the house for something, she was there in various stages of undress. The final straw was when he entered the house, only to hear her call his name. It sounded urgent, so Chris jogged up the stairs to see how he could assist, just as he had with Perry.

When he got to her room, she was posed, completely nude, in her doorway. She grabbed him like a spider and pulled him into her body, holding him close. She breathed into his ear words that he had never heard being used about him, and in a moment of weakness, he let her pull him into her lair.

The sex was a production on her side, but the satisfaction just wasn't the same as it had been. There was no emotional connection or passion from him. Instead, he went through the motions until the act was over. Then, feeling ashamed, he went to the kitchen, grabbed the meals he'd originally come there for, and also snagged a bottle of wine. He was beyond asking Kara if it was okay for him to take her expensive bottles. To Chris, she was no longer his employer's wife, but someone who saw no issue with chewing him up and spitting him out. If she could take from him, he could take from her. He was extremely stressed out over all of this.

After that incident, Kara seemed temporarily placated. She wasn't as emotional around Chris, and at times was calm and levelheaded. When the two passed each other on the property, she was quiet, but cordial. When Chris suggested they see Perry, she was reluctant, but agreeable. She didn't whine on the drive there, but talked about how she was thinking about joining a friend in the city for some philanthropic work in the next year. At the hospice that day, she got nowhere near Perry, but she sat and listened as the hospice nurse gave an update. She waited patiently as Chris asked questions about his current state, and then quietly requested that they leave after an hour or so. Chris was impressed with her change in behavior, until they drove home.

"I've been doing some research," she said, turning toward Chris as he drove her home. "Given all of Perry's assets being in different places, it could take months after Perry dies before I have access to any money. I could sell some of our belongings to free up cash for me, but that's way more work than I want to do on my own. I thought about selling one of the cars or the boat while we're waiting, but we would need Perry's signature to transfer the title."

"Do you need money?" Chris asked.

"Yeah, kind of," she said sulkily. "We don't know how much longer Perry is going to live. The nurse said that he's really hanging in there, as far as his body goes. His brain is gone, and I don't think it's coming back. He's essentially a vegetable, but a really healthy one. Part of me worries that he's never going to die and that I'm not going to be in control of the assets so I can liquidate them and start over."

Chris wanted to roll his eyes. He had no idea how much money Kara currently had access to, but he guessed it was more than he could ever imagine spending in a lifetime.

"I think it's time to do something," she said gravely.

"Kara," Chris warned.

"I'm done being patient. It's been weeks now. What if he hangs on forever? What if we spend years of our lives visiting this place every day? You've got to want more for your life than this. I've told you what I want to do when I have my freedom. You hardly ever talk about what you want to do."

"One day at a time, Kara, and you know his arrangement was for ninety days."

"I don't care anymore. I'm done, Chris. Don't you see that?" she huffed. "Don't you have any future ambitions?

There must be something. What would you do if you were free from this place tomorrow?"

"I don't know," Chris said, raising his voice. "It's different for me. You have money and connections. You could try something out, and if you failed, you'd be no worse for wear. You'd still have people by your side, ready to pick you up and help you with the next idea. I don't have that. I have a couple of people who might be willing to help me out in a pinch, but my career as I knew it is over. I can't work as a mental health provider anymore."

Kara looked like she had been smacked across the face. "I just think that we would both be in a better place if we can move on. You know that I'll take care of you, even if we're not together. Perry's in that place to wait out the rest of his life. No one would think anything of it if he passed."

"You don't think they'd do an autopsy on him after getting so much attention from the police department?"

"Then we do something that won't leave a mark," she suggested. "Smother him when the nurses are busy. Inject air into his IV. Give him something that will make him really sick, but won't show up on a drug panel. There's got to be something. We can do some research—"

"Stop doing research on anything that looks suspicious," Chris said harshly, though he wondered why he was bothering. "If you think about typing something that you wouldn't want the police to see, don't type it. If they have cause, they could get a subpoena and search your devices. It's just plain stupid to search anything that could make it look like you're concerned with assets, let alone murder."

"I'm no better now than I was before," she huffed.

Chris made the turn onto the country road to head back to the house. "You said Perry was beating you," he said dryly.

"If that's the case, then you're much better off. You can still do whatever you want to do."

"No, I can't," she complained.

"You just went to the city to stay with friends," he retorted. "You have people come in and give you massages. You go to salons to have your hair and nails done. It's like your life hasn't changed at all except you can fuck college kids in your house without Perry knowing."

She shot Chris a glare, so mean that he could almost feel her eyes burn through him. "Yeah, well, you didn't have any complaints when we were sneaking around."

He knew that he had lost that argument when he brought up affairs. He felt foolish for bringing up the mover guy, as if Kara had cheated on him, not her actual husband.

"The point is, you're not being careful enough," Chris said. "One slipup can send us both to prison. I want you to stop researching this stuff and get the idea of killing Perry in the hospice out of your mind." He couldn't allow her to do something like that.

She rolled her eyes as they turned to drive up to the property. Darryl's car was at the front of the house, so Chris wanted to end their conversation then and there. He just had so little hope that Kara was actually listening to what he was telling her.

"You talk like you never wanted to kill Perry in the first place. I don't know if you remember this, but when I first brought up the idea, you seriously considered it. That was even before you saw my bruises. You completely bought in. You helped me with the plan and were the one to cause him to overdose. What is different now? Why do you suddenly act like it's wrong to finish the job and put a brain dead man out of his misery?"

Chris pulled into his parking spot and turned off the car. "I can acknowledge that I made a mistake," he said, feeling his voice about to break. He took a sip of the cold coffee they'd picked up on the way to the hospice. "I think it's normal to look back on a poor decision and feel regret."

Kara stared out her window and twirled a strand of hair around her finger. "Do you regret being with me?"

Chris knew the answer in his heart, but had the good sense not to voice it. "I didn't support you staying in that marriage. The two of you were not a good fit, and it wasn't healthy for either of you, especially you. You clearly need your freedom. You're young, and you know exactly what you want. Perry has his flaws, but I don't think that means he should die. He was always good to me, and I would be lying if I said I didn't feel a tremendous amount of guilt.

"I'm also seeing that I'm not as anonymous and innocuous here as I thought. It's a small area, and the police know Perry. They've found out that I was fired for negligence, and someone died because of it. If they continue digging, they'll find out I've developed a bit of a drinking problem and that we are together. That's about all the evidence they need to make sure I never work in the field I have a passion and talent for ever again. I can live a pathetic life as a drifter if I have to leave this place. I've done it before. What I can't do is live in jail. That's not a life, and it's something I won't be able to handle."

"You're not going to jail," she said flippantly.

"I could. So could you. You have no idea how hard life would be for you in prison. Most of the women in there have had really terrible lives, and they'd love to terrorize a privileged woman like you. Your skin would break out and wrinkle from the hard water and lack of skincare products.

There would be no supplements and healthy meals, and your Pilates studio is now an open yard. The worst part is that everyone you know will go on with their fun and glamorous lives while you waste away in prison with no hope of ever seeing the outside. If you do, you'll be old, and everyone would have moved on without you."

"Stop." Kara grimaced.

"Am I finally getting through to you?"

"No, you're annoying me. You're being overly dramatic, and it's not doing us any good. If you hate being here so much, leave."

"I can't," he said, frustration in his voice. "If I leave, how does that look to the police?"

"Like you don't have any work to do," she replied. "If you hate me so much, go and let me deal with this myself."

She got out of the car, and Chris quickly followed her, worried that she would do something they both would regret.

"Kara," he said gently, "I'm sorry. I don't hate you. I'm just looking out for you—for both of us."

"I'll be fine." She sniffed. "I just have this feeling that everything will work out. Please relax and follow my lead."

Chris nodded, though he had no intention of leaving things up to Kara.

After giving Kara a head start, Chris went into the house, but trotted to the basement while Kara went upstairs. Darryl was in the prep area, washing and peeling vegetables for Kara's green juice.

"Any change with the boss?" Darryl asked, hardly looking up from his work.

Chris watched as the polished knife worked through a cucumber. "Nope."

"That's a shame," Darryl replied. "I was reading up on homemade feeding tube formulas if he ever had the chance to come home for his care. I feel like I'm losing a little part of my life. I know it's just a job, but it's not very often that you get to work with the same crew of people for this many years. It's pretty rare for chefs to have one household to take care of. Even if I find another family to work for, this house feels like home. I'm not ready to leave."

"I hear you," Chris said, as his mind wandered to the cottage and everything he would have to do to pack up his life and move out in the middle of the night if need be. "It does feel like home."

Darryl rummaged around the counter and filled up a cardboard takeaway box with food before handing it over to Chris. "We might as well take in the benefits of being here before it's all gone. There's about twenty dollars' worth of organic produce in that salad." He went back to the range and ladled something into a cylindrical container and sealed it. "And here's the best lobster bisque you've ever had."

"Thanks," Chris said. "I'm surprised Kara eats this."

"She doesn't," Darryl said with a small smile. "I'm dealing with my inevitable layoff by creating the best meals I can for the staff. Kara isn't watching my grocery budget. It might be wrong, but I'm going to squeeze every last joy from this place while I can. I suggest you do the same."

"Thanks," Chris said again. "I'll do my best, though it's hard to even think of how I'd begin to do that."

"I'd start with the liquor collection," Darryl said with a wink.

## 31

The next day, Chris made his pilgrimage to the hospice center on his own, as Kara had informed him that she was leaving for a shopping trip. Chris couldn't find the words to respond before she took off in her black Mercedes SUV, but if he had gotten his head put on straight, he would have told her that while it was a bad idea for her to be frivolously spending her husband's money, he was relieved to see her go.

After going on a short jog, Chris showered and put on a pair of jeans and a golf shirt and drove the familiar route to the hospice center. He had made the trip so many times that he wanted to close his eyes and see if he could get there without even looking at the road.

It had been a while since he had made a solo trip to see Perry. He always wondered what the nurses thought when Kara was on her worst behavior, but also wondered what they thought when Chris showed up solo. He understood that it was unusual for anyone to have their own private mental health nurse, and stranger that he continued to show up even when Perry was no longer in his care. Everything about their situation was odd.

"Not a lot of change for either of us, huh?" Chris asked Perry as he took his seat near the bed. "The nurse at the front desk told me that you're going to your sister's house tomorrow. Even if they didn't need the extra beds, I think that will be a safer place for you. I'd go with you, but with the investigation going on, I don't think it would be right. It's all a matter of optics, I guess. Kara said she's not a fan of your sister, so I guess she'll have a good excuse not to visit you. Sorry if you wanted her to grovel at your bedside, but I don't think that's happening. She's going to be so happy to hear that she never has to come back here. It's almost disappointing to me that she doesn't have to go through the unpleasantness, even though it was a pain in the ass for me to get her here at times."

Chris looked to Perry, whose eyes were shut, though he could see the faint movement of his eyes underneath their lids. And was that a quirk of his lips? "It feels weird to talk to you, knowing that you won't talk back. I hope you're happy to know that I'm doing all I can to keep your house in order. I'm sorry to say that a bunch of your stuff is in a storage facility, though I've tried to convince Kara to keep it and not sell it."

Chris felt an immense amount of guilt every time he looked at Perry. He felt the urge to apologize for everything he'd done with Kara, but it wouldn't be good to bring that up at this particular time.

"I don't know if there's anything else to say right now. Kara went on a shopping spree. Darryl wanted to help in some way, so I'll tell him to prepare a few frozen dishes to take to your sister's house. I'm sure she would appreciate it."

Chris looked out the open door and watched families mill about the entrance. It was such a sad place, and he was glad that he wouldn't have to return anytime soon.

"Well, I guess I should get going now," Chris said, out of things to say aloud to someone who did not respond. "I'll get in touch with your sister to make sure she has everything she needs. I probably won't get to go to the house, but I'll make sure she is taken care of. I know you wouldn't want to be a burden on her. I'll see to it that you aren't."

Chris gave Perry an awkward pat on the shoulder and watched his face for a moment before going out to the nurses' station to let the nurses know that he was leaving.

"Are you going to be there for the medical transport?" a young nurse asked.

Chris shook his head. "I'm not going to be part of Mr. Bryant's medical care going forward."

She gave a knowing nod. "I imagine it's not easy doing this. Has to be so stressful for you to do all of this. What are your next plans?"

He shrugged. "We'll see."

"Would you ever consider working here? We're always short-staffed. If we got another nurse, I might be able to see my family once in a while," she joked.

Chris smiled politely. "I don't know if you want me to work here. I'm bad luck, as it turns out. If I knew how to do anything else, I might try to quit the profession altogether."

"I get that," she said. "It can be rewarding, but most of the time, it's soul-crushing. If you ever change your mind, this place is often hiring."

"I'll keep it in mind," Chris lied, knowing that he couldn't take that job. He gave the nurses a wave before heading out of the hospice for the last time.

The detectives intercepted him before he had a chance to cross the parking lot.

"Hiya, Chris," the older one said cheerily. "Mind if we have a word with you?"

"Sure," Chris said without emotion.

"We just wanted to suggest that you have a word with Kara about our investigation. We know that she is only with Perry for the money. If we can get evidence that she wanted something bad to happen to him, then we can close this case without too much trouble."

"I'm not talking to Kara much these days." Chris sighed. "To tell you the truth, she's been in a bad mood, and I don't make a habit of lingering around women in a mood."

This caused both detectives to chuckle.

Chris couldn't share in the levity. He felt his hands tremble every time he was near them. Their presence set him on edge, as if they were always one gotcha moment away from cuffing him and stuffing him into the back of a patrol car.

"We need you to get her to talk about her role in this in a way that could be delivered to a jury as evidence. You could send texts or record a conversation. She's no genius, nor is she a career criminal. She wouldn't even think twice about incriminating herself."

Chris swallowed hard. Part of him still wanted to protect her. "I don't know. She's not home right now, and I don't know when she'll be back."

"Look, we know you've got a plan; this is part of it. You've got to do your part and get her to confess," the lead detective said, flipping his business card toward Chris. "We'd really appreciate if you could make this happen sooner rather than later."

"So you aren't focused on me?"

"You know we aren't. It's her we're after, though you know who you can thank for that."

Chris nodded. He was fully aware that he should be grateful and helpful to them. "I'll see what I can do," Chris said, but he had no idea how he was supposed to record Kara talking about everything. And on top of that, he wasn't sure if he was a good enough actor to pull it off. He wasn't even sure how he'd been able to pull this off so far, but then it helped that Kara was always wrapped up in herself. Still, he needed to try to do what they were asking.

The police left him for the hospice center.

Feeling on edge from the encounter, he made a right turn where he would usually make a left to get back to the country road that led to Perry's house. In the next small town over, there was a restaurant that Kara occasionally went to when she had friends staying over at the house. She called it a quaint place to brunch outside of the big city. Chris knew that it was the one place in the vicinity where no one would give him a funny look if he was drinking before noon.

He asked the hostess for a table in the corner of the patio and ordered an egg white omelet, toast, and a Bloody Mary.

When his order arrived, he slipped his sunglasses on and took a pull of the spicy tomato cocktail, waiting for his hands to stop trembling. He was getting tired of feeling on edge—he couldn't pinpoint many days in the past year in which he felt calm and comfortable. Most of the time, he felt like he was in a nightmare, running away from a monster that was always two steps behind.

"Would you like another drink?" the young waitress asked over the raucous laughter of a table of twenty-somethings who were draining a mimosa tower.

"Please," Chris croaked. While he waited, he picked at his meal, which he had little appetite for. He looked at his phone and debated calling Kara, but then he remembered what the cops had said about getting her to talk and recording her.

He was fairly confident that selling Kara out entirely would absolve him of his sins in the eyes of Perry as well as the state of New York, but he was utterly paranoid that someone in the department of justice would see his past and put some sort of permanent black mark on his name despite him doing what was right and cooperating fully. It was bad enough that the cops knew about what had happened in Omaha, but it would be worse if every other potential employer who ran a background check in the future knew his dirt.

He thanked the waitress after she set the glass down, then pulled out his phone.

> Just saw Perry. You remember that he's being moved to his sister's, right?

Kara always had her phone on her. Chris imagined her picking it up the second it buzzed. The fact that seconds had passed without a response told him that she was either thinking about how to respond or ignoring his question.

He was halfway done with his drink when his phone buzzed.

> I know. I'm at a friend's boutique right now, but I'll call you when I'm done.

He wasn't going to wait for that. Kara had a way of forgetting other responsibilities when she had something else that she'd rather do. He finished his drink, munched on the toast, and paid his bill. He was feeling a little better after the meal, but still couldn't shake the uneasy feeling the cops had given him. It felt like a bad cold that lingered on for too long.

Kara called as Chris was driving back to the house. When he glanced at his phone, he was annoyed to see a video call. Grumbling to himself, he answered it and propped the phone on the gear shift. Since he was driving, there was no way to find the recording app before he answered.

"Hey," she called, too cheery for someone whose husband was being moved out of hospice. "What are you up to?"

"Driving," he said abruptly. He glanced down at the phone to see Kara strutting down a city street. "We can talk later if this is a bad time."

"No, it's fine," she said breezily. "Chris, do you ever have moments where everything just feels so clear to you? Like you know exactly what you need to do with your life, and you can almost reach out and touch everything that you want and deserve?"

"No," he said flatly. "I don't know if I can relate."

"Well, it feels good. And it's been too damn long since I felt this way," she said with a hair flip. "Whenever I'm with my people in the city, I feel like I belong. It's like I'm a cat living in a house filled with dogs. I need to be with other cats. Do you know what I'm saying?"

"Not really, Kara." Chris took a deep breath and prepared himself for the conversation that he knew they needed to have. "I wanted to talk to you because the cops basically told me today that they know that foul play was involved with Perry's health. It's only a matter of time before someone is taken away in handcuffs. Best-case scenario, we're looking at attempted murder. Worst-case—"

He had a hard time saying the words. He was one bad decision away from going to jail, and the idea of that was keeping him on edge. His mind kept playing back alternate realities where he didn't make the decision he had actually made. Realities where he got the girl, realities where he went to jail... He started to hyperventilate.

"I know, I know," she said quickly, pressing her earbuds further into her ears, as if people on the street could hear their conversation.

Chris cleared his mind of the what-ifs playing through his head and refocused on the conversation. Again, he wished he'd found a recording app before answering. "Have you talked about what happened with anyone?"

"No."

He was suspicious of the fact that she was saying no. "Not even to your closest friends? Not even to the ones who you think might understand and support you?"

"No."

"How about the police?"

She opened her mouth in disgust, as if he had said something dirty. "When would I have done that?"

Maybe he was pushing her too far right now, but he needed to keep going. "I don't know. While you're in the city? While you're away from me and the house?"

She looked annoyed. "Don't be stupid. We're going with the attempted suicide story. It's perfect. It's foolproof."

Chris shook his head. Hadn't he just explained that the cops knew something was off? "It's not."

Her face fell. "It'll be fine. I need you to stop stressing me out about it. I'm not an idiot. We can make this go away."

"I don't think we can. I think you should get home. You'll need to make an appearance to see Perry at some point."

"I told you, his sister hates me. I'll be home later today."

"Fine." Chris sighed, figuring that was probably enough pushing for now. "I'll see you soon."

As Chris made his way back, he wondered if there was any way for him to pick up recording equipment and set it up before she got back—just in case.

## 32

"All of the medications Perry needs will be in the green tote from the hospice," Chris said into the phone as he paced around the dining room in the main house. "The instructions are on the bottles, and it's all pretty easy to keep track of. If you have any more questions, don't hesitate to call. You can also call his doctor, but I'm easier to get ahold of because I don't have much going on at the moment."

"Okay, thanks, Chris. I know this isn't easy for you, but it will work out," Gisele said. "Oh, and tell Darryl thanks for the food. We appreciate it."

"I will."

Kara crept down the stairs as Chris wrapped up his conversation. He could hear her making her way over to him. He hung up and slipped his phone into his back pocket.

"Who were you talking to?" she asked, folding her arms over her chest.

"Perry's sister," he said nonchalantly. He figured she

already knew the answer. "She had a question about his care."

"Then why don't you just go over there to make sure everything is okay?" Kara asked, sounding worried. "You would know who comes over to the house and what Gisele says about me."

Chris narrowed his eyes. "She hasn't said anything about you on the phone. Why do you think she's talking about you right now?"

"She might not be talking about me at the moment, but she's definitely talking about me. I don't like the idea of her having Perry at her house. She's bound to bad-mouth me, and it's making me crazy to think there's nothing I can do to stop it."

Chris shrugged. "You didn't want Perry here because you didn't want to be responsible for his care. Gisele offered, and it seemed like the best solution. If you're so worried about her bad-mouthing you, then you could go over there."

She quickly shook her head. "You know I'm not capable of taking care of him. Besides, Gisele and I don't get along, and she didn't offer, she insisted. If I went over there, she would only try to make me miserable. Have I told you about everything leading up to the wedding?"

Chris knew her story would take a while, so he went to the liquor cabinet and helped himself to some of Perry's fancy whiskey. He took his glass to the living room and got comfortable.

"When Perry and I got engaged, I had a party to celebrate, and I encouraged him to invite Gisele because they don't have other close family members. Everyone had a great time except for her. When she smiled, it was totally fake. I thought that maybe she was feeling left out. I asked her if she would like to be part of the wedding party, like a guest book attendant, but she said no. I figured she was being shy because she didn't know me. When I started planning everything, I sent her a bunch of my plans and asked her again if she wanted to be part of the wedding."

"What did she say?" Chris asked, trying to look like he cared about the story.

"She said no. Told me that she was feeling uncomfortable about us getting married and preferred to just attend as a guest to support her brother." Kara looked at Chris, obviously expecting a reaction out of him.

He didn't know Gisele, but thought it sounded like a reasonable answer. "How have things been with her since then?"

She huffed and rolled her eyes. "I see Gisele maybe once a year, and she's cold toward me every time. Perry has never seemed to notice or care that we don't get along."

"Perry doesn't notice a lot of things," Chris said absentmindedly.

"Sometimes that's a blessing," Kara grumbled. "And other times it's not."

Kara picked at the skin around her fingers, which Chris noticed as being an unusual behavior for her. She spent so much time and money getting her nails perfect that she rarely did anything that would mess them up.

"What are you worried about?" Chris asked, trying to cut to the chase.

"What aren't I worrying about these days?" she responded, flopping back down onto the couch. She pulled a crocheted throw pillow over her lap and wrapped her arms around it, squeezing it tightly.

Chris recognized that he was now playing the role of mental health counselor whether he liked it or not.

"Perry's health," he said with a smirk.

She rolled her eyes. "I'm worried that all of this will be for nothing. You should be worried about that, too. We did this in order to have a better life. I would be free to live the life I've always wanted, and you would have the financial freedom to make choices based on what you wanted to do, not what you had to do to survive. I think you've lost sight of that."

Chris shook his head. "Kara, I'm keenly aware of what's at stake. I'm surprised that your biggest concern isn't prison. I feel like I'm always bringing up how scared I am of having the police dig too deep into my life, and it's not something you seem concerned about."

She squeezed the throw pillow tighter. "We come from different worlds. People like you get in trouble for accidents, mistakes, minor crimes—people in my social circle don't. I can't even tell you how many friends of friends have done things that would put other people in jail, and they get away with a slap on the wrist."

Chris stared at Kara. She truly believed that she could get away with the crime because she was pretty, rich, and connected. She was so far removed from the real world that Chris didn't know if he should be disgusted by her or take pity on her for being so clueless.

"Let's face it, Perry is more connected than you are," Chris said matter-of-factly. "I think you could attribute most of your connections to him. The police are on his side, and that's really all that matters here."

"Politicians matter, too. They have pull, and I have friends who are in league with senators and congressmen."

There was no use talking sense into Kara. She lived in her own world where she chose to believe whatever suited her.

"It's the money that worries me," Kara murmured. "Gisele has some money, but not anywhere close to what Perry has. I could see her wanting to make a play for it and leave me high and dry. If she finds any wrongdoing on our end, I'm sure she could petition for some sort of seizure of Perry's estate. She's his only family apart from me. Things could be contentious, and even if I end up winning what is mine, it could take a long time to get things straightened out."

"You're married to him, so I don't know if that's a real possibility." Chris didn't know what New York's laws were in that regard, but if Perry had a will leaving it all to Kara, then she probably shouldn't be concerned about it. Well, apart from the facts that Perry wasn't dead, and Chris was working with the cops to get her to confess on tape to all of this, not that she was aware of that. At least he hoped she wasn't.

She pursed her lips and looked away for a moment before turning back to Chris. "I think she might be using you to get back at me and take his estate for herself."

It took Chris a moment to process what she was insinuating. He had talked to Perry's sister a few times on the phone, but had never met her in person. He didn't know much about Gisele other than the fact that she agreed to take Perry in and take over his care, alongside his medical team, until this was all over. He had certainly never given her information that would lead to Gisele getting Perry's estate for any reason.

"If that's all you're worried about right now, I can put those fears to rest," Chris said. "Gisele and I talk about

Perry's health and his care. That's it. There is no scheme for her to take his money when he dies."

She looked furious, which was illogical to Chris.

"But you see why I would think that, right?" she asked, her lips curled like she was ready to bite off his head if he said the wrong thing.

"No, I don't," he replied, feeling tired from all of her questioning.

"It's simple, really. You don't have feelings for me anymore. I don't know exactly when that happened. Things were so good for a while. I felt genuinely content because I knew that Perry wasn't solely responsible for my happiness. I could have stable finances through him and the affection I desired from you. It was perfect. Then it wasn't. Things were never the same since the night that we carried out the plan."

Chris wished that he were recording their conversation for the detectives; it would save him a lot of time and energy. It was too late now, though. Kara was fully locked into Chris, and getting out his phone now would be suspicious.

"Yeah, well, it did change things," he admitted. "There are things that I regret now. I can't tell you how exhilarating it was to be with you. Honestly, it brought more joy to my life than anything I can remember in the last few years. It was an escape, and it was blissful at times, but I understand on an ethical level that it was wrong. I was sleeping with my boss's wife at his home. Regardless of your relationship with Perry, we can both admit that it was wrong."

She didn't respond. Chris couldn't tell if it was because she knew it was wrong and didn't want to admit wrongdoing, or that she genuinely thought what they did was acceptable.

"I think that deep down, you know that you need me more than I need you, and that scares you," Kara said. "If we didn't end up together, I would be fine. I've had famous actors and musicians hit on me and ask me out. It wouldn't take much for me to get into a relationship. I'm out of your league, and you'll probably never so much as date someone like me in your lifetime. You know that if I carry on without you, you'll need a backup plan."

"What? The only thing I'm trying to plan is how I'm going to get out of this mess without getting into serious trouble that will affect the rest of my life." There was more to it than that, but he couldn't share that with her for obvious reasons.

"And that's why you're talking to Gisele," she said, with an eerie calmness. "She's not seeing a lot of people right now. She's cute, but she's plain. If you can make her feel pretty and special, I'm sure she would eat that up. You'll show up in a time where she feels helpless and confused and lend a helping hand. You'll show concern and ask her how she's feeling. She'll open up to you because you're good at getting people to talk about their feelings—the ones they usually don't talk about. Then, when she's good and vulnerable, you'll seduce her. You're an attractive man, and lots of women find a sensitive guy to be very sexy. You'll sleep together and convince her that she loves you, and then you'll tell her exactly how to get Perry's money. And she'll be so thankful that she's taking it away from the blonde bitch who married her clueless brother that she'll cut you a check."

"Come on," Chris said in disbelief. This story sounded so well thought out that he wondered how long she had spent constructing it. It scared him to hear her say these words, as if they were true. Who else had she told this yarn to? And did she suspect he'd already set a plan in motion? Not one that included him getting with Gisele, but one where he didn't go to jail.

"You don't love me anymore," she said morosely. "There was a time where I saw us living together and going out on real dates. Now, I feel like there's not much I can do. How can we get back to where we were, but without the constant worry about Perry catching us?"

Chris sighed. "I don't know if that's possible. The last few weeks have been pretty awful. We're not the same people as we were back then. Things changed. I think we just have to do our best to get through whatever comes next and then go our separate ways."

Tears came to Kara's eyes, something Chris hadn't seen in a long time. Her primary emotion had been disgust as of late. It was rare to see her truly sad, though she probably wasn't really; still, she was good at making it seem like she was.

"You wouldn't part ways with me without taking what you deserve, right?" she asked, joining him on the other couch.

Chris felt stiff and uncomfortable, as if he had to be ready to fight her off at any moment. She was a wild card, and there was no telling what she might do next. "What do you mean?"

She lightly placed a manicured hand on his shoulder. "We made a plan. We were going to take Perry out of the picture so he couldn't hurt me anymore, and in the process, I would be in control of our estate. For your help, I was always going to make sure you were taken care of, even if we weren't together. Seeing as things are strained between us right now, I still plan on honoring that agreement. I don't know if anyone else in Perry's life would do that for you if the money changed hands. I know you, Chris. I know that you've had bad luck these past few years. I know that things are harder for you going forward because of it. I know that money would make all of those troubles manageable. No matter what happens, I promise to take care of you."

Chris had only had one stiff drink, but he felt completely out of it. Kara's thoughts were in so many different directions that he couldn't possibly keep up. He was afraid he was going to slip up and give something away. He wanted some fresh air. He wanted to get away from Kara so he could think clearly. It had been a while since he had really thought about what their relationship was like when things were at their best, and it was tearing him up as he thought about what could have been.

He shook his head. It was too late for what could have been.

"Kara, I can't talk about this anymore. Not right now," he pleaded, trying to keep himself composed. He suddenly felt like crying, which was something he rarely did.

"But I need you to understand that we will be linked through this forever whether you like it or not," she said urgently. "We have to stick together. Please tell me you understand that."

"I understand," he replied. He got up and placed his empty glass on the bar in the dining room.

"Where are you going?" she asked as she got up from the couch. She acted as though she expected more from him.

"I'm going out."

"Where?" she asked, fear emerging from her voice.

"I'm going to the bar in town," he admitted. "I'm not going to talk to anyone about this. I'm going to order a few drinks, maybe get some food, and stay to myself. I just need to get away from the house for a little while."

"I can go with you."

"No, I want to be alone. I'm going to turn off my phone for a few hours and pretend like I'm someone else." Chris went back to his cottage and grabbed his car keys and wallet before locking up.

He looked toward the house before he got in the car and noticed that Kara was watching him from the window. It was a good trade-off for her to be scared now. It was what Chris had been feeling for weeks as she planned how she would spend her fortune—the fortune she was set to make for the murder of her husband.

## 33

"Anything for last call?" the older bartender asked.

Chris had already had too many drinks, but he was free from Kara, so he stayed on his barstool and ordered another. "Yeah, I'll have the same whiskey, but mix it with Coke this time."

"You got it, boss," the graying man said with a smile and a wink. He sloppily poured the booze into the glass and hit it with a splash of soda, then slid it to Chris. Then he printed a receipt for Chris to sign. "Thanks for coming out tonight."

Chris gave a half-hearted smile and nod, then took his drink to a quiet table in the corner. He felt a pang of loneliness as he watched the couples and groups of friends talk and laugh, then head off into the night together. There were just a few singletons in the dive bar, but they all looked like regulars. Chris wondered if he would ever look that way—old, weathered, and either void of emotion or over the top with it.

Chris took a sip of his whiskey. He knew that he shouldn't drive, but he didn't have any other options. He went to the water station and filled a plastic cup, then chugged it alongside his cocktail. He needed to sober up some before getting behind the wheel.

Being around Kara was exhausting, he concluded as he tried to process some of his feelings. When things were good, they were extremely good. When things were bad, she was a nightmare to be around, and at times he felt physically sick at some of the things she said and did. He couldn't believe the mess he had gotten himself into, but then again, it all felt par for the course these days.

By now, most of the bar patrons had left, and Chris didn't want to be the last poor soul to trickle out before the door was locked behind him. He got up and walked to the door, testing his drunkenness. He reasoned that if he could make it outside without losing his balance or acting visibly drunk, then he would be good to go. The drive home was simple. All he had to do was drive on a few empty roads, make a couple of turns; then he was back on Bryant territory. He could drive in a straight line. He would even go the speed limit.

Once the other cars had left the parking lot, he slowly crept out to the main road, then gently accelerated until he was up to speed. He turned the radio down low and turned the air conditioning up high, chilling himself into sobriety. The painted lines blurred in front of his eyes, causing him to feel nauseated. He focused on the road ahead and his steady breathing to keep both symptoms in check. He made one turn to the left, signaled early, and made a textbook ninety-degree angle turn. Farther from civilization, he started to relax his tense muscles a little, and began to let his guard down.

Then something darted out in front of his car. He couldn't tell if it was a skunk or a possum, but his instincts told him to turn the wheel to avoid it. Then he overcorrected, sending him into the shallow ditch. His car jumped back onto the road, and he skidded to a stop on the gravel.

His hands shook as he put the car into park to survey the damage. The front bumper had some chips and scratches, but other than that, there was no major damage done, as far as he was aware. He worried about mechanical damage but didn't want to call a tow truck to take it to the shop. He just wanted to get back to Perry's property before the cops caught him on the road. They were already watching him, and this mistake would be enough to put him in the doghouse for real.

He got back into the car and fastened his seat belt, but before he could put the car into drive, tears started leaking from his eyes, clouding his vision. Every negative feeling he had experienced over the past month had caught up to him. Loud sobs came from his mouth as he pitched forward and rested his forehead on the steering wheel, in between his hands, which gripped the leather. Tears poured down his face, but he didn't attempt to mop them up. It wouldn't matter anyway; more would follow in their tracks.

"I want to go home," he muttered. Then he repeated the phrase louder and louder like a mantra, as if wishing would transport him from Upstate New York back to eastern Nebraska. In the back of his mind, he knew he no longer had a home there, but it was the idea of returning home that appealed to him. He didn't want to talk to Kara, he didn't want to talk to Perry's sister, who was in over her head, and he didn't want to talk to the police, who silently judged him for his past even though they believed him now. He wanted to leave the estate but knew that he couldn't. He'd made a promise to carry out a plan, and he had to see it through.

Eventually, the tears slowed, and his breathing returned to normal. He took the sleeve of his jacket to his face and wiped it down. He looked around the car to see if anyone was coming. Luckily, it was a quiet night, and no other cars were on that road.

Before he pulled back onto the road, he noticed that where he drove off the road was just yards away from where he rescued a stranded Perry Bryant in the midst of a mental breakdown. The coincidence was not lost on him, but he wished that there had been someone to pull him out of his car and take all of his worries away. After a moment, he realized that it was his job, once again, to put a broken man back together. He had to rescue himself.

He returned to the property and immediately went into his cottage and poured the last few ounces of alcohol from their bottles. Feeling empowered, he then went into the main house and trudged down to the basement, where he put Darryl's bottles of various alcohols into a box, attaching a note that begged Darryl to take them out of the house the next time he came by with groceries. Darryl rarely used them for cooking anyway, and he never stuck around to have a drink at the end of a workday.

Then Chris marched back upstairs, where he started pulling the expensive bottles that he once lusted after down from their displays on the mahogany bar. One by one, he twisted the caps off, pulled out the stoppers, and poured the amber liquids down the kitchen sink. He gently laid the bottles in the trash can, trying not to create a ruckus that would cause Kara to get up and question him.

When the cabinet was empty, Chris washed the final drips off his hands, grabbed a snack and a sports drink from the fridge, and went back to his place to sober up. He chugged water and recovery drinks and snacked on vegetables and crackers while he watched TV. When the room stopped spinning, he got into the shower and turned the water up as high as he could stand it to purge the toxic drink from his pores. Once his skin turned pink, he brushed his teeth, climbed into bed, and prayed that the next day would be better. It would be hard, but if Chris could give up sex with Kara, he could give up drinking.

He just needed to get his head right in order to carry out the plan. Then there was no telling where his life would go.

## 34

Chris woke to the sound of someone knocking on the front door of the cottage. The sun was shining through his window blinds, meaning that he'd slept much later than he normally would. With Perry being out of hospice, he had no reason to wake up early anymore. There were no responsibilities left for him regarding Perry's care.

His first thought was that the police were getting impatient and were ready to push the plan forward. He dressed quickly and padded barefoot across the kitchen floor to answer the door, and was surprised, and almost relieved, to see Kara there instead.

"I wanted to apologize," she said before Chris could get a word out. "I've been acting crazy, I know. I've been stressed, and I realize now that I'm taking it out on you when you don't deserve it. I know we probably won't go back to how we used to be, but I want to make amends."

"Kara, I— "

"Just hear me out," she said, a coy smile forming on her

lips. "I've planned a few things, and all I ask is that you follow along. If you decide you hate me afterward, fine. I just want another chance."

Chris took a deep breath and put his hands on his hips. "What do you want me to do?"

She grinned. "Follow me," she said, grabbing his hand and leading him toward the main house.

"Kara, let me at least put some shoes on," he replied, finding himself about to laugh. It was an odd change. There hadn't been lightness with Kara in such a long time that the feeling was almost foreign to him.

"Oh, right." She laughed. She gave his hand a squeeze.

He didn't have the urge to pull her in close and nuzzle her neck like he might have a month ago, but the physical connection felt nice.

She led him to the dining room of the main house, where there was a massive breakfast spread waiting for him. Chris felt his stomach growl as he realized that he was starving.

"I pulled some strings and had breakfast made for us," she announced, pulling out a chair for him.

Chris looked over his shoulder. "Is Darryl still here?"

"No, he had to go somewhere else—another job, maybe? Anyway, I told him to do a little bit of everything, and I think he delivered."

Chris smiled and nodded as he sat down. Darryl had prepared all of his favorites: bacon, hash browns, and fried eggs with yolks that were just the slightest bit runny. He dug in before Kara had a chance to sit down across from him. In front of her seat, she had a tall glass of green juice and a bowl of mixed fruit.

"So let me tell you what I've arranged for today. I know it

might not sound like your thing, but all I ask is that you give it a try."

"Okay, what do you have planned?" he asked, feeling his spirits rise. He hadn't eaten anything so good in a while. Any trace of the hangover he had was disappearing.

"You've been tense lately, so I thought we could do an at-home spa day together. I have a masseur coming in, and he's bringing his acupuncturist friend. Then my esthetician will give us facials while my manicurist touches up our nails."

"Kara," he started to complain. He wasn't the type to get special treatments done, and the thought of someone coming in to do all of those things made him uncomfortable.

"You said you'd give it a try," she said, looking disappointed. "I promise that you're going to feel a lot better once you've taken care of yourself."

He sighed. "But how do you think it looks to have all of these people come into the house for what appears to be a couple's spa day?"

She waved her hands dismissively. "It's not like that. First of all, I know these people. They work for some pretty high-profile clients, so they know better than to dish dirt. It would cost them their livelihoods. Secondly, when you're in that profession, you're basically a therapist—you just don't talk about your clients. Finally, I explained everything when I booked it. I told them that you are Perry's medical attendant and you've been going through it lately. They thought it was very sweet of me to set this up for you."

"Okay," he relented.

She was right—the stress was getting to him, and the only way he was really coping with it was by drinking. Maybe if he tried things her way, he'd be able to get through the day without drinking half a bottle of liquor. Who knew she could be so helpful?

Kara answered the door as he finished eating, and let in a whole host of visitors, greeting them with hugs and kisses. They went downstairs to the gym to set up while Kara returned to the table to finish sipping her juice. Then she briefly disappeared and came back with a white terry cloth robe, which she flung at Chris. "Get changed. They'll be ready for you in a few minutes."

Feeling very uneasy, Chris slipped out of his shorts and T-shirt and wrapped the robe around his waist. He walked downstairs to the dimly lit yoga studio and stood awkwardly in the doorway. Soft music was playing, and it smelled perfumed, but in a good way. Thankfully, the masseuse talked him through everything that they were going to do, so he felt less clueless.

Chris's apprehension melted away after a few minutes, and he allowed himself to fully relax. After the massage, he sat in a padded chair while a woman scrubbed the calluses from the palms of his hands and buffed his chewed fingernails. She even used tiny clippers to cut away his cuticles, which he didn't know could be done. When she was finished, she brought him a hot cup of tea, plopped his feet in a steaming tub, and repeated the process on his feet. Apart from the pumice scrub, which was unbearably tickly, he was amazed at how much he was enjoying the process.

Then it was time for the facial, which Chris was the most uncomfortable with because it seemed like something only women did, and he didn't want anyone to scrutinize his skin, which he took no care in keeping youthful. However, he found it relaxing to have hot towels draped over his face, darkening the room even more. He allowed himself to fully surrender into relaxation as the world melted away.

Finally, the acupuncturist inserted a few tiny needles into various spots on Chris's body, explaining what the different spots did. Chris wasn't sure if he believed in alternative medicine, but he couldn't deny that he felt better in some way, as if he had returned to his twenty-year-old self.

"What do you think?" Kara asked smugly as they watched the crew pack up their cars after the session was over.

"I can see why you do this on a regular basis," Chris replied, still feeling like he had melted, but in a good way.

"You feel good, don't you?"

He nodded. "I do feel a lot more relaxed. Thank you. I see now that you were right about this." That was true, but he knew it was all a manipulation tactic on her part.

This pleased her. She took his hand in hers and gently swung it. "Let's go on a walk. It's a nice day."

They filled two tumblers with the tea the crew had left behind and walked around the perimeter of the property. The sun felt warm on Chris's skin, but not so hot that any physical exertion would cause him to sweat. He wasn't holding Kara's hand any longer, but he wouldn't have minded if she hadn't let go, and he hated himself for that.

"Have you talked to Gisele lately?" she asked. Her voice was soft and concerned, not accusatory like it had been in previous conversations.

"Not since the last time you heard us talk on the phone," Chris replied. His guard was up, but his defenses had been weakened by a very peaceful morning. He shouldn't have allowed himself to get so relaxed; there was too much at stake.

She nodded. "I know I sound crazy, but would you mind letting me know if you two talk? Think of it this way—imagine that I was having casual phone calls with the police. After all, some of the officers know Perry pretty well. I bet you wouldn't feel comfortable hearing me have those kinds of calls and not fill you in on what was being said."

"Yeah, I guess so." He knew what she wanted to hear.

"I'm going to try not to ask too much of you. I've already asked way more than I have of anyone. But I want you to keep me in the loop. If you talk to someone related to Perry or the case that the police are working on, I want to know who you spoke to and what was said. In return, I'll do the same for you. We're linked now. If we go down, we'll go down together. If we make it out of this mess, it will be because we put up a strong united front."

"I hear you," Chris said, feeling like she was manipulating him, or trying to at least. He supposed he'd let her think it was working, though his stomach churned with all his subterfuge.

She put her hand on his shoulder and let it gently fall down to his wrist. "No matter where the two of us end up, we'll always be connected by this. We are a part of each other's life now, for good. I don't want this to be a bad relationship, like a messy divorce. I want us to be like a chill separated couple who hangs out in the same friend group."

Chris couldn't help but laugh at this analogy. He had one ex-wife already—he didn't need another when marriage wasn't even involved.

"I'm not going to close the door on us," she said earnestly. "There's a reason we ended up here together. I think the universe knew I needed someone sweet, caring, and down-to-earth. I needed someone different than Perry, and that's you. Being around you is truly a breath of fresh air. You're a good person, and not just because you want something in return. So many people in my life are purely transactional; they treat you kindly because everything is a power play. You're not like that. You're probably way too good for me."

She brushed a strand of hair behind her ear, then leaned down to pluck a daisy from a garden bed. She twirled it in her fingers as she walked beside Chris.

It was a departure from the previous day when she insisted that she was way out of his league. Then, she was a cruel bitch. Now, she was an ethereal angel, practically glowing under the midday sunlight and speaking kind words. He had to wonder what she was up to.

"I appreciate what you did for me today," Chris said honestly. And he was appreciative, but that didn't mean he was going to go back on the plan. "I was feeling really bad, and this helped."

"Literally, anytime," she beamed. She took a step closer to Chris, brushing shoulders with him.

Goosebumps involuntarily crept up his arms.

"Can you promise me something?" she asked.

"What's that?" he asked, not ready to commit to anything.

She paused in her tracks as they came up to the cottage. Kara faced Chris and looked him straight in the eyes. "I know that the police will try to play us against each other. I'm not going to say a word to them. But if you're asked, please don't tell them that I had anything to do with Perry. Please, can you promise me that you won't sell me out even if it means that you'll get in trouble?"

Chris's stomach suddenly hurt. He couldn't believe he

was embroiled in all this. Acting was never his great ambition. He'd never been one to want center stage, yet here he was, putting on the performance of his life. "I won't say anything to the police. I think you're right—we shouldn't say anything at all."

"But if you're faced with a really good deal, you'd turn it down to protect me, right?" She looked desperately at him, clearly hoping to hear the words that she needed to hear to feel safe.

He gave them to her, but they were all lies. "Of course."

Kara abruptly pulled Chris in for a hug, momentarily knocking him off balance. "Thank you. You don't know how much peace of mind this gives me."

"I know you'd do the same for me," he replied as she released him. That was a lie too. He knew she'd toss him to the wolves the moment she got the chance.

"Let's talk later," she said as she started walking to her house, pleased with her work. "Oh, and let me know if Gisele calls again."

"Will do," he said, gritting his teeth.

He gave her a wave and went back into his quarters, fighting off a sudden wave of nausea. Playing games caused a visceral reaction in his body that told him he would never be up to Kara's level, but he had to outplay her if he wanted things to work out for him. It was nice of her to treat him to a relaxing day, but it was all part of the game. He knew that she wouldn't have set everything up for him that day if there wasn't something she wanted in return.

He hated lying to her face, but it had to be done. He had to win this war.

## 35

Around eight o'clock that evening, the knock on the door that Chris had been expecting finally came. Detectives Johnson and Matthews looked just a little too pleased to be in his doorway, which rubbed Chris the wrong way. They were supposed to be investigating an attempted murder, and they rolled up as if they were on their way out to the bar.

Chris slipped on a pair of shoes and followed them onto the concrete slab in front of the cottage. "To what do I owe the pleasure?" he asked, though he already knew since they'd planned this all out.

"We're going to ask you and Mrs. Bryant to come in for questioning."

"That's not going to go over well," Chris replied.

"We're going to ask out of courtesy," Detective Johnson said. "Perry is a friend of the department, and we'd rather not put his wife in cuffs and drag her in without the confession. It's all part of the plan. Do you think you can talk her into staying calm about things?"

Chris shrugged, knowing that if Kara was worked up, there was little he could do to calm her down. "I can try, but I can't guarantee it's going to work."

Chris followed the detectives to the main house, but unlocked the door for them and let them into the foyer. He called for Kara, who came up from the basement in her gym clothes, a cropped top and matching pair of leggings. She was breathing hard, but still looked perfect, as always. However, there was a look of shock on her face that Chris hadn't seen before.

"What's going on?" she asked, panic in her eyes.

"Ma'am, we'd like for you and Mr. Abrams to come to the precinct so we can ask you a few questions," Detective Matthews said.

"The police station?" she cried. "If you have questions, you can ask them here. Better yet, you can direct them toward my lawyer."

"Mrs. Bryant," Detective Johnson said, "it's best if you two come with us."

"Why?" she asked indignantly.

"Because people will see us go into town, and it's better to be seen in the front seat, not the back seat," Chris answered. "I'd rather not do this now, but I think it's best just to get it over with. You can tell them that Perry attempted suicide until you're blue in the face, but we have to comply."

"Whatever," she barked, slipping on her designer sandals, and snatching her purse from the kitchen counter.

Kara insisted that Chris ride in the same vehicle as her, probably because she was still paranoid of him flipping on her, and she should be. So, much to his dismay, he sat in the back of the elder detective's car while Kara sat up front with her arms crossed. Neither of them said a word, so the detective turned up the radio. Chris was trembling slightly, so he tapped his toes along to the classic rock to ease his nerves. He was playing a dangerous game, and he still wasn't sure if it was all going to work out in his favor.

When they got to the police department, reality must have set in for Kara, because she refused to get out of the car and go inside. Chris fully understood that it was bad news to be taken away from the house for questioning, and seeing the entrance to the county jail didn't help.

The younger detective went to her door to try to coax her out.

"I changed my mind," she said stubbornly. "Take me home."

"We're already here," Matthews said. "Let's just step inside, where we can have a private conversation."

"I don't know why I'm here," she complained. "I didn't do anything wrong. I already told you everything I know. Perry tried to kill himself. If I were there, I would have stopped it. It's sad, but there was nothing I could do. If you think I'm happy that my husband is a vegetable, you're out of your mind and, quite frankly, sick in the head."

Chris winced. It was never a good move to insult a police officer. She was about to cause a scene, and he didn't want to be trapped in the back seat of a cop's car while she did it.

Detective Johnson's patience seemed to be wearing thin. He motioned for his partner to get into the back seat and close the door.

Kara looked satisfied, as she assumed that she would be taken home.

"I'm going to level with you," Johnson said to Kara. "People close to you have been talking to us about your relationship with Perry."

"Who?" she demanded, immediately looking back at Chris.

He was just as surprised to hear this as she was. Of course, he shouldn't be surprised. It was all part of the plan, and he had talked to them about Kara, but he wondered who else might have been. Had they spoken to Morrie or Darryl? What had they said? Chris wondered. Had they told them their suspicions that Chris was with Kara? That thought had his blood running cold.

"You know I'm not going to name confidential informants," Johnson answered. "We've had multiple people who spend time around your home reach out to us after they heard the news about your husband's hospitalization. We called a few people to verify their information, but the majority of interviews we held were requested by the witnesses."

"And what did they say?" she challenged, though her face was tense with fear.

"Some said that your relationship with Perry was rocky. You'd get into huge fights and wouldn't even care that there were people around to hear it. They said that you never acted like a real couple. You only spent time together when you had to make appearances. Otherwise, Perry spent all of his time working, and you spent your time away from the home. Is it true that you even sleep in separate beds?"

She shot the detective a nasty look. "Is my marriage on trial here? Find me a couple who doesn't fight. Are you married? Do you agree with everything she says?"

Detective Matthews stifled a laugh.

Johnson smirked at him, then said to Kara, "And several people mentioned that you had affairs with men at your home, most of whom were employed by your husband. This includes his caretaker, Mr. Abrams."

Chris's face turned beet red at this mention. He should have known all of the dirty laundry would come out, but for some reason, it was so shameful and embarrassing to hear it out loud. Guilt consumed him, and he wished he could go back in time and stop all of this before it even started.

"That's a lie," she murmured.

"Some people thought that your behavior seemed odd after Perry was hospitalized," Johnson went on. "It sounds like you went about your normal life, packed up his things, and partied in the city with your friends, even flirting with men in clubs. No one saw you act sad or talk about how you were concerned about your husband. Hospital staff noted that you were rarely there to visit, and when you were, you seemed in a hurry to go."

"I don't like hospitals," she argued. "Is that so crazy?"

Chris noticed that she had nothing to say about the other observations about being around other men. He was oddly jealous when he heard she was getting cozy with guys on her trips into the city, which was completely demented.

"People have contacted the department with concerns that you were involved in Perry's overdose." Detective Johnson continued pushing her. "Like any lead, we look into it, and we think, given what we've heard, that this could be a likely scenario."

Rage washed over Kara's face. She kicked the glove compartment in the detective's car and screamed, "I'm going to fucking fire everyone and sue their asses. I'm going to sue this police department for illegally detaining me when I did nothing wrong."

Johnson reached over to move a drink up before Kara

smashed it, but he got too close to her tantrum, and she brought her fist down on his hand, causing him to drop the cup to the floor.

Chris had known she had a temper, which was why he'd been trying to get her to confess by using gentleness, but it seemed the detectives were going to go another route.

The other detective swiftly exited the car, opened the passenger door, and put Kara into cuffs.

"You can't do this," she squealed. "It's not my fault that people are jealous of me and want to bring me down."

Detective Johnson shook his head like he couldn't believe what he was dealing with and gestured to Chris to get out of the car and go into the station.

Chris wanted to bolt—run as fast as he could and hitch a ride back to his car so he wouldn't have to deal with the mess, but he knew better. They had a plan. It was going to work. He prayed that it would work. He followed the detectives and Kara into the building, where Kara was placed in an interrogation room, and Chris got a hard plastic seat in a waiting area.

"There's a bathroom down the hall and a vending machine around the corner," the younger detective said to Chris. "But don't go anywhere. When we're done talking to Mrs. Bryant, we're going to need to speak with you."

"I'll be here," Chris said flatly, staring at the clock on the wall in front of him. Immediately, he accepted that he would be there all night.

He could hear muffled shouts coming from the interrogation room but couldn't make out any words. He already had a good feeling what Kara was saying anyway. For someone who had just pledged to stay silent if questioned about Perry's overdose, she was awfully loud.

## 36

Waiting was a police tactic, Chris decided as he sat in the stiff chair that was used to break down even the most hardened criminals. Hours had passed since they first entered the police station. Kara's lawyer showed up about thirty minutes into her stay in the interrogation room, dressed in a dark suit and wearing a watch that Chris estimated cost more than his car.

The detectives were in and out of that room several times, and each time they crossed paths with Chris, they hardly even acknowledged his presence. They brought a variety of beverages in for Kara and her lawyer, but didn't so much as offer a bottle of water to Chris.

As he studied a brown stain on the carpet in front of his feet, he felt his composure slowly dissolve. For their plan to work, he understood that he could very well be there all night, as he had been in this situation before. It didn't make it any less hard.

After his patient's death, he had been brought in to the police precinct in Omaha, along with a small team of lawyers, to give the detectives all of the information they needed to know. It was not a quick process, either. Every few minutes, they were interrupted by a cop who needed to talk to one of the detectives, or a lawyer needed to make a call. Every time they took a break, everyone stepped out of the cold, dimly lit room except for Chris, who had nothing to do but sit there with his thoughts. He knew that he was ultimately responsible for the death of his patient, though he knew in his heart that it was purely accidental and out of his control. He thought about the girl's family and friends and how he could possibly face them in a courtroom. In the interrogation room, there were no distractions where he could take a slight reprieve from the terrible thoughts. He had nothing to do but focus on the hurt he had caused, not only in the patient's family, but within his own.

Now, he wondered whom he had caused harm to, beyond Perry. His boss didn't have many family members or friends, but he could tell that his sister was struggling with her new role as caregiver. From his sessions with Perry, he knew that Gisele hadn't been born until Perry was already out of the house. They were both academic types, but his sister had inherited more neurotypical traits, and they ended up living different lifestyles. After their parents' deaths, they found few reasons to stay in touch. Perry never saw the need to take on the role of protective older brother, and easily got lost in his own world and forgot to check in on her. They would talk on the phone a few times a year, and see each other at least annually, but they just weren't very close.

Chris could pinpoint Gisele as someone who was hurt by the ordeal. He could also recognize that some of Perry's clients, business partners, and employees were negatively affected by all of the turmoil. Then, there were all of the healthcare workers and police officers who had to deal with Perry on top of their already busy workloads.

Then, there was Perry, who was a decent man and deserved nothing that had happened to him. Initially, Chris had reasoned that his affair with Kara was a victimless crime. While cheating was wrong, he found moral ambiguity in the fact that Kara and Perry were on the rocks, and that Perry didn't have much interest in having sex with Kara to begin with. When Chris swooped in, it was as if he were only helping himself to leftovers. Why couldn't he have some if no one else wanted any? But now he fully understood that he shouldn't have had that mindset in the first place. He would have been wise to steer clear of Kara from the start.

The waiting room was still, save for the occasional ring of a telephone and voices down the hall. Computer keyboards clacked as dispatchers and office workers pecked in reports.

Chris was overcome with a sudden sense that this was his time to confess to all of the wrong he had done in his life in order to clear it from his conscience. He wasn't a religious man, but he felt deep down that this was the opportunity for him to turn his life around. Unlike how he'd felt when he met Perry, Chris desperately wanted to live, and he wanted to live a life that didn't cause trouble for himself or others. He wanted a fresh start. He thought he'd find it at Perry's mansion, but it was more of the same—stupid mistakes that led to massive trouble and regret.

Chris prayed that if he could make it through this nightmare in one piece, that their plan would work, then he would make a concerted effort to be a better person. He would be careful about his work, wouldn't manipulate anyone to get what he wanted, and he definitely wouldn't sleep with anyone who was already married.

Finally, Kara and her lawyer were led out of the room. The lawyer gave Chris a quick glance, and Kara didn't even acknowledge him.

The detectives wordlessly ushered Chris into the same interrogation room, the scent of Kara's perfume still lingering in the air.

"Need something to drink?" Detective Matthews asked as they got set up for his round of questions.

"I thought you would never ask," Chris said with mild sarcasm. "I would love a cup of coffee, if you've got it."

While Detective Matthews went to get Chris's coffee, Detective Johnson opened his notebook to a full page of sloppy handwriting and tapped his pen on the table.

"For someone who kept saying she had nothing to tell us, she talked a whole bunch," the younger detective said. "Luckily for us, her lawyer urged her to tell us what happened. Usually, the lawyer tells clients to say absolutely nothing, so this was a real treat for us."

"Happy for you," Chris said dryly as the other cop returned with a steaming Styrofoam cup.

"Where do we start?" Detective Matthews asked as he pulled his seat up to the metal table.

"Well, we could read back everything that Mrs. Bryant said, and Chris could comment on it," the other detective proffered.

"Sure," Chris said, knowing he had to let this play out; they had to make it look good. "I guess it's good to know what I'm being accused of."

"Settle in, then, because there's a lot to cover." Detective Johnson flipped back a page in the notebook and pulled out a pair of reading glasses. He slipped them on and looked down the bridge of his nose to report what he had found. "Mrs. Bryant alleges that you were solely responsible for Mr. Bryant's overdose."

Chris knew that this was coming, but it still hurt to hear. It felt like rejection, as if he had been passed over on a big job application or told he would be a better friend than love interest. He sat there for a moment, pondering the unusual feeling as he took a sip of his coffee. It was almost surreal sitting here, knowing a plan was in place, but still being made to feel like a criminal.

"Well, let's start from the beginning to give you the timeline of events according to Mrs. Bryant," Johnson said. "She admitted to having an affair with you, starting several months ago. She said that she was experiencing a rough patch with her husband and that you came on to her. She only gave in because she was feeling momentarily unsatisfied with her sex life and was weak. She reported that she told you it was a bad idea and that it was risky, but you insisted many times that you two would never be caught and convinced her the affair wouldn't carry on for long."

Chris took a deep breath and slowly let it out. Even if he denied the creative liberties Kara took with her story, the affair was very real and couldn't be disputed. Besides, they were already aware of the affair because he'd told them before all of this even started.

"She said that shortly after you started seeing each other, she noticed that you were acting strange around the house, and that she was suspicious early on that you were jealous of Perry. She said that most people who come to their home do become envious, and that's why it's hard to keep staff on board for more than a year."

"Then how do you explain Morrie?" Chris said curiously.

"She did mention that," Johnson said, flipping through his notes. "She said that Morrie didn't understand their lifestyle and had no use for money, as he was just a very simple man with a simple life. He was able to work there because he liked having an easy job where he got paid a decent salary to do little work. However, other people who worked there, including some maids, looked at what Kara had, and it made them so upset that they quit. She said that you were showing signs of wanting more money than what Perry paid you for your work."

"I actually think the pay was fair," Chris said casually, offering a rebuttal. "Especially since I was also living there."

"She said that you would talk about what it would be like if she left Perry, took her half of his money, and lived with you. It was like a fantasy you had. She said you were very frustrated when she told you that she loved her husband and wouldn't leave him and that it was impossible anyway, because she signed a prenup that would leave her with nothing if they divorced."

While this was mostly true, in the beginning he had wanted her to leave Perry, he didn't think they were good together. She'd proven that to be true. He shook his head and just waited for the detectives to finish going through her statement. They seemed to be enjoying themselves, and he just wanted to get all of this over with.

"This is where things escalate. She claims you asked her if you had a chance with her if something happened to Perry. She thought this was a hypothetical question and answered that if she were back on the market, she would consider dating you. You took this as a sign that you needed to get rid of Perry for good. You caused him to overdose on his pills, unbeknownst to Kara.

"When she saw the paramedics working on him, she became very upset. She said that something inside her head snapped, which explains why people thought she was acting strangely. She avoided going to the hospital or hospice because of a prior fear of hospitals, along with the fact that she couldn't see her husband in that condition. When she went, she had a hard time seeing Perry because she was afraid that something would happen, and she would be there to witness his death. That is why she was so distant and eager to leave, which lines up with all of the witness statements we collected."

"Oh," Chris replied, as he wondered if Kara had come up with all of this on her own, or if her friends had coached her through it.

He thought back to when everything was happening to see if he could provide evidence that would dispute her claims, but little came to mind. It was largely her word against his, and she fully understood that, which made him glad he'd prepared for this eventuality and had agreed to the plan.

"When it was all said and done, she said that you confessed that you tried to get him out of the way, and that you would bring her down with you if she said anything. She was scared to death and didn't understand the law, so she kept quiet. It was only when we started investigating that she talked with a lawyer and realized that there was enough for a strong case against you, so she wouldn't have to worry about retaliation. She said because it's likely that Perry will die, she wants to make sure his estate is not taken away by jealous lovers who want the money for their own."

"Okay, wow, that's some tale she's telling," Chris said, finishing his coffee. It didn't make him feel any more awake than he had been when he went into the interrogation room.

"That's it?" Detective Johnson asked with a snicker as he set his notebook down and took off his glasses. "I thought you'd have more to say about her statement."

"I honestly don't know what I could say," Chris replied. He'd known she was going to throw him under the bus, but then so did the detectives. "You already know the truth, so me saying anything isn't going to do much, is it?"

The detectives shared a smile.

"I thought you'd have a lot to dispute," Detective Matthews said. "She made some pretty serious allegations against you."

"Yeah, she did, didn't she?" Chris replied. "I guess I'm completely speechless. I don't know if I've ever been truly speechless in my life."

"A first for everything, I suppose. And now it's a first incarceration for you, but if you take Mrs. Bryant's word for it, you should have already had one of those under your belt."

"That's uncalled for," Chris said, feeling exhausted. He might not be the best guy on the planet, but he'd never intentionally hurt anyone.

"Sorry, you're right," Detective Johnson said, correcting himself. "Are you ready to do this? I'm not going to lie to you; it's going to be difficult. I'm honestly surprised you agreed to do it."

Chris had known it was a possibility that they might have to go to such extremes if he couldn't get Kara to confess on tape, but he'd hoped it wouldn't come to this. Who wanted to spend time in a jail cell? Certainly not him.

Granted, it was temporary. Just something that had to happen so the truth could come out. But it didn't make it any easier.

Chris gave them a bland look. "Let's get this over with."

"You really don't have anything else you want to put on the record right now?" Detective Matthews asked as his partner took out his handcuffs.

"Really?" Chris said, rolling his eyes as he stood up and turned his back to the detective.

"You're no fun. If it were me she said all that shit about, I'd be livid and giving away all her secrets."

"Pretty sure you know everything I know." Chris shrugged.

He was cuffed and led from the interrogation room down a long tile hallway toward the jail. As they went through the lobby, which was planned so that he'd be seen, Chris caught a glimpse of Kara in the entrance with her lawyer, who was talking to an officer.

She avoided making eye contact with him, but he could still see her face. She looked relieved, and why shouldn't she? Kara had already made it abundantly clear that she was too pretty, rich, and connected to get into any trouble. All she had to do was present the police with a perfect suspect, and then she was off the hook. Chris was in cuffs, and she was free. She had gotten away with everything; at least in her mind she had.

Chris tried to think of something snappy to say to Kara as he was led to the jail, but nothing came to mind. He wanted to leave a hint that she would soon get what she deserved, but he didn't want to speak too soon. He wanted to tell her that he knew everything she said to the detectives about him, but he didn't think that she would care. No, his reward would come later when she was the one behind bars and not him. He just had to be patient.

Kara examined her nails as her lawyer talked to someone at the front desk. Even in the midst of an attempted murder investigation, her focus was squarely on her and her physical appearance. Chris wanted to feel pity for her, as her appearance was the only thing of value she possessed, but he knew that she was satisfied with this truth. She thought she was winning. The system was perfectly designed for a person of her stature to stand impatiently in the lobby of a police station while she was under investigation for the attempted murder of her husband. It was set up in a way that allowed her to scream at police who were doing their job, and then have them apologize to her for inconveniencing her. She was highly skilled in getting people, especially men, to bend to her will. Why would the justice system be an exception to this rule? Of course, she wasn't going to get away with it, and that made him smile inwardly. He just had to put up with a little more stress, and then everything would fall into place.

After a whispered conversation between Detective Matthews and the officer who came to collect Chris, the new officer took him over to the jail. There was a series of heavy, reinforced doors to get through, which were opened by someone out of sight. With each beep, there was a clunk of a lock releasing, then a whoosh of air from the next chamber.

The detectives had quickly explained in hushed tones what the next steps would be for him, but it was all a blur, and Chris just allowed the officer to guide him into a room to change into a blue-gray outfit that felt like cheap pajamas and escort him into a cell. Chris was also given a small bag that contained a toothbrush, a roll of scratchy toilet paper, and other things he would have to look at later. He thought of how rough the night would be in a cell and immediately thought of how comfortably Kara would sleep that night in her king-sized bed, and the leftover pills from Perry that made sure she never even had to feel sorry for what she had done.

He was grateful that the detectives had made sure he would have a cell to himself, though, and that Kara's freedom was going to be short lived.

At least he prayed that was going to be the case.

## 37

Chris understood that jail was not meant to be comfortable, but he really struggled to relax to the point where he could sleep that night. It was late, though Chris didn't know how late it was because he didn't have access to a clock. He only knew that he had been brought into the police station in the evening, spent several hours there, then was taken to jail, where it was already dark.

Though he was alone in his cell, he wasn't alone in the jail. Vents in the door exposed him to the main hallway, which was fully lit throughout the night, though his individual cell was darkened. The quiet of the night was punctuated with loud snores, footsteps in the hall, and the occasional yell from a drunk or disgruntled prisoner. Just as he could see out into the hall, it meant that anyone in the vicinity could see in, which made it particularly hard to use the small, metal toilet adjacent to his bed after the interrogation room coffee had run its course through his body.

Having nothing to do but sleep and being in impossible

sleeping conditions felt like a mild form of torture. Chris took a few squares of his allotted toilet paper and created plugs to jam into his ears. This didn't block all sound but muffled it a little. He lay back on his thin mattress that covered the metal frame and pulled the scratchy, threadbare blanket over him. He wasn't the first, nor would he be the last, to shiver himself to sleep in his clothes and bedding. It was one of those nights where he felt as though he woke up every time he drifted off to sleep, though there was no way for him to prove the passage of time.

Eventually, the lights flipped on, and Chris heard the squeaks of bedsprings as the other men in the jail got up. Chris opted to remain in bed, until he was informed by a guard that this wasn't an option. He left his cell and followed the other men to the showers, where tattered plastic curtains covered approximately half of the stalls. As he waited in line, Chris kept his eyes on the tiled floor, in case he accidentally looked up and caught a glimpse of someone using a toilet without a stall door, or be accused of watching someone shower. Chris managed to get into a shower with half of a curtain, and rinsed off, dried his body, and tugged his clothes back on within the small space. Depending on how long his stay ended up being, he considered asking around to see how one acquired soap and shampoo.

Then the group was herded to the cafeteria, where he stood at the back of the line for breakfast. Men shuffled to grab a tray, then waited for scoops of beige slop to be delivered to separate compartments.

When it was his turn, he gave a faint smile to the two workers in hairnets, who completely ignored his pleasantries. Instead, they scraped the bottom of the metal containers and gave him what they had left of a sticky substance that appeared to be oatmeal, watery scrambled eggs, and a piece of toast that was both burnt and soggy at the same time. At the end of the line, he picked up a plastic container of orange juice that was an odd burnt orange color and a straw to jab through the foil lid.

Some of the incarcerated met up with certain people, but most sat at the cafeteria tables with as much space around them as possible. Chris found a spot at the end of a table and tried not to shake it as he took his seat on the bench. He was relieved that no one attempted to talk to him. He knew in some ways, he was just as bad as some of the people there, but some of the men looked rough, which frightened Chris. He didn't know the rules of jail and didn't want to find out the hard way if he made a mistake.

The meal was tasteless and hard to stomach, but Chris didn't know when the next meal opportunity would be, so he finished what he was given, then returned the plastic tray to the kitchen. He tried to go back to his cell, but was stopped by a guard, who gave him a look like he was out of his mind.

"You can't go back in that hallway right now," the guard said, as if Chris should have known better. "You need to go into the recreation room or library until after lunch. Then you're permitted to go back in your room."

"Really?" Chris asked, not challenging the guard, but more out of curiosity at how the system worked.

"The rooms need to be turned over for contraband," the guard explained. "You can't go back until that's completed."

"Okay," Chris said, accepting the rules.

The guard walked down the hall with the cells.

Chris followed a few men to an atrium that opened up into several small rooms. One looked like a hospital waiting room, with old chairs and a small television hanging on the wall. Another room had decks of cards and board games on a shelf, along with a Ping-Pong table. The third had several rows of bookshelves, along with a few tables and chairs, and the fourth was completely empty. The TV room was full, and the game room would require human interaction, so the library seemed like the best bet.

Chris grabbed a newspaper and found a seat in the corner of the room. He scoured the paper from cover to cover, searching for any information about Kara's arrest or his involvement in the attempted murder scheme. Afterward, he felt foolish for thinking that the paper would have already told their story, as it was still not finished. However, he knew that before long, his name would be in the paper along with Kara's and Perry's, considering how outrageous this whole affair was.

After a long and boring morning, his guard announced that he had visitors, and he was led to a small room. Upon entering, he noticed Detectives Johnson and Matthews.

"We're going to have to make this quick," Detective Matthews said, holding up a thin black wire.

Chris nodded and stripped off his shirt. Within a few minutes, a wired microphone was taped to his chest, and when he put his shirt back on, it was out of sight. "You think she's going to show up?"

Detective Johnson nodded. "She's on the move, so we want to be prepared."

Chris hoped they were right.

Detective Matthews knocked on the door, and the guard reopened it. The guard said, "Phones are available if you need them, or you can return to your cell."

Suddenly, Chris remembered his sister, the only person he chatted with on a semi-regular basis. What if Laura called his cellphone and was met with voicemail for an entire day? She understood that Chris's mental health had taken a dive after the accident in Nebraska. In recent weeks, Chris had spared her the details, but explained how things weren't going well at his job. She could also connect the dots and realize that his employment with Perry was miraculous and that finding a job with his history wasn't an easy task. Paired with unanswered phone calls or texts, it painted a worrisome picture, which might cause Laura concern.

Now, Chris had no proof that his sister would try to contact him, but seeing as he wasn't sure how long he'd be in the jail, he couldn't help but wonder if he needed to make a preemptive jailhouse phone call to assure her that he wasn't well, but very much alive. Then again, if she wasn't worried about his whereabouts, then a call from jail would be extremely jarring, and there was no way he would be allotted enough phone time to fully explain everything. Ultimately, he decided that now wasn't the time to call Laura, and instead, he would push that anxiety to the back of his brain to deal with later.

"Cell, please," he answered.

The guard led him back to his tiny room, and he sank down on the threadbare mattress to wait. He didn't have to wait too long for something to happen.

"Try to make it quick," a deep voice said softly from just beyond Chris's cell. "You're technically not supposed to be here, and I could get into big trouble if a superior comes in and sees you."

"No one will notice I'm here," a sweet voice promised.

Chris's heart started pounding as he stood up and lunged toward the door of his cell. The detectives were right. He would recognize Kara's voice anywhere, especially the way she used it to get what she wanted. Sometimes, it was sultry. Other times, it was childlike. Occasionally, it was stern and intimidating. She was well versed in manipulation, and talking was one of her many tactics.

The guard let her into Chris's cell, and she waltzed in and sat on his mattress as if she lived there. She smiled, though she was sitting two feet away from a toilet, and one foot away from the man she had put in this cell through her lies.

"How's it going?" she asked, as if she were visiting an old friend.

"Not great, Kara," he replied coldly. He scooted a few inches away from her and placed his toiletries bag to his side so he wouldn't sit on it. "If you haven't noticed, jail is terrible. I didn't sleep at all last night, and the food is giving me a stomachache. My leisure activities include reading newspapers or watching TV with thirty other men. It sucks. It sucks not knowing how long I'm going to be here. What I'm having a hard time understanding is why you're here."

She looked over her shoulder and then back at Chris, as if she were confused. "I slipped the guard some cash and told him I needed a few minutes to talk to you."

He shook his head and looked down at his shoes, willing himself to keep his patience. He knew that if he raised his voice, the guards would notice and come to rescue the pretty young woman from the "criminal" in his cage. He'd been told that the guards weren't in on things because the detectives had said they had to make things look real.

"No, I'm referring to the fact that we were in this together from the very start. I can accept that I'm here right now because I did a bad thing. I can't accept that you're not on the women's side of this jail because you were in on this plan.

You were the one who came up with the idea, and you were the one who begged me to help you. So please explain to me why you aren't in jail right now, and don't give me that same shit you gave the two detectives."

She grinned and snickered. "Because I always win. You kept asking me why I wasn't worried about getting in trouble. The reason is because I orchestrated things perfectly from the very beginning. From the moment we first spoke, I knew that you could be turned into a pawn for me. I wasn't sure how I'd use you, but then the opportunity presented itself in the most useful way."

"From the very beginning?" Chris asked, trying to sound incredulous.

For the first time in a long time, he was able to speak to her with some honesty. There was no reason to be gentle or careful with her feelings. Not now when she thought she was untouchable and couldn't be brought down. Getting her to out herself was the goal.

She nodded. "I will be honest with you, though, the sex was pretty good. I know that I can put on a show when I need to, but I enjoyed myself and looked forward to our meetings. At first, it was just for fun—something to make the days more exciting. Then I realized that if I kept things up, you would be willing to do anything for me. When I finally had a purpose for you, things went even better than I could have imagined."

"So those times after we attempted to kill Perry when you wanted sex and I didn't want it, you did that because—"

"I had to do some maintenance on the relationship," she said. "You were all mopey afterward, and I was worried you were going to freak out and go to the cops before I could give my side of the story."

"But do you see how it's unfair that you came up with the whole plot in the first place and you're not in any trouble?"

She shrugged. "I don't see how that matters."

"You were the one who wanted Perry dead. You wanted to get his money and not have to deal with a divorce."

"Yeah, so what? You also wanted me to be single and have cash because you saw me as an opportunity to live your wildest dreams. Remember all of those times that we were in bed together and you talked about how good our lives were going to be? You fully bought into the idea of having a hot girlfriend who would spend a lot of cash on you. Your life was going to be so easy. I was willing to bankroll that for your help."

"But do you know that I actually like Perry?" Chris said.

"You didn't like him when I showed up with bruises," she replied.

"Were those part of the act?" He knew they were.

"Of course," she said casually. "I got a really deep massage and didn't want the bruising to be for nothing. I added a few extras with makeup to complete the look. You were convinced."

He wasn't. "What was I supposed to think?" he asked. "You said you were fighting with Perry, and then you're bruised."

"You were supposed to think that I needed help. You were hesitant, sure, but then you went right into action to save me. Want to know the best part?"

"What's that?"

"I technically didn't do anything wrong."

"How do you figure?"

"I came up with the plan, but I didn't carry out the deed. You did. You were the one who gave Perry the pills and got him to take them. I wasn't even in the same room when it happened. You're the murderer, not me."

"As far as I know, Perry's alive at his sister's house."

"For now," she said coldly. "To be honest, I'm still pissed at you for not fully committing to the job. I could be waiting months to be free. It wouldn't have taken that much more work to finish the job."

"How?"

"You visited him a bunch of times in the nursing home. You could have unplugged a cord or slipped him something to make him sick. He was already brain-dead, so it wouldn't have taken much to finish him off. You could have gone to his sister's and finished the job. Gisele wouldn't have known any different."

"You could have," Chris suggested. "Why didn't you? You had the same access to him as I did."

She looked frustrated by this questioning. "Because I would have been liable. If you would have gone to Gisele's and injected him with poison, it could have shown up in an autopsy. The police would have a suspect because you were at the scene. I wasn't, so I'd have an alibi and wouldn't go down for it."

"So it was always about me doing the dirty work?"

"Pretty much, yeah."

Chris shifted in his seat on the hard mattress. "You don't think I would sell you out? You don't think that when this thing goes to trial, I won't tell the court that you planned this from the beginning?"

"Why would you?" she asked, as though it were a stupid thing for him to question. "It's not going to help you. You're still going to jail regardless of any deal you try to make. The detectives told my lawyer that you had nothing to say, even after they told you everything I told them."

Chris shrugged. "What else was there to say? You embellished the story, but some of the things you said were true. Plus, we had made a deal to say nothing when we spoke to the detectives. We made a pact to stay silent and get through things together."

"Yeah, well, I saw a better way out. You can't blame me for looking out for myself. In this world, there are winners and losers. If there weren't both, then the whole system wouldn't work. I am a winner. I exude confidence, and I make sure things work out for me. Don't take this the wrong way, but you're a loser. You let bad things happen to you, and then you just feel sorry for yourself. Instead of doing things on your terms, you follow other people's plans and let them tell you what to do. You take the bait, you get in too deep, and then you take the fall. It was always going to turn out this way. You were always going to be in here, and I was always going to be out there."

"You really think you're smarter than all of the cops in this town?" he asked, already knowing her answer.

"Yes," she replied proudly. "It's my attention to detail. Here, try me. Think of something I did that you might tell the cops about in order to get me in trouble."

He didn't want to play any more games, but he was curious to see how far her hubris went. "The moment that Perry overdosed. You can't prove that you weren't in the room with me. What if I said that you administered the pills?"

She smiled, ready to explain her brilliant chess move. "If you look at my call log, you would see a long phone call with a friend in the city. If the police asked her, she would tell them that we often speak for hours at a time, and on that night, like I have on many occasions, I fell asleep during the call while she just stayed on the line. My friends know that the police are sniffing around, and they would all provide me with an alibi, even if I wasn't with them. My ride-or-die friends would do anything for me."

"Like lie to the police?"

"Anything."

"So they know that you're involved in Perry's attempted murder?"

She smiled. "No, they know that *you* are. They're happy that I'm slowly getting my life back, but they're also shocked to learn that the help tried to murder his boss. I have a designer friend already drawing sketches for my funeral dress. We're going to turn the event into a very classy affair. The funeral will be all-black attire, veils, hats, the whole thing. Then there will be my freedom celebration where my friends help to release me into the world again. It's going to be a full year of partying and travel. If Perry's slow death has given me anything, it's planning time to really do things right."

Chris didn't want Kara in his cell anymore. He was disgusted by the way she casually talked about all of the things she would do once Perry succumbed to the supposed injury she'd orchestrated.

"What if I tell the detectives everything you just said? What if I tell them to check the security log and tapes to see you enter my cell to talk?"

She shook her head. "First of all, they won't believe you. Secondly, I'm still willing to treat you right. Who's going to fund your commissary in prison? You know you'd never ask your sister to send you cash to pay for new underwear and toothbrushes. I can keep it fully funded."

"Bribes don't mean as much if I'm already in prison," he retorted.

"Then how about a threat? You have a history of killing people you're supposed to give mental health treatment to."

"You want my money?" Chris laughed. "That's rich."

"No, I would sue everyone who knew that you were working without a license. I know you talk to your sister, and she knows what you're doing here. I could sue for damages. Do you know how much it costs to keep Perry in the hospital? I'd get medical costs and funeral expenses paid by her, because she knew what you were doing and never spoke up."

"Fuck you," Chris spat. "You are easily the worst person I have ever met. You might be the shittiest human in the entire world."

She promptly got up and clutched her tiny leather purse in her hands, then slid her round sunglasses over her eyes. "Have fun in prison." She smirked. She pounded on the door twice.

Within seconds, a guard came and escorted her out, locking Chris in his cell.

Chris wanted to scream. He wanted to drill his fist into the cinder block wall. It was one thing for Kara to brag about how she was getting away with attempted murder and didn't care who went down for her crime. It was another to threaten someone's poor sister who had nothing to do with the plot, and take her money while Kara needed none of it. Instead of lashing out in rage, since none of that was likely to happen, Chris bit his tongue to the point where he could taste the metallic tang of his own blood. Then, after a while, he started to relax in his cell, knowing that the game wasn't over yet.

There was one knock on the door, and then it swung open. Detective Johnson stood in the doorway with his hands on his hips. "Did you get what we needed?"

Chris opened his shirt and took off the wireless recorder that they'd attached to him. He handed the entire thing to the detective, who looked like a proud coach after a game.

"Yeah, I got it," Chris said as a chill went down his spine. "I have way more than I could have anticipated."

As he was escorted out of the jail to change back into his street clothes, he felt like he was well on his way to righting wrongs and making amends.

## 38

Detective Matthews suggested that Chris stay in jail for another night or two to keep up the act, but after seeing his pleading eyes, Detective Johnson made some calls and got a nonsmoking queen room at the Hampton Inn.

Though it was all a careful ploy to get Kara to talk on record, Chris couldn't shake off the feeling of being in jail for a day. Some parts of the process were fake, he did not have to submit to an invasive search upon getting to jail, nor did he have to have his mug shot or fingerprints taken. He knew that he would get out of there the moment the detectives had what they wanted, in contrast to the other inmates, who were there for an indefinite amount of time. He even had the detectives' word that though the guards weren't exactly in on the plan, they would take extra caution to keep him safe, which couldn't necessarily be said about the other men in that jail.

Other parts were very real. While it was nice to be in a single cell, the cuffs placed on him left bruises on Chris's wrists, which ached whenever they rested against his body. He felt like garbage from lack of sleep, and his back ached from spending so much time on that lousy bunk passed off as a bed. His mental health hadn't been great going in, and that tiny stint in jail didn't do much to help. He felt violated by the whole experience. He was glad that Kara had exposed herself for who she truly was, but felt a little resentful that he had to be used as bait. Then again, it was all part of his penance. He couldn't say no, especially after having an affair with her.

After a long, warm shower and a sandwich from the grab-and-go bar in the lobby, Chris was starting to feel more like himself. He flipped on the TV and tucked himself into bed a little past nine o'clock and slept until the phone on his bedside woke him the next morning.

"Hello," Chris croaked into the hotel phone, resting it on the side of his face. Sunlight was streaming in through the cracks in the curtains. He felt dehydrated and knew that he had been asleep for far too long.

"Morning," Detective Johnson said casually. "Is everything fine at the hotel?"

"I think so," he replied groggily. "I've been asleep for a while. Everything okay with the case?"

"It's good," the detective said, sounding satisfied. "I wanted to run through a few points that the team has been wondering about. How about I swing by in a few minutes and pick you up?"

"And go back to your offices?" Chris asked, not eager to sit in a cold interrogation room for hours at a time.

Detective Johnson must have heard the hesitation in his voice. "How about a diner? I know one that is a little out of the way. We can still keep your cover."

"Yeah, okay," Chris said, peeling himself from the bed.

"Great. I'll leave now and be there in a few."

Chris hung up the phone and scrambled to his feet. He instinctively reached for a dresser drawer to put on fresh clothes, then remembered that he only had the clothes on his back. He snatched his crumpled jeans from the floor, gave them a sniff, as if there was something he could do about the smell, and pulled them on. He went to the bathroom, splashed some water on his face, brushed his teeth, and called it good. As he briefly studied his reflection in the bathroom mirror, he wondered if he had been getting old for a while, or if the stress of the investigation was finally getting to him, altering his appearance as a permanent reminder of this stage in his life.

The detective was whistling a jaunty tune when he came to get Chris and didn't stop with the melody until they were nearly halfway to the diner.

"How was the recording quality?" Chris asked when Johnson stopped whistling. He wasn't sure if he had already asked that question or not.

"Pretty good," the detective replied. "Oh, by the way, I forgot to give these back to you." He handed over a zip-top plastic bag containing Chris's wallet and phone.

Chris was surprised to realize that he hadn't missed the items. He powered on his phone and checked for frantic messages from his sister and Cole, who might have noticed he had gone MIA. There was nothing. With an odd mix of relief and disappointment, he slid his phone into his front pocket, and his wallet into his back.

"When can I go back to the cottage?" Chris asked, acutely aware that he was technically homeless until he was given the all clear to return.

"That's what I wanted to discuss with you," Johnson said as he pulled into a gravel parking lot for the roadside diner. "With any luck, you'll be back in your own bed tonight."

Chris raised his eyebrows in surprise as he followed the detective into the diner and slid into a booth in the far corner, next to the window.

"Order whatever you want," he said. "My treat."

Normally, Chris would order conservatively on another's dime, but he felt that he had earned the privilege to get exactly what he wanted.

While he waited for his full spread to be delivered, Chris cupped a steaming mug of black coffee between his hands and listened to the detective's plan.

"The office has been working on the case through the night, and I think we'll be ready to make our arrest this afternoon. The team will go in after Kara's been arrested and search for any additional evidence that will help our case. If all goes according to plan, then the scene should be clear for you to return by tonight—assuming you're still going to stay on the property."

It was a question Chris didn't know the answer to. He didn't have anywhere else to go, but seeing as Kara was being arrested and his role in the sting was over, it felt weird to return to the property. Especially when Perry wasn't there.

"I'm still shocked by how easily the plan worked," the detective said cheerily as the meals were brought out—steak and hash browns for the detective and waffles, eggs, and bacon for Chris. "How did you know it was going to work?"

Chris shrugged as he swallowed a mouthful of food. "It was always going to be a gamble. Perry knows her better than anyone, and he suspected this was what would have to happen. I think having her see me in a jail cell gave her enough closure. She thrives when there's a power dynamic. She had the expensive lawyer and got your approval when she sold me out. I had no one, and I was stuck in jail. To her, that meant the whole saga was over, and that she had gotten away with it. It was a done deal, so it didn't matter what she said to me. She wanted to prove she was as powerful as she's always thought she was."

Johnson shook his head. "I still don't understand how Perry got with her in the first place. I haven't heard a positive thing about that woman."

"You heard what she said about me," Chris mumbled. "She said she turned me into a pawn for her. That wasn't a lie. It's extremely embarrassing now, but she really does use her charm to convince men to do things for her. You don't see someone like Perry enjoying attention from a beautiful woman who is at ease in social situations?"

"I guess."

"She's very skilled at being appealing," Chris replied. "From what Perry said, she charmed him, and he didn't really listen to anyone who had anything negative to say against her before he married her. Then he just tried to do his best to keep her happy. I don't think there's a man out there who wouldn't fall victim to her charm when she turned it on them."

"A blind man, perhaps," Detective Johnson said as he wiped his mouth with a napkin. "I will say, having her confess in her own words will make all the difference with the jury when this goes to trial. If they put her on the stand, the jury will fall in love with her. If you let them hear how nasty she really is, no one will feel sorry for her. Not a bit."

The two finished their meal, and the detective paid the bill.

As the pair walked back to the detective's car, Chris asked something that the cop never informed him about. "So what am I meant to do until I can go back to the property? I don't have anywhere to go. My car is on the property. If I get dropped off somewhere around town before you make your move, someone might tip off Kara."

The detective started the car and pulled out of the parking lot, driving back toward town. "It's a little unconventional for me to suggest this, but seeing as you've already become an informant, here's what I've got in mind. How about you ride along with us? You'll have to stay in the car because it's police business, but I get the feeling that you'd like to see Kara when she gets put in cuffs."

He was correct, but Chris didn't know if it was wrong to admit that he did want to see Kara go down for her crime. He'd love even more to rub it in her face, but he knew that there were rules to arrests, and he didn't want to jeopardize the case for his own personal benefit.

"Yeah, I'll come along," he replied, and thought about how relieved he was going to feel to see the case come to an end.

Detective Johnson had to attend a briefing first, which Chris wasn't privy to, so he sat in the detective's car and played games on his phone until it was time for them to move in.

On their drive to Perry's estate, the detective explained how the arrest was going to work. "If we expect the suspect to be dangerous, like have weapons and a propensity to use them, we'd have more cops come along."

Chris noticed the small parade of police cars, marked and unmarked, following.

"We'll need at least a few guys to cuff her and take her

into custody. We wear cameras in these situations now, but you still don't want to be accused of any bad behavior. We already know the suspect is a manipulator, so we don't want to risk it. We'll double-check to make sure all cameras are functional before we go in. Then we'll have a few cops on scene to comb through the house and collect any evidence."

"What kinds of stuff?" Chris asked.

"Oh, it's hard to say before you get in there. For this case, I'd pay special attention to potentially toxic materials or anything that suggests Kara was ready to move on from Perry."

"She's got a storage container filled with his things," Chris said with a snort.

"We're already onto that," Detective Johnson said.

Chris felt butterflies in his stomach as they pulled up to the estate. He squinted, trying to catch a glimpse of Kara standing in the window, watching the processional. Then again, she thought she was off the hook. She wouldn't have expected the police to return. In fact, Chris was surprised that she wasn't holding a party or out of town celebrating her victory.

"Hang tight," the detective said. He got out of his car and joined the group of cops on the driveway, making their final preparations.

Chris took a deep breath and held it as he watched a uniformed officer knock on the door, and saw Kara open it. She looked confused as the officer spoke; then her expression quickly turned to rage. She started screaming, stomping her feet, and then flailing her fists.

The officer talked to her; then she was led down the stairs to the driveway. Now, she was close enough to the car for Chris to hear her. Unable to contain himself, he cracked the door open.

Two uniformed officers asked if she had anything dangerous on her, which she refused to answer, causing them to ask again so they could search her without worry. The detectives stood in their plain suits on the front step, discussing their next moves while Kara remained completely noncompliant.

Detective Johnson looked toward his car and saw the passenger door ajar, which brought a wry smile to his face. "You can come out, but just stay by the car," he called to Chris.

Chris unbuckled his seat belt and stood beside the car, leaning on the frame. He wanted Kara to see him. For her to realize that she was going to jail, and he was out of jail, would tell her everything she needed to know. He wanted her to know that she was caught in a setup, and that she had lost the game by a long shot. Like the detectives said, the case wasn't finished until the jury gave their verdict, but it was okay to quietly celebrate small victories when they could.

"Why is he here?" she screamed. "This is a huge misunderstanding. Whatever he told you to get out of jail is a lie. I gave my testimony. That's the truth. He is dangerous and needs to be behind bars. He tried to kill Perry."

At the mention of her husband's name, the back door of a different detective's door swung open, and Perry got out.

## 39

Perry looked well rested and less troubled than he had the last time Chris had spoken to him. A younger woman, who had his same facial structure and light hair, got out of the other side, peeking curiously around the car. Seeing them made Chris grin.

Kara blinked with her mouth slack for a few seconds as she processed that not only was Chris out of jail, but Perry was conscious and doing well. Not that he'd ever not been doing well. Mix in Gisele's presence, and her brain completely short-circuited. This caused a new wave of screaming and cursing at everyone on the property.

Perry winced and covered his ears when she reached a new octave. Gisele said something to him, and they both got into the car and closed the doors.

"You fucking set me up!" Kara raged. "You can't do this. This isn't legal."

"It is," Detective Johnson said as he joined Kara and the other cops on the driveway. He sounded like he was growing bored of her antics. "It's all very legal and carefully planned out. At the end of the day, you played yourself, so don't forget that."

"I'm not telling you anything," she snarled as officers tightened handcuffs around her wrists. "I want my lawyer."

"You'll get your lawyer," Matthews said. "Hell, I don't care if you talk to us or not. I think you already said more than enough when you visited Mr. Abrams in jail. We really enjoyed hearing your take on the situation. And don't worry, we won't tell Perry what you said."

"But he'll probably hear it when this thing goes to trial," Johnson responded.

She was marched into a car and carefully stowed away. Johnson gave the patrol car a wave, and then they were off to the county jail, where Kara was sure to have the worst night of her life. Jail would be torture for Kara, who required an entire staff to take care of her.

Chris smiled at the thought of her arriving at the cafeteria and asking for an organic green juice.

"I don't think evidence will take more than an hour, so I'd recommend staying out of the buildings until you get the all clear. Feel free to leave, as you've done your job, and we won't see you again until the trial."

"Wow," Chris breathed. "That's it?"

They nodded. "You've done a good job."

Chris shook his head. "I've done a bad job, but I think I've redeemed myself."

"Absolutely," Johnson said. "Best of luck in your future endeavors."

The detectives smiled and walked to the other car to talk to Perry.

Chris watched the house as a few cops with gloved hands and cameras entered the home. Chris checked his phone. He had an hour to figure out what his future entailed before he either packed up his things and left or settled into his cottage.

Chris was a little surprised to see Gisele and Perry get out of the car and wave goodbye to the detectives who worked the case on his behalf.

Though Chris had spent plenty of time with Perry over the past few weeks, he was always either sedated or pretending to sleep. Chris had talked to him, but Perry never gave a verbal response. It felt like seeing an old friend he hadn't talked to in a long time, as well as someone he had only spoken to on the phone but was aware that he'd made her life difficult for a short time.

"How are you feeling?" Chris asked Perry.

Perry looked better than he had in the hospice center. He suspected that Gisele had convinced him to go outside and get a little sun. His short salt-and-pepper hair had grown out a bit, which suited him. He was thinner than usual, but it still looked like a weight had been lifted off his shoulders.

"I'm ready to get back to work," he decided, looking over Chris's shoulder toward his house. "It's been really hard lounging around when I could be doing things."

"Well, you've got fewer interruptions now," Gisele said. "I think you'll be able to work in peace."

"I can get used to that," Perry replied with a small smile. "I think I'll go for a walk around and check on things. Care to join me?"

Chris joined Perry and his sister on a stroll around the perimeter. It was not lost on him that the last time he'd walked that path, Kara was planning on selling him out. Now, he had successfully done the same to her.

. . .

Shortly after the last police officers left the property, Chris realized that there wasn't much food in the house, and he wasn't an expert on Perry's preferred meals.

"Should we go out for dinner?" Chris asked, causing Perry and Gisele to shoot him a confused look. "My treat," he added before breaking out into laughter. Perry was finally home. There was no way he would pry him away from the house for any reason. Perry would go days without food before subjecting himself to a restaurant.

"I never told the staff," Chris said. "I tried to tell everyone to stick around a little and not get too attached to any other work, but I don't know how things ended up."

Perry nodded understandingly. "I think it would be best if you made the calls and explained everything. I imagine it would be quite a shock for my staff to get a call from me right now considering they all believe that I was in a coma."

Chris wanted to refuse this job. Hadn't he done enough to redeem himself? Now, he had to call everyone he worked with and tell them that Perry's illness was an elaborate plot to pin Kara for conspiracy to murder, a long story that included Chris sleeping with the boss's wife. He didn't know some of these people very well, which would make it hard to explain why their job was in danger, and now it wasn't. He imagined there would be angry responses to his explanation.

"I'll start with Darryl," Chris said as he got out his cell phone. "I think the others can wait until tomorrow."

Chris strolled a few feet back toward the walking path while Perry and his sister headed toward the house. As he listened to dial tones, he felt nervous and embarrassed. He kept reminding himself that Kara was the one who would be on trial for her misdeeds, not him. He was already paying the price for what he did.

Chris told Darryl that Perry was home and awake and asked him to make dinner tonight. He answered a few of Darryl's questions with as much brevity as he could muster, then hung up the phone.

How many more phone calls like this would he have to make? How much time would he spend explaining to everyone who washed windows, cut grass, and added pool chemicals that Perry was alive and well and had never been in any danger? Well, aside from Kara wanting him dead. Chris would have to talk Perry into having a meeting at the estate so everyone could hear the story once and get the questions out of the way.

Darryl showed up with remarkable speed, having gone to the grocery store immediately after ending the call with Chris. He brought in boxes of food to the kitchen, eyeing Chris all the while, but not asking questions. Darryl chopped vegetables and whipped up sauces while Chris stacked food on the pantry shelves and cleaned out the refrigerator, all in silence. Neither man knew what to say to each other.

At dinnertime, the four sat down at the dining room table as Darryl passed around the different courses. Perry ate as though nothing had happened, while Darryl and Chris acted as though they were sharing a meal with a ghost. Gisele, the odd woman out, seemed just as uncomfortable.

"Very delicious," Perry remarked as he ate his lightly seasoned chicken breast. "I've missed enjoying your cooking firsthand while I've been away," he said, as though he had only returned from an extended work trip. "Oh, and thank you for sending those meals to Gisele."

"May I ask what happened?" Darryl questioned.

Chris and Perry shared a look. Perry was smiling, but Chris was not—not genuinely, anyway. He had his mouth stretched into a grimace.

"Why don't we start from the beginning?" Perry said, reaching for his water glass.

"Please do." Gisele spoke up. "I don't think I've heard the whole story, and I have some questions."

Chris looked to Perry, yielding the floor to him. He didn't want to be the one who said how the saga began.

"A few months ago, I started to suspect that something in the household wasn't right," Perry said, looking toward Chris. "Kara was happier than she usually was, and Chris was quiet and would ask me strange things about my marriage when we had sessions together. I sent him to take a short vacation and get his head together. When he got back, I noticed he was distracted and out of sorts, so I asked him about it. He told me Kara was having an affair and wanted me dead. I was of course very upset, as I quickly realized he meant he was the one having the affair with her, and the guilt was eating him up. The details he gave me about Kara's plot allowed me to come up with a plan to turn the tables on her."

"Morrie had mentioned something was going on with Chris and that he didn't trust him," Darryl added.

"Morrie shared his concerns about Chris with me as well," Perry replied. "But at the time I'd suspected that it was professional jealousy. Turned out he was right to be suspicious, but of Kara, not Chris."

Darryl's eyes widened. He might have had his suspicions, but Chris believed that most of the staff thought Perry's hospitalization was either an accident or a suicide attempt.

"While I was away, she came to my hotel covered in fake bruises, claiming Perry beat her up," Chris said, taking over the story. "She wanted me to give Perry too much of his medication. She wanted him to overdose and die at home and then discover him once it was too late. Kara wanted to stay in her room while it was happening. I'd wait until it was time to give Perry his normal dosage, and then trick him into taking more, or even just inject him with sedatives."

"And what was the point of this?" Gisele asked. "Why didn't you just go to the police?" She looked at Perry. "Wouldn't divorce be easier?"

"Maybe I should have, but I didn't want her to win. I suppose she didn't want to divorce me because we had a prenuptial agreement," Perry replied, staring at his plate. "If we divorced, we would both retain our assets. That would leave her with very little, and she requires a lot. She reasoned that if she got rid of me, she could have the benefits of being single while having my money."

"Damn," Darryl whispered.

Perry looked up and met his sister's gaze. "You were right. She was a gold digger."

"Yes, I thought so," Gisele said. "So why not settle it differently? Tell her that you would be fine separating, but you would leave her a trust or an allowance."

"She would want more," Chris suggested. "I'm sure whatever number you would give her wouldn't be enough."

"And honestly, I didn't want a divorce," Perry said. "She was very skilled at the social aspect of my work. She attended events and put on a good show when I needed her to, because she understood that it would mean more money for us. Without her, she would have no obligation to help, and I would have to take on more of that load that I'm simply not good at, nor want to do."

"Still sounds better than being with someone who wants you dead," Gisele said. "I didn't know her well, but she always acted like she was the one pulling the strings."

"In some ways, I think she did pull my strings," Perry admitted. "Once Chris started talking about her manipulation tactics, I started recognizing it in my own life, but in different ways. She tries to seduce men like Chris, but she tries to aggravate me to get a response. Chris thought I was an abusive husband because of the way we fought. We only fought because she knew how to trigger me. I wish I could be better about controlling myself, but it's a daily struggle, and she knew it. She knew exactly which buttons to push to get the reaction she wanted out of me."

"And then she painted on marks to make it look like Perry hurt her," Chris added. "She knew how to play me. I was fooled by a lot of things."

"But not when it counted," Perry said with a glimmer in his eye. "So, seeing as my wife had a very real plan to murder me, we discussed the options. First, we did talk about filing a police report."

"But that fell through quickly because there was no evidence," Chris interrupted. "If the police came and talked to us, they would hear a crazy story and have no way to prove it. That would leave Kara free and angry, and we worried about what she would do if she got very desperate. Accusing her with no proof wasn't an option, so we continued our discussion."

"So it was back to the drawing board," Perry continued. "We talked about Kara's mental state and concluded that she was a danger. If I made a sweet deal with her to give her what she wanted, she would go on to abuse and manipulate someone else. Both Chris and I were hurt in this situation, and I know that over the years, she has treated our staff poorly. It wasn't so much about teaching her a lesson as it was preventing her from doing this to someone else. I don't know exactly how we got our plan figured out, but it came together."

"I'm still shocked we pulled it off," Chris said. He instinctively reached toward the open wine bottle sitting on the table, but swiftly withdrew his hand and picked up his water glass instead. "I didn't realize that a person could convince a police department and multiple medical centers to pretend that someone was dying. I guess it helps to have connections."

"Why not just fake his death?" Darryl asked, completely absorbed by the drama.

"It would have been easier." Perry laughed. "But we worried that Kara would want to verify it herself. I can pretend to be unconscious, but I can't convincingly play dead. Plus, she wanted the money as soon as possible. With no body to bury and no real death certificate, she wouldn't have gotten it, and would have been suspicious. That was actually a suggestion by the detectives."

"They knew what they were doing," Chris admitted, though he thought they treated him rougher than they should have. At times, Chris really felt that he was in trouble and occasionally feared that they had changed the plan without notifying him and were going to charge him too.

"And everyone was on board right away?" Darryl asked. "It took me a while to understand that Perry's okay. How did you convince everyone to go along with it?"

"The police were first," Perry said. "I explained the situation and told them our tentative plan. I know some of those guys pretty well, and they like me. They thought it was an interesting idea and gave me some suggestions. They saw the real danger Kara posed and wanted to give it a try. Then I talked to my main doctor. She thought it wasn't a good idea, but I explained that it was happening whether she helped or not, so she talked to a few providers and set up rooms where only certain people would go. The ambulance knew that they were just transporting me to a room in the hospital, where I would be given light sedation so I would sleep for a long time. When I had visitors, I slept. When they left, I ate meals and watched TV. At the hospice, only a few key nurses went in to perform fake tests when Kara visited. Chris stayed in touch with them as a means to put on a show in front of Kara, as well as receive updates on the plan. Eventually, we felt as though we had overstayed our welcome, and Gisele agreed to let me spend some time at her house until we got the confession we needed."

"Which was harder to get than I originally thought," Chris said. "The detectives were very clear that rushing things would cause us to get sloppy and make mistakes. They prepared us for a few weeks of playing games, but even they were surprised at how long it was going to take to make a case. I don't know about you, but I was losing hope toward the end."

Perry gave a solemn nod. "I wasn't sure when I was going to get my life back, if ever. If Chris hadn't gone into jail and gotten that recording, I don't know what I would have done. Gisele knows that there were moments where I wasn't doing well."

"Chris helped me through some of it," she said kindly.

"But it was never meant to be a long-term change," Perry stated. "I need to be at home in a familiar place where I can settle in and work. My doctor was getting ready to pull the plug on the whole operation because I wasn't getting the regular care I was used to. I tried so hard to keep it together because if I didn't, then it was all for nothing."

"Same," Chris echoed. "It was really hard for me to keep a straight face and lie to everyone who works here when Perry was taken to the hospital. I knew that it would be hard for everyone to stick around while it seemed like your jobs were in jeopardy. I just couldn't say outright that things would be better in a month, and to enjoy a slower-paced day until Perry came back. I know we might still lose staff who have gone on to get other jobs."

"Like Morrie?" Darryl asked.

Perry shook his head. "Morrie knows. I called Morrie shortly after I was transferred to the hospice. I explained the plan and why we were doing it. I told him that he could have a few weeks of paid vacation, and then he could come back when everything settled down. He didn't take me up on my offer."

"Really?" Chris asked, surprised to hear that Morrie wasn't interested in a paid vacation of that length.

"No. He said that he was getting tired of the drama," Perry said. "I told him that it was just a little dramatic, but I think he disliked splitting work with another nurse and wanted to do things his way. He told me that our plan was idiotic, and he had no interest in playing along. I wished him luck and gave him two paid weeks anyway. After talking with my doctor, we decided that one medical attendant on duty was probably enough, so I had no trouble letting him go."

Chris had no trouble with Morrie's departure either. He was a crotchety old man, and Chris thought that his old-school tactics weren't helping Perry's mental state. He was not sorry to see Morrie leave, nor was he upset to hear that he would not be returning.

"Damn," Darryl said as he took a swig of wine. "So does that mean that Kara's in jail for good?"

Perry nodded. "She is currently in the county jail, awaiting her trial. The judges around here are very strict on bail, so I would be surprised if she gets out, given the circumstances that brought her there. If she gets bail, it will be exceptionally high, and I will not allow her to use our funds to get out. She has wealthy friends, but I doubt that they will be willing to embarrass themselves by associating with her. I know the press is going to run with this story, and her friends are going to desert her."

"Or exploit her for press," Gisele interjected. "I'm sure they would love to be featured in a documentary as someone who knew her from before her jail time."

Chris didn't want to be dragged out into the spotlight on what was certainly a colossal story that people would eat up.

"I don't want any part in that," Perry said. "I'm not saying more than I have to, and I'm definitely not signing away any rights. I would prefer it if everyone kept it that way. I have no problem with people knowing the truth about Kara, but I don't want my private life to become media fodder."

This was reassuring to Chris, who imagined his résumé appearing in news articles and his past life being discussed in podcasts. He had no interest in becoming a pop culture figure for five seconds. He just wanted to live a normal life.

"But she's going to be out of your life for good, I hope," Gisele said to her brother.

"It sounds like she'll be in prison for a while," Perry said. "Which was hard to think about at first, but if you put it in the context of my life in exchange for her payday, I think it's fair."

"It's more than fair," she said with a shudder. "Murder. I can't even imagine. What kind of person would even consider a thing like that?"

Chris took another bite of his dinner so he wouldn't have to look at Perry or his sister. Though he hadn't admitted it to Perry at the time, there had been a split second when he'd imagined how he'd benefit from that outcome. It had been a fleeting thought, wrapped up in his intense infatuation with Kara, but the fact that he'd considered it was a secret he'd take to the grave.

"It's just good to know she can't hurt anyone now," Chris said softly.

"I'll drink to that," Darryl said, raising his glass. "Hey, do you mind if I relay this information to a few of the guys who have been asking about their jobs? I think they'd be glad to know they can come back for good, but I don't want to tell your story."

"Be my guest," Chris said, feeling relief wash over him. "If I don't have to tell this story over and over again, I'd be a happy man."

"I'm sure you'll be called to testify at the trial," Gisele reminded him.

"That will be the last time I tell the story, then," he concluded. "Then I'd like to live a different life—a less complicated life."

"I'm with you on that one," Perry said to Chris with a smile.

## 40

At first, life around the estate was somewhat tense for Chris as he and Perry tried to return to normal. Chris was grateful that Perry was willing to keep him on staff because even in his downtime to consider his options for employment elsewhere, he came up short. While the police were skeptical about his ability to perform the services Perry had hired him for, Perry convinced them that Chris didn't do anything a good friend wouldn't, and that all medical advice was given by his doctor, not Chris. This was enough reassurance for the police department, which was set to receive another major donation from Perry's estate once the case had been settled.

In fact, Chris was so racked with guilt that he started working with his own therapist online. It was hard to explain the affair over and over again, but he found it helpful to hear another voice in his head tell him that he was making up for his mistakes by being a good friend to Perry after the fact.

After a few months of working with the therapist, he was learning to forgive himself for his past mistakes and see a path ahead where he didn't have to carry the burden. It was a daily struggle to not blame himself, and to avoid drinking so he could forget his past, but he was making great strides in bettering himself. However, there was always a reminder in the back of his head that he was indebted to Perry for giving him a job and a home when no one else would and keeping him around when he had done something terrible. He didn't know if Perry was a saint or just too trusting.

Part of Chris's apology tour included difficult phone calls to Laura and Cole, to explain why he had been so secretive and withholding in some of their calls, and then distant. Laura was disappointed, then horrified to hear what Chris had done. She was relieved that he wasn't hurt and amazed that he'd managed to stay employed. She repeated her refrain of her long-standing offer to stay with her if things were too weird for him in New York, but he insisted that he was doing well—better than he had been in a long time.

Cole was also shocked by Chris's story, but he was more interested in the nitty-gritty details than Laura was. He was amazed that something so scandalous could happen to his plain friend from back home. Chris wasn't proud of it, but after talking to Cole, he did realize how the undercover mission had been brave, considering just how crazy Kara was. Until Cole brought it up, he'd never considered Kara harming him in order to reach her ultimate goal.

Chris walked away from those conversations relieved that the two people he was still in contact with from his old life still had his back. Laura even promised to come to New York to support him during the trial.

For the most part, Perry was doing surprisingly well, given the ordeal he had gone through. His biggest struggles, to no one's surprise, dealt with a fear that people were out to get him for his money. Kara was safely behind bars, awaiting her trial, but that didn't mean to Perry that others wouldn't take up her crusade. Suddenly, he was extra suspicious of people he did business with and wanted to hire extra lawyers to ensure that he wasn't going to get ripped off. Most of Chris's sessions with Perry involved conversations about how his money was well protected, and apart from his megamansion and partial staff, he generally lived below his means.

There were some issues Chris was worried would arise from Kara's betrayal, but that didn't seem to be the case. Perry didn't care that his marriage was over, and had no concerns about being lonely or stressing about finding another partner. In fact, he seemed more relaxed around the house, as he knew that there was no one who would purposely trigger his anxiety or sensory disorder. Overall, Chris thought his mental health was better in the months following Kara's arrest than in the time before the plot went into motion.

However, both Chris and Perry had a tense few weeks once Kara's story broke to local news media and a few enterprising journalists arrived in hopes of staking their claim on their big story. Everyone in the household received frequent calls, emails, and run-ins at the grocery store in search of a comment or tiny morsel of information that hadn't been given by the local news blurb.

It wasn't until Chris met a group of journalists at the gate of the home and explained that their prying was actively harming the victim that they backed off. Actually, it was only Chris's insistence that he would name the pushy journalists as individuals harassing the victim that caused them to take a step back. He heard from other staff members that he was anonymously mentioned on podcasts as a silencer of independent journalism, but it kept people away from Perry, which was good enough for Chris.

It was Darryl's idea for Perry to prepare a statement for the local paper once the trial was over. The editor of the local paper knew Perry and understood how difficult the whole case was on his well-being and could be trusted to give the facts in an ethical manner. That way, they could get the truth out there without having to deal with constant nagging from strangers who only wanted to make money off of their misfortune.

So, over the course of several days, Chris and Perry wrote a memo that included the outline of the event in a straightforward manner. There was no judgment of Kara, nor anyone else related to the case, but an objective look at what happened. Perry emailed the memo to the editor, who took a look at it, asked a few clarifying questions, then promised to keep quiet and stick to the script when it was time to go to print. Once that was sent off, Perry relaxed some, and the hounds at the gate ran off with their tails between their legs when Chris told them that they'd already told their story to a local paper.

Eventually, it was time for the main event. The trial had been in the back of everyone's minds since Kara's arrest, but it was always talked about as something that was a future concern and not something to dote on. Before he knew it, Chris was called to be a witness for the prosecution. He met with the prosecutor a few times to go over the facts and practice how he would tell his story to the court. He was unfortunately familiar with this process, which saved the lawyer a lot of work in preparing him as a witness.

On the first day of the trial, Chris woke up feeling nauseated. In the past, he would have added a splash of Irish crème to his coffee to settle the nerves, but these days, he was living without alcohol. Instead, he went for a run, took a cold shower, and put on the new suit he'd purchased for the occasion.

He drove Perry to the courthouse and dispensed a small dosage of anti-anxiety medication to get Perry through the morning. Chris was worried about how Perry would handle the commotion and hoped they could make it through without an outburst. It certainly wouldn't look good for the prosecution if Perry looked like a madman.

He was concerned that catching a glimpse of Kara would trigger an anxiety attack in Perry, but he seemed calm when she strutted into the courtroom in a designer suit and heels that made her look impossibly tall and lean. Light brown roots were growing in along her hairline, and her face looked rougher than usual without her expensive moisturizers and serums. Her expression was stony until the jury entered. Then she looked small and meek, as if she were a child and not a grown woman who had conspired to kill her husband for his money.

To no one's surprise, the defense created a case that made it appear that Perry was a danger to Kara, and that she was constantly terrorized by him. He was older and manipulated a young woman into a loveless marriage when she was blinded by a fairytale wedding. As tough as they were on Perry, they were a hundred times tougher on Chris, who was made to look like a stalker who would do anything to get Kara's attention, including killing her husband.

In their story, Kara went to Chris to tell him about how terrible Perry had been, and Chris took it upon himself to be a white knight and take Perry out of the equation. When they were finally forced to acknowledge Kara's jailhouse confession, they told the court that she was under duress and afraid of what would happen to her if she didn't say what Chris wanted her to hear. It was a forced confession, they claimed, and it should be regarded as such.

The defense's case was weak, and everyone knew it. An older couple, who Chris assumed was Kara's parents, sat in the back of the courtroom on the first day, but didn't make another appearance for the rest of the trial. None of her friends showed up to support her. Her lawyers didn't allow her to speak on her own behalf, likely because they knew that she would either perjure herself or come off as unsympathetic to the jury.

The defense tried to get Chris flustered when he took the stand, but after admitting to many people that he had done something wrong and did his best to make up for it, he had little issue telling the court that he was guilty of sleeping with Kara, but he told Perry about her idea immediately and had no plan to harm Perry. Given that Perry was in on the whole plan from the start, it was impossible to prove that he wanted Perry dead.

In the end, the wire confession was all the jury needed to make their decision. It painted Kara as the sole conspirator, and her silent tantrum during the playing of the tape suggested that she was in no way under duress when confessing, but in fact on a high from beating Chris in their game. After a quick thirty minutes of deliberation, the jury gave their guilty verdict, and Kara was sentenced to thirty years in prison. She would be up for parole in five years, but seeing as she would never be truly repentant of her crime, she would likely be denied.

Chris watched Kara as she was led from the courtroom

in tears, swearing under her breath. He knew that jail had been hard on her, as the creature comforts Perry's money had provided for her were gone, and the other women didn't fall for her manipulative ways. They had no time for a rich bitch, even when she tried to bribe them with gifts from the commissary. She was living her greatest fear: irrelevance and being forced to live out her best years away from the spotlight.

By the time of her release, she would be in her late fifties, with no money and no prospects. If she was lucky, another wealthy man would fall for her charms and give her a life, but even that was uncertain, seeing as though she was miles away from her athletic trainer, plastic surgeon, and stylist. Time would tell if her appearance would keep up without her resources.

Once the trial was over, life settled down. With a strengthened relationship, Perry was in more frequent contact with Gisele, who threw a small celebratory party at her home the day after the trial. Initially, it felt wrong for Chris to attend, as it wasn't so long ago that Kara had been planning her celebration for when Chris was in prison and Perry was under the ground. But once he got there, he saw that it was a small gathering of family and close friends who supported Perry and were happy to see that he was in a new chapter of his life.

During the gathering, Perry found Chris, who was sipping on a bottle of sparkling water in the kitchen, away from the rest of the guests. He had felt out of place and awkward but wanted to be there to support Perry.

"It was strange seeing Kara in the courtroom," Perry said, as if he were relaying an observation in an objective manner. "There was a time where I looked at her and saw the face of someone I admired. Then there was a time where the sight of her would make my blood pressure rise. I realized yesterday that I don't feel anything when I see her."

"I just saw regret and a waste of human potential," Chris admitted.

"You don't see her as the bombshell we used to see?" Perry said with a small, sneaky smile.

Chris shook his head. "I will never look back on that time with good memories, even when things felt good at the time. I will only see hurt and deception."

Perry gave him a pat on the back. "I want to thank you for all of your help. I do believe that even if you weren't involved in this, if you never even worked for me, I'd be in this position at some point. If it weren't you, it would be someone else. If there was no one else, she'd find a way to get what she wanted. I appreciate you setting aside your wants for me. Deny it all you want, but you could have gained a lot by getting rid of me. I understand that, and I will always remember it. I know you want to leave the past in the past and move on, but I think you need to understand that I am just as indebted to you as you are to me. It was pure chance that we met that day on the highway, but I feel very fortunate that we have found each other."

Chris smiled. Perry didn't do sentiment often, but when he did, he had no idea the impact it had on Chris's guilty conscience.

"I think I've had enough of this party," Perry said. "Do you think it would be all right if we left?"

Chris patted his boss on the shoulder. "I don't think Gisele would mind. You'll be back for Thanksgiving anyway."

"We both will," Perry added as he went to the closet to retrieve his jacket.

The men gave Gisele a wave goodbye, then stepped into the early autumn air.

As Chris let the cool breeze wash over him, he couldn't help but feel as though he had finally achieved the new life he had been desperately searching for. The path was unconventional, but the result was everything he had needed for so long.

Finally, Chris had his win.

# THANK YOU FOR READING

Did you enjoy reading *The Honey Trap*? Please consider leaving a review on Amazon. Your review will help other readers to discover the novel.

## ABOUT THE AUTHOR

Theo Baxter has followed in the footsteps of his brother, best-selling suspense author Cole Baxter. He enjoys the twists and turns that readers encounter in his stories.

# ALSO BY THEO BAXTER

**Psychological Thrillers**

The Widow's Secret

The Stepfather

Vanished

It's Your Turn Now

The Scorned Wife

Not My Mother

The Lake House

The Honey Trap

The Detective Marcy Kendrick Thriller Series

Skin Deep - Book #1

Blood Line - Book #2

Dark Duty - Book #3

Kill Count - Book #4

Made in United States
Troutdale, OR
09/18/2024